More praise for
Aaron Elkins and
A DECEPTIVE CLARITY

A DECEPTIVE CLARITY

Aaron J. Elkins

FAWCETT GOLD MEDAL • NEW YORK

A Fawcett Gold Medal Book
Published by Ballantine Books
Copyright © 1987 by Aaron J. Elkins

All rights reserved under International and Pan-American Copyright Conventions. Published in the United States by Ballantine
Books, a division of Random House, Inc., New York, and simul-
taneously in Canada by Random House of Canada Limited, To-
ronto. Originally published by the Walker Publishing Company,
Inc. in 1987.

Library of Congress Catalog Card Number: 86-22450

ISBN 0-449-14900-5

Manufactured in the United States of America

First Ballantine Books Edition: January 1994

"It's eleven-fifteen," Tony Whitehead announced peremptorily to the assembled curatorial staff of the San Francisco County Museum of Art. "We've been at this for over two hours and we don't seem to be getting anywhere. I don't know about you, but I've had enough talk, and now I want some action. By next Wednesday morning I expect to see each department's preliminary budget on my desk with three scenarios: current-year allocation, five-percent reduction, and ten-percent reduction."

He waved away the rumble of protest. "We don't have any choice. I'll do my best with the board. That's all." He shuffled his papers together and glanced at me. "Chris, you stay, please."

While the rest of the staff glumly packed up their file folders and made for the door of the conference room, the director nodded them cheerfully out, remaining plumply ensconced in his customary Duncan Phyfe lyre-backed chair at the head of the oval, deeply polished Queene Anne table. The conference room, like most of the administrative offices in the building, was filled with handsome furnishings from the seventeenth and eighteenth centuries. Access to the storerooms for office decoration is one of the pleasantest, least-known perquisites of curatorial rank in an art museum.

"Chris," Tony said, folding sleek, square hands on the table and peering earnestly over them, "I'm worried about you. You didn't say a word in the meeting."

1

"Sorry," I said. "I don't think budget reallocation arouses me."

"I know, but I can always count on you for something constructive. Besides, you've been down in the dumps for weeks."

Months was more like it. I mumbled something and waited for him to continue. Anthony Whitehead was no casual socializer. Whenever he began a conversation in that vein—in any vein—there was a particular and well-defined end in mind. And that end was almost always to extricate himself from one of the political or administrative squeezes that pretty much constitute a museum director's life. Still, to give him credit, he was a good boss, not just a politician and a fund raiser, and eight out of ten times he had your interests in mind. Well, say six.

"I think you need a change, Chris," he said, as if he'd discovered something I wasn't aware of. Smiling, he leaned back in the chair and studied me. He picked up a pencil that had been left from the meeting and tapped it slowly on the table—first the eraser, then the point, then the eraser again.

"I've got an idea," he said with a sense of dawning wonder, as if he'd just thought of it. He laid the pencil carefully on the gleaming table. "How'd you like to spend a month or two in Europe? Salary and expenses?"

I hesitated, which may seem strange, but overseas travel is nothing extraordinary for a curator (another one of those little perks). Besides, there were some personal problems keeping me in San Francisco.

I shrugged gloomily. "I don't know, Tony. I'm not—"

The ringing of the telephone cut me off. Tony picked it up. "Yes, he is." He held it out to me and made a pious face. "Miss Culletson. For you."

Miss Culletson's telephone manner was as crisp, cool, and businesslike as her person. "I have a call for you, Dr. Norgren. Rita Dooling. I thought you might want to be interrupted."

"Oh, Lord," I muttered. I knew by now that no call from

your lawyer ever turns out to be good news. Not when you're in the midst of long, messy divorce negotiations. Norgren's Law, I was thinking of calling it.

"Did you want to take it in your office, or shall I have it transferred to the conference room?"

"No, I'll go to my office."

"I thought you might prefer that," Miss Culletson said in a neutral tone. "I'll ask her to hold."

"My lawyer," I said to Tony. "Can I get back to you later?"

"Make it before twelve. I'm tied up all afternoon."

I nodded, trotted to my office, picked up the telephone, and punched the appropriate button.

"Chris, we're almost there," Rita barked with her usual bluff optimism. "Bev's agreed to everything; our entire counteroffer."

I'd heard this before. "But," I said.

"Well, yes; but." She cleared her throat. "She's tossed in a new wrinkle. Nothing we can't live with when you think in terms of the whole picture."

Our counteroffer . . . nothing *we* can't live with. . . . It was certainly nice to have a lawyer who suffered through these things with you.

"What she wants," Rita continued, "is nine-and-three-quarters percent of the royalties on your book."

"Nine and . . . of *Jan van der Meer van Delft*?" I was surprised and angry in about equal measure. What right did Bev feel she had to any part of the Vermeer book? I'd put together almost all of it in a twelve-week burst of desperate energy during the bleak, miserable period right after she'd left me fourteen months before. "No," I said, "absolutely not," and caved in immediately. "Maybe five percent."

"Well, now, Chris, I don't think we should—"

"Why exactly nine-and-three-quarters percent, for Christ's sake? Why not ten?"

"It's a little complicated," Rita said with a laugh, relieved that I wasn't rejecting the idea outright. "From what she told her attorney, you and your publisher got together on August twenty-sixth last year to lay out the idea of the book. Does that sound right?"

"I don't know. I suppose so." Bev, I had been learning, to my cost, was seldom wrong on dates or figures.

"And the manuscript was submitted on March twenty-seventh? Is that correct?"

I agreed that it probably was, although how Bev knew, I had no idea.

"All right," Rita said, "the thing is, exactly forty-two days after that first meeting with your publisher, you and Bev separated; October sixth."

That date I could vouch for. Black Saturday. Rita was being kind when she used the word *separated*. Bev had simply up and left me. I'd gotten back after a couple of hours at the museum—I'd wanted to look over a fine Mantegna Head of Saint Paul that we'd just gotten from Geneva—and she just wasn't there. No notes, no arguments, no civilized adult discussions, no nothing. At breakfast she'd been the same as usual; we'd laughed over coffee and even talked about going to dinner in Chinatown. It took two wretched days—contacting the police, the highway patrol, every hospital within fifty miles of San Francisco—before I found out where she was: in Marin County, living with a stockbroker I'd never heard of.

I hadn't suspected a thing, hadn't known anything was seriously wrong. We'd had nothing remotely resembling a fight for years. Afterward, one of my friends, a relentlessly well-meaning psychotherapist named Louis, tried to explain things.

"I'm not surprised, Chris," he'd said soberly. "You have a lot of trouble legitimizing authentic confrontation, you know, particularly in dyadic interrelationships." Well, Louis was right. Facing up to interpersonal problems wasn't my long suit. I wasn't sure I'd faced up to this one even yet.

"Anyway," Rita was saying, "August twenty-sixth to March twenty-seventh is two hundred fifteen days, and forty-two is nineteen-and-a-half percent of two-fifteen, and nine and three quarters is fifty percent of nineteen and a half. Community property. *Capisce?*"

"Sort of, but why is she making a point of it? It's not exactly going to be a best-seller; if it earns two-thousand dollars, it'll be a miracle. Does she really care that much about . . . what would it be, two hundred dollars? What happened to her big stockbroker boyfriend?" I bit my lip. Did divorces make everybody childish, or just me?

"It's not the money. She's very strong on the principle of the thing, Chris."

I sighed. I was learning more about Bev in divorce than I had in ten years of marriage. "Rita, tell me something. Is this what divorces are usually like, or is Bev being a little, well, strange?"

Rita's beery chuckle rumbled over the telephone. "Yes and yes. This is what they're usually like, and you better believe people get a little strange. Including you, if you don't mind my saying so. Look, Chris, don't you think we can afford another two hundred bucks and be done with it?"

Yes, I said, I supposed I—we—could afford another two hundred dollars, but I doubted if we were done with it. Rita said I was getting awfully mopey and pessimistic, and why didn't I shape up? And, oh yes, there was one other little glitch.

"Ah," I said.

"She knows you love Murphy, and she wants you to have him."

"Mm," I said. Murphy was the dog.

"She says if you let her keep the car, she'll be happy to let you keep Murphy."

"She . . . she . . . a new, eight-thousand-dollar car . . . and I get the *dog?*"

"I thought you were fond of him."

"I am, I am, but how could she . . . I mean, does she think I'm a, a—"

"I figured you might not go for it."

"Rita, I thought all that was finished, settled. We worked out the car months ago."

"It's not settled until you both sign that piece of paper, my friend."

"Well, I'm not agreeing to it," I said truculently. "Anyway, where does she come off having anything to say about poor Murph? She abandoned him too, you know. No warnings, no good-byes—" I clamped my mouth shut. Rita was right; I was getting pretty strange.

"Well, look, Chris, here's what I think we should do. I think we ought to get us all together again, sit down, and talk through these things like rational adults. I think you need to try to see Bev's side a little. From her point of view, this is all a way of affirming her adulthood, her independence as an integrated human being, not just a—"

"Rita, I've got to go now. I'll be in touch."

I caught Tony as he was slipping into his coat to leave for lunch.

"I'd love to go to Europe for a couple of months," I said. And meant it.

I had known from the start what he'd been referring to. A year earlier, the museum had bid for and won a contract from the Department of Defense to organize and administer Treasures of Four Centuries: The Plundered Past Recovered. This was to be an extraordinary exhibition of twenty paintings lent by Claudio Bolzano, an eminent Italian collector. Bolzano often lent and sometimes gave his paintings to public galleries, but this, as far as I knew, was the first show totally devoted to his pieces. All twenty had been seized by the Nazis in World War II and then, after the war, recovered and returned to him by the U.S. military, in some cases after decades of diligent investigation. The Plundered Past would be shown at six American bases in Europe, and each showing would coincide with a "good neighbor" open house at the base.

The idea of this show was the brainchild of an army colonel named Mark Robey, and the object was to provide some favorable exposure for U.S. forces in the face of an increasingly hostile European press. The San Francisco Museum had contracted to supply an exhibition director who would be responsible for compiling the catalog, providing expert consultation, and "performing other duties as required during the course of the project."

The impetus for this unusual undertaking had been the amazing discovery of a cache of three Nazi-appropriated old masters that had disappeared forty years before without a trace. The treasure had been uncovered by the American military, true enough, but not by the celebrated MFA and A—the army's Monuments, Fine Arts and Archives Unit. It had, in fact, been found completely by accident.

A twenty-year-old soldier named Norman Porritch, stationed at McGraw Kaserne in Munich, had spent the weekend in Salzburg, and on Saturday he had taken a guided tour of the famous old salt mine in nearby Hallstatt. Porritch, a gangling spelunker from Kentucky, had had a flashlight with him, ready for whatever opportunity might arise, and, ignoring the guide's instructions to stay with the group, he had wandered off into a beckoning side tunnel. There, he had been drawn by a black hole in the wall seven feet above the mine floor. He had clambered up, and with his first step knocked over an old, lichen-encrusted wooden crate, which tipped over the two crates behind it like so many dominoes.

The resulting clatter had brought the guide scurrying and shouting, and by the time the fuss died down a few days later, Porritch's homely grin was familiar around the world. Signor Bolzano had come forward with tears and gratitude (a new Alfa-Romeo for Porritch) to claim the Vermeer, the Titian, and the Rubens that had been "liberated" by the fleeing Nazis from his palazzo in Florence in August 1944.

Colonel Robey, a high-ranking member of the army's European Community Relations staff, had recommended that the three great paintings be the nucleus for an exhibition of art tracked down since the war by the American military, and that Bolzano, a beneficiary many times over of the MFA and A's work, be asked to lend several other paintings to complete the show.

When the contract had been awarded to the San Francisco Museum six months before, Tony had asked Peter van Cortlandt to take the job. This was as it should have been. Peter was the chief curator of art, my immediate supervisor. An internationally respected authority on nineteenth-century painting, with thirty years' experience overseeing major exhibitions, he was the man the Defense Department had had in mind from the beginning, and he had gone to Europe on eight months' leave.

And now, Tony explained to me, the Defense Department had funded a deputy-director position to take some of the work load off Peter's shoulders, and I was just the man for it. From Tony's perspective—not that he said so—it meant he would be saving my salary for a couple of months, which would help in the new budget, and he would be getting my temporarily gloomy and unproductive self out from underfoot.

From mine it meant a deeply needed respite. I was suddenly tired to death of budget reallocations, tired of San Francisco, tired of my lonely Victorian off Divisadero, tired of the endless, petty squabbling with Bev. This last was done almost entirely through Rita. Bev and I had spoken only twice since she'd left, and both times I'd wound up shouting at her, practically foaming at the mouth. That had shaken me, if not her. I couldn't recall ever having been truly, quiveringly furious with anyone else in my life, and certainly I'd never been reduced to incoherent raving. The divorce was teaching me a few unwelcome things about myself too.

All in all, a few months in Europe sounded like just what I needed. Moreover, as Tony was quick to point out, Peter had already done the hard work.

"Everything's going smoothly, as far as I know," he told me. "Oh, they've got a few minor problems, of course, but nothing special."

"What will I be doing, exactly?"

"You'll be the deputy director."

"I know, but what am I supposed to *do*?"

"Well, you know, assist Peter, provide technical advice to Robey, that kind of thing."

"Thanks. That's very instructive."

Tony shrugged a little further into his coat and began to button it. "Look, to be perfectly candid, I don't really know what you'll be doing. As far as I can see, there's barely enough to keep one man busy, let alone two. I think you're going to wind up with an all-expenses-paid vacation, but what the hell."

"What the hell," I agreed. "So what do I do first?"

"Just show up in Berlin Wednesday. That's where it opens next."

"You mean *next* Wednesday?"

"Sure, why not? What else have you got going?"

"Are you kidding? All kinds of things."

"For example."

"Those budget scenarios, for one thing."

"Forget them. I'll take care of them. You know I'm not going to cut your department. And you know Sawacki can run Renaissance and Baroque for you for a couple of months. What else do you have to do?"

"What else? Well . . ." But what else was there, aside from putting Murphy in a kennel and having the mail held? My life at the time was not exactly overfull. "Maybe I can make it. Where in Berlin do I go?"

"Tempelhof. You know where it is?"

"No, but isn't that where—"

"The planes came in for the Berlin airlift, right. It's an American air base now, and the show's going to be in the officers-club building—Columbia House, I think it's called." Tony looked importantly at his watch, as if a hundred more urgent things pressed him. No doubt they did. He put a few papers into his attaché case and zipped it up. "Well."

"Wait a minute, Tony, I still don't know anything. What about those problems you mentioned? What kind of problems?"

"Not to worry. Minor problems. The usual thing," Tony explained helpfully. "You'll do fine."

Louis, my trusty psychotherapist friend, once told me that I had a low tolerance for ambiguity. At that moment I was inclined to think he was right, because I was uncomfortable with Tony's vagueness. Vacation or not, whatever I was responsible for, I wanted to do a good job of it. (Louis has also pointed out to me that I have an obsessive-compulsive attitude toward work, probably the result of an anal fixation. Louis furnishes me with much useful information of this kind, all free.)

Having been a civil servant at a county museum for five years, I was also a little wary of that "performing other duties as required," but not enough to think twice about going.

Berlin wasn't one of my favorite cities, being too frantically, resolutely decadent for my taste, but there was a lot I liked about it: Nefertiti at Charlottenburg, the Dürers and Rembrandts at Dahlem, the wonderful zoo, the Tiergarten. . . . Best of all, it was over six thousand miles away, where people in San Francisco (lawyers, for example) would not be able to reach me by telephone whenever they liked, bearing counteroffers and other unpleasantnesses.

Messages would arrive days or weeks late, sapped of their urgency, to be dealt with in my own good time; not sandwiched between budget reallocations and deaccessioning meetings, but at my ease, perhaps over a Scotch, when things could be pondered. Maybe, under conditions like that, I could look at what had happened between Bev and me in a reasonable light, try to understand, maybe even . . .

A hundred bristling, angry obstacles sprang up at the thought. I wasn't ready to be reasonable yet; maybe I never would be. No, the heck with Bev and her nine-and-three-quarters percent and her integrated independence. And her stockbroker. I needed to get on with my own life, to find my stride again, and a couple of months in Europe would be a terrific way to do it.

Had I but known, as Miss Sibley taught us never to say in Creative Writing 201.

2

"What's this thing supposed to be?"

The guard at the entrance to Columbia House looked at the card in my wallet, and then up at my face, with equal skepticism.

"My ID."

"Take it out of the wallet."

I handed the flimsy plastic-encased card to him with sinking confidence. It had been issued the day before, at Rhein-Main Air Base, near Frankfurt, where I'd been instructed to stop on my way to Berlin. The sergeant who gave it to me had assured me that it would get me into any American military installation in Europe, but I had been doubtful even then. It wasn't very official-looking—my name, photograph, and a few details on one side, and on the other a small-print list of twenty-nine varied "privileges," some of which I was shown as entitled to, others not, according to some esoteric and unfathomable guidelines. (Mortuary services, officer-NCO club, and credit union were okay; laundry, dry cleaning, and postal service weren't.) It was about as impressive as my library card.

That's what the guard thought too. "This ain't no ID."

"It was issued yesterday at Rhein-Main—"

He shook his short-cropped, beret-clad head and signaled me to take the card back. "This ain't no ID. I can't let you in. Sorry."

I set my jaw. "Look, it says GSE-fourteen, right? That's equivalent to a light colonel." I wasn't sure what a light

11

colonel was, but that's what the sergeant had told me, and the sergeant had sounded impressed.

The guard didn't. "Yeah, well," he said, patient but unyielding, "don't expect nobody to salute."

"Well, well, Chris, having a little trouble? Nothing we can't work out, I'm sure."

I turned, and there was Peter van Cortlandt, genteel, smiling, his patrician face as smooth and ruddy as ever, his thrust-out hand as well manicured, his suit as flawlessly and conservatively tailored.

"Now: What seems to be the difficulty?" Peter addressed himself pleasantly to the guard, and I watched admiringly as he straightened things out within seconds.

Peter van Cortlandt was one of those people with command presence, but of a quiet, unaggressive sort, and he usually got his way. Although he was nominally my boss at the museum ("nominally" because there was only one functioning boss, and that was Tony), I knew little about him. Peter had that aristocrat's knack of being unfailingly cordial and courteous, yet maintaining a cool, objective distance, physical and psychological, between himself and others. What I did know of him, I liked. Although he accepted deference as his due, he managed to do it in an unassuming and considerate way. Moreover, he was an art historian of great erudition, and he had always shared his knowledge freely—not something you ran into every day in the art world.

By the time Peter had finished with the guard, the young man was smiling and apologetic, and even saluted me through the doorway.

"Do you want to go up to your room, Chris?" Peter asked. "Wash up, perhaps?"

"No, I'm fine." I looked around at a lobby much like that of a hotel, with reception desk, worn but good carpeting, and comfortable-looking armchairs arranged in informal groupings. "Nice place."

"You sound surprised. Were you expecting something more along the lines of a Quonset hut?"

I laughed. "I guess I was."

Peter motioned to a couple of upholstered chairs in a window alcove. I draped my suit bag over the arm of one and sank into it, facing the window and the blustery green plaza outside.

"The Platz der Luftbrücke," Peter said. "The Germans called it the air bridge, not the air lift, which makes more sense, don't you think?" He sat facing me and rubbed his hands briskly together. Not many people could do it without looking like Uriah Heep, but Peter could.

"Well, Chris, I'm glad you're here. We can make good use of that sensitive touch of yours that so impresses us all."

From someone else it would have been banter, but Peter never—absolutely never—poked fun at anyone. Nor, for that matter, was he effusive with his compliments.

Flattered and caught off guard, I was embarrassed. "Something need a sensitive touch?"

"It well may. As you know, Bolzano continues to threaten to pull out. I've calmed him down twice this week on the telephone, but I'm not sure I can successfully keep it up. You might be able to do better if push comes to shove."

But I hadn't known there was any trouble with Bolzano. And if Peter's formidable persuasive powers couldn't resolve it, what was I supposed to be able to pull out of my hat, sensitive touch notwithstanding?

"But what's the problem, Peter? Does Bolzano really want out?"

Peter looked startled; that is to say, his right eyebrow rose all of an eighth of an inch for an eighth of a second. "Do you mean to say Tony didn't tell you about it?"

"Not that I remember. Must have slipped his mind."

"Hm. Well. Bolzano's quite concerned about security, for one thing. He seems to think we're not taking adequate precautions. And he's worried that we may not be giving proper care to packing and transportation, and he's afraid . . . well, just worried. He genuinely loves those old paintings, you know."

"And is there really anything for him to worry about?"

"I don't think so. The army has quite a professional operation mounted here, as competent as you'd be likely to find in the United States. And if the Defense Department isn't expert in security, well, who is?"

I nodded. "What makes you think I'd carry any weight with him? I've never met him."

"I know that, but he thinks very highly of you. He's read that monograph of yours on the Spanish mannerists in the new edition of Arnoldi, and he was telling me all about a highly complimentary review of your new book in the *Bollettino d'arte*. He's impressed with your scholarship— told me so very frankly. And of course I agreed with him— very frankly."

Two compliments from Peter van Cortlandt in one day. Surely a record.

"But let's not worry about signor Bolzano right now." He smiled at me somewhat mischievously, which was not a typical way for him to smile. "Tell me, what did you say when Tony told you about the, ah, forgery I seem to have uncovered in the midst of The Plundered Past?"

"The . . . ?" I couldn't help laughing. Good old Tony. What was it he'd said? "The usual little problems"? "That must have slipped his mind, too. You know Tony; he tries not to get too involved in details."

After a moment Peter laughed, too. "Yes, I know Tony." He looked at his watch. "Well, that can wait, too. Chris, I have to catch a plane in a couple of hours. What do you say to lunch? Do you like Kranzler's?"

I left my bags at the reception desk, and twenty minutes later we stepped out of a taxi in downtown Berlin in front of the Café Kranzler. I hadn't been inside it for four years, not since the last time I'd come to Berlin. It had been at a table on the balcony that I'd tried unsuccessfully to talk Wildenberg into lowering his price on a carved, fifteenth-century Riemenschneider tryptich. I hadn't been sorry I'd failed to get it for the museum, and in fact I hadn't tried as hard as I might have. Riemenschneider was one of those great artists (one of those many great artists) whom I soberly appreciated, but whose work I just plain didn't like. That was true, I'm afraid, for the grim, grotesque German Gothic as a whole. It's not that I don't recognize great art when I see it, you understand; it's just that I know what I like.

A hell of an attitude for an art curator.

The Kranzler hadn't changed at all, not a bit. Gaudy in a decorous, old-maidish way, a bit too self-consciously grand and sedate, it was an institution, the only one of the great old cafés on the Kurfürstendamm to have survived the war, and to enter it was to walk into the Berlin of the twenties.

It was quite crowded, largely with elderly women in green hats who commanded their tables with a distinct air of de-jure possession. One of them, presiding over a *kännchen* of coffee and a *Deutsche Zeitung* provided by the café, nodded regally as we passed. I returned the gesture respectfully. Probably remembered me, I thought. No doubt she'd been at the same table four years ago in 1982. Given reasonable odds, I would have bet she'd been there in 1922.

"Upstairs?" Peter suggested.

"Fine."

We climbed the spiral marble staircase, winding past a central pillar of white and gold mosaic, and found a table at the window. I sat looking east along the Kurfürstendamm, toward Berlin's riveting memorial to the destruction of war: the black, gutted stump of the Kaiser Wilhelm Memorial Church, cowering so incongruously among angular, modern buildings of glass, like a bewildered dinosaur that had wandered into the twentieth century and didn't know how to get out. Closer, the Ku'damm was lined with chic stores and garish theaters with four- and five-story marquees. (*INDIANA JONES UND DER TEMPEL DES TODES!!!* proclaimed twenty-foot-high green letters directly across the street.)

"Peter," I said, "this forgery you mentioned . . ."

"Yes?" He looked at his watch. "Let's order first, shall we? My flight leaves Tegel at two-fifteen."

Among Peter's many impressive qualities was his ability to attract the attention of a waiter or waitress when he wanted it. This was difficult enough in the United States; in Europe, where it was a maddening part of the waiter's art not to "intrude," it was near-marvelous. Without moving his calm gaze from my face, he raised a casual, elegant hand.

The sleeve of his dark gray jacket slipped away from his wrist, showing a taintless French cuff of palest ivory. Peter van Cortlandt had the cleanest shirt cuffs of any man I knew. There had been a time when I'd suspected that in the privacy of his office he slipped a pair of accountant's celluloid cuffs over them, but the answer turned out to be much more characteristic of the fastidious Peter: He changed his shirt every day before lunch, and then again when he left the museum at four.

"*Bitte?*" The waitresses wore black dresses with frilly little pink aprons and pink bows in their hair, so that they looked like French maids in a play. They did not, however, look silly; for the Kranzler it was just right.

I ordered Wiener schnitzel, *Pommes frites*, salad, and a large beer.

"Hungry?" Peter asked.

I shrugged apologetically. "No breakfast."

His urbane face wouldn't show it, of course, but I knew he didn't approve of my eating habits. Peter never ate fried foods, and he had once told me without any attempt to be facetious (Peter was rarely facetious) that he had never had a McDonald's hamburger, never had a Hostess Twinkie, never had beer from a can. He thought he had once had a taco, and it hadn't been too bad, but it had been a long time ago and he wasn't really sure.

Without bothering to look at the menu, he ordered Rhine salmon with asparagus and a half-bottle of Riesling. "Now," he said, "while I'm in Frankfurt you can familiarize yourself with the files. We've got Room twenty-one-hundred of Columbia House as our office, and Corporal Jessick—he's our clerk—will know who you are."

"All right. What takes you to Frankfurt, by the way?"

"Oh, there's a small problem with a Greco that the Frankfurter Kunstmuseum is lending us."

"The Kunstmuseum? I thought everything in The Plundered Past was from Bolzano's collection."

"It is, but this one had been on loan to the Kunstmuseum for the last four years. So, in effect, we're borrowing it from them, and that's complicated things. The show's opened and closed in Naples without it, and now we open in Berlin in just a few weeks."

"But what's the problem?"

Peter's lips thinned slightly. "Insurance. I'm meeting with them at ten A.M., and I have every hope of bringing the painting back with me when I return."

"Ten tomorrow? But why not fly out in the morning? It can't be more than two hours to Frankfurt."

Peter smiled. "I'm afraid I'm not much of a shuttle diplomat. No, I prefer to arrive the evening before, have a good dinner, relax at a decent hotel—and be fresh and rested when it comes to business the next day. It makes good sense."

So he had told me before. So Tony reminded me whenever I was reluctant to spend too much of the museum's money when traveling. I must be the only person in the world who gets chewed out regularly because his expense account isn't extravagant enough.

"Anyway," Peter said, sipping the wine, which had just been placed before him, and according it a brief nod of acceptance, "I'd like to stay in Frankfurt through Friday and do a little museum-hopping. Can you believe that I've been here five months and I've yet to visit the Städel? Can you manage without me until Saturday?"

"Sure." I took a long swallow of my Schultheiss, rediscovering with pleasure how large a large beer is in Germany. "Now how about telling me about this forgery—"

This time it was the waitress who interrupted, setting down our lunches.

"Ah," Peter said, "shall we tuck in? I'm hungry myself."

I was happy to. The veal was succulent and tender, like nothing you can get in the States except at restaurants I can't afford. The potatoes were crisp, the *gemischter Salat* aggressively Teutonic—not thrown together willy-nilly, French-style, but with the marinated vegetables set in orderly ranks, each in its place. For a while we were content to attend to our food, chatting easily while Peter filled me in on some of the routine aspects of The Plundered Past.

"Well," he said, leaning back expansively a few minutes after we'd been served coffee, "that was splendid, and I can't tell you how glad I am to have you here with me. It's been wonderful—"

"Now hold it, Peter. You don't have to leave for half an hour yet. You're being evasive."

He looked at me benignly. "I, evasive? What a thing to say. What would you like to know?"

"You told me—I think you told me—that there's a forgery in the show." He continued to regard me tranquilly. "Well," I said, "that just isn't possible."

"Is it not?" Peter's occasional and uncharacteristic excursions into archness were not among his most endearing habits. "Then I suppose I must have made a mistake."

"That I doubt."

"But you just said—"

"Never mind what I just said. Which one is it?"

He shifted his coffee to one side with the back of his hand and leaned closer over the table, suddenly excited, his eyes glowing. "I may be wrong, you understand. I'm not a hundred percent certain. In fact, I'd like your opinion before we go any further. It's right down your alley, Chris."

"My alley? Peter, I'm no forgery expert. You know that."

He chose to remain irritatingly silent, merely smiling enigmatically. It was all very much unlike him. I opened the exhibition catalog that Tony had given me to study on the airplane, and began to leaf through it, reading aloud.

"Hals, *Portrait of the Saint George Militia Company*, 1633; Reynolds, *Lady Raeburn and Her Son*, 1777; Corot, *Quai at Honfleur*, 1830. . . . This doesn't make any sense. Everything here has a provenance a page long."

"Really? Then it looks like I *am* wrong."

"Come on, Peter," I said in a rare flash of annoyance at him, "how can . . . Wait a minute! It's got to be from the new cache, doesn't it? They've been out of sight for forty years—the Rubens, the Titian, the Vermeer. . . ."

But he only smiled some more and shook his head, amused. "How unlike you to leap to conclusions, Chris."

I frowned. "But the others—there isn't one of them that hasn't been authenticated a dozen times."

"Surely it isn't necessary for me to point out to you that authenticity and authentication have not been invariably correlated where art is concerned. But that's beside the point."

He poured the last of the coffee from his *kännchen* and turned serious at last. "I apologize; I've been enjoying myself at your expense, haven't I? But what I found last week is so remarkable that . . . so fantastic . . . so . . ." For the first time that I could remember, the suave and articulate Peter was too excited to finish a sentence that he'd started. And if he'd really come upon a fake among the previously uncontested masterpieces of the Bolzano collection, I could hardly blame him.

"You're serious, then?" I said.

"Oh, certainly! And, truly, I haven't been trying to tease you." He collected himself, sipped his coffee, and smiled. "Well, maybe just a little. In any case, here's what I'd like: You'll need the next two days to get oriented, so just go ahead and do that. Then, after I come back, you and I will walk through the collection, and I'd like you simply to look it over and see if something doesn't strike you very, very peculiarly indeed. Really, I'd tell you more, but I want your unbiased opinion before we take it any further. Will you do that?"

"Of course, if that's what you want. Tell me one thing,

though. Are you suggesting that Claudio Bolzano himself is aware of this? That he's—"

"Perpetrating a fraud?" Peter looked scandalized. "Definitely not. I should say that of all the people in the world he's the last person likely to know about it. And his son is equally above suspicion—the scholarly Lorenzo, whom I believe you know."

"I'm not sure I understand," I said, understating greatly. "If you think Bolzano has a fake in his collection and he doesn't know it, don't you owe it to him to tell him?"

"Of course, but it isn't as simple as that. He's not very well, you know. He's been having a terrific time of it with gallstones, has finally had them out, and hasn't been having a very smooth recovery. I don't want to excite him until I'm absolutely sure of my facts. With your help, that should be only a few days more."

He finished his coffee reflectively. "You know, I just might call him from Frankfurt, though, and ask a pertinent question or two—in a subtle way, of course." He nodded to himself. "That might be a good idea." He dabbed at his lips with his napkin and tossed it on the table in a way that indicated lunch was over.

I was far from satisfied. "I don't understand why Tony didn't tell me about this."

"Possibly it seemed unimportant."

"Unimportant?"

"But he had nothing to tell, you see. I told him no more than I've told you—quite a bit less, actually, and only in passing. In fact, *no one* has any idea what I've found . . . what I think I've found." His eyes flashed briefly with private excitement. "I'll see you when I get back, and we'll go over it at length."

Like it or not, I had to settle for that. Peter left for Tegel Airport, and I took a taxi back to Tempelhof through the intervening miles of gray, blank-faced apartment buildings.

3

A driving, sleety rain had begun to fall by the time we reached the Platz der Luftbrücke. I gave the driver a ten-mark note and dashed under the elegant blue canopy that stretched from the curb to the building. Columbia House, U.S. Air Force Open Mess, it said in English, Tempelhof Central Airport.

I threaded my way between staggered rows of waist-high marigold-planters-cum-car-bomb-barriers, and approached the bullet-proof sliding glass doors for the second time that day. Fortunately, the same guard was still on duty, and he not only let me in, he saluted. Heady stuff for a mild-mannered thirty-four-year-old museum curator who'd been rejected by the army during Vietnam (heart murmur) and who'd had no dealings with the military since.

I was itching to see the show, of course, and I went directly to the Clipper Room, the big room on the ground floor where it was to be held, but there were no pictures, only a couple of carpenters nailing up partitions. One of them told me that the paintings were still in the storage room, and as far as he knew, they hadn't been uncrated yet, or then again maybe they had. I could find the storage room by taking the elevator to the basement and turning right.

The basement of Columbia House was a long, dreary, curving corridor with concrete-block walls. At its end was a battered but formidable steel door, once beige but now so nicked and dented that the orange undercoat showed rustily through the paint in a thousand places. In front of it a guard leaned casually against the wall. When he saw me, he straightened up, shifted the stubby black rifle slung barrel-down over his shoulder—an M-16 automatic, I've since learned—and watched with half-closed eyes as I came up.

I smiled confidently. "I'm Dr. Christopher Norgren, deputy director of the Plundered Past exhibition. I'd like to have a look inside, please."

This try at a command presence of my own was not wholly successful.

"ID," he said woodenly.

I sighed, doing my best to seem bored with this routine triviality, and held my breath as I handed him my pathetic yellow card.

He stared hard at it, turned it over to see the back, and then examined the front again, as if this were a type of object wholly unknown to him, unlike anything he'd ever seen before.

"Issued yesterday at Rhein-Main," I said. "Department of Defense prerogative."

This, whatever it meant, had its effect.

"Okey-doke," he said. He shifted his rifle a little farther around his shoulder and turned to operate the combination padlock. When it opened with a sharp click, he pushed the handle down with his clumsy farm boy's hand, leaned his shoulder against the metal door, and shoved.

The heavy door groaned over the concrete floor, and a weak shaft of light from the hallway slanted diagonally into the otherwise dark room. I could see some large picture crates standing on end, and I leaned to one side over his shoulder to get a better look at them as he pushed the door fully open against an inside wall. This was, after all, my first sight of the collection of masterpieces I was going to be responsible for.

It was a good thing I did, because it saved my life.

There was a hoarse, boarlike grunt, then a scraping noise, and from the darkness hurtled something that I thought in momentary confusion was some kind of vehicle rushing out at us. What it was was one of the crates, flung end over end through the doorway, so viciously that it splintered with a wrenching groan against the concrete-block wall of the corridor. Had I not been moving to the side, it would have struck me full in the face; as it was, it caught my right shoulder with enough force to whip me around and slam me face-first into the concrete.

The last time I'd seen stars, I had been fourteen years old, trying out the high-school trampoline. The first bounce had gone beautifully, but on the second I came down on the metal rim, smack on my nose. It broke then, and it broke now. (The crunch is audible.) The first time it happened, I passed out, and this time I came close. There was a sickly, growing dimness at the borders of my vision, like rose-colored ink spreading on a blotter. I felt my jaw go slack, my eyes begin to roll up, my cheek start to scrape down the rough, cold wall. But this time I managed to fight the darkness off. The pain helped—for a relatively insignificant organ, the nose is awfully well supplied with nerve endings.

Tears streaming from my eyes, blood from my nose, I pushed myself away from the wall and turned, blinking and queasy, to see the guard just inside the storage room, his back against the door, struggling with a man in blue workman's clothing. The man was short but frighteningly massive, built more like a gorilla than a human being; virtually neckless, with a huge chest and long arms as thick as thighs. One thick-wristed hand was on the M-16's barrel, the other on its stock, and he was leaning hard, pressing the rifle into the guard's throat. The guard, husky as he was, was helpless. Crimson-faced and gagging, he was flopping about like a Raggedy Ann doll, banging his elbows impotently against the door.

There was a second man too, no less evil-looking, with a face like a skull: tight, shiny skin; a long, fleshless mouth; hard, mean, bulging eyes. He was hovering to one side like a deadly mosquito seeking just the right place to bite. There was something flexible and metallic in his hand; it looked like the top ten or twelve inches of an automobile radio antenna.

I probably would have been petrified if I hadn't been too stunned to think clearly. Instead, I made for them, none too steady on my legs. Somehow I managed to get one hand on the rifle barrel, the other over the gorilla-man's chin, and tugged with all my strength, digging my fingers into the soft flesh of his mouth. For a moment the three of us strained soundlessly and almost motionlessly, as if locked in a multiple arm-wrestle. The only movement was a pathetic screwing-up of the guard's eyes in my direction, in a purpling and otherwise rigid face. Then, as I got my feet under me and leaned forward, I felt the gritty jaw twist away under my hand, felt the rifle barrel give just a little, so that the guard was able to turn his head to the side and suck in a strangled breath.

That was the high point. From there things slid rapidly downhill. Skull-face turned his attention from the guard to me, lashing out in a precise little movement with the antenna thing, snapping it like a tiny whip. It caught me on the outer bone of the right wrist. The pain was so astounding that I yelped and let go of No-neck's face. Another concise little movement and the antenna flicked my left wrist, same place. I gasped and let go of the rifle. The antenna rose again and quivered like a terrible dragonfly. I ducked quickly sideways to avoid it, to get under his arm and ram him in the chest with my shoulder.

That was the plan. As it happened, No-neck intervened. It was like being charged by a rhinoceros. He rammed me against the doorframe, got one clublike hand on the neck of my shirt, the other one tangled around my belt, and actually lifted me off the floor while I pawed at him with numbed hands.

At this point my memory loses its customary acuity, but I think he simply tossed me through the doorway and across the six-foot-wide corridor. I know I banged into the concrete wall a second time, just about where I'd hit it before, but backward this time.

Of the two impacts, I'd have to say the back-of-the-head experience was less painful, but only marginally.

Again the dimming vision, again the sickening pinpoints of lights, and again I worked hard to keep from going under. The floor was undulating under my feet, and it was all I could do to stay upright with the help of the wall. I forced my eyes to focus and saw a repetition of what I'd seen before: The guard was propped against the door, the M-16 jammed savagely into his throat, his fingers plucking weakly at the barrel, but no match for No-neck's powerful hands.

The other one hung to the side again, lifting the antenna thing, holding it poised and vibrating over the guard's head. I tried both to shout and to move, but nothing happened. The metal cracked against the guard's temple and his whole body jerked. I heard his heels rattle against the floor. No-neck flung the rifle clattering down the hallway, grasped the boy by the shoulders, and dispassionately rapped his head against the steel door. Instantly the uniformed body went flaccid and collapsed bonelessly into the corridor.

Skull-face stood in the shaft of light, seemingly studying me, considering whether I merited another application of the antenna, or perhaps worse. I was too woozy to do anything. What I remember thinking in a bemused way, in fact, was how remarkably much his raw, open mouth and hollow, malignant eyes made him look like the shrieking bug-eyed man on the bridge in *The Scream*, that nightmare on canvas by Edvard Munch.

I guess I didn't pose any immediate threat, because he decided to let me be. He slid noiselessly back into the darkness of the storage room and let his strong-man friend slam the thick door home. I still couldn't move, and while I continued to sag wretchedly against the wall I heard a bolt shoved into place on the other side of the door. Then a crash—a crate being knocked over?—and feet scraping over raw concrete, running up steps. Obviously there was a back way out of the storage room, maybe to the street. . . . Definitely to the street; an engine started up, followed by a lurching squeal as the car—truck, probably—jerked forward before the parking brake was released. Another roar of the engine and they were gone.

There didn't seem to be any pressing reason for me to stay on my feet, so I got slowly to my knees and lowered my head, gingerly shoving some wadded tissue into my nostrils to stop the bleeding. When I felt that I could dare to move away from the support of the wall, I crawled on my hands and knees to the guard and touched his shoulder. To my relief he stirred and moaned.

"Hoo," he said. "Hoo boy." He hauled himself to a sitting position against the wall and kneaded the back of his head, his eyes closed. "Jeez."

I stared into his face. "You all right?" I had the impression he was in better shape than I was.

My voice startled him. His eyes popped open to see my blood-smeared face a few inches from his own.

"Ock!" he said. "Jeez!"

"It's not as bad as it looks. Just a broken nose, I think." Just, indeed.

"Lean your head against the wall, man. You're gonna bleed to death." Frowningly solicitous, he put a hand on my forehead and gently tilted me back, beginning to take charge, which was fine with me. I had begun to tremble, which seemed to me a very reasonable reaction, considering.

"I better get on the brick," he said.

From a holster on his belt he produced a toy-size black radio with a stubby little antenna. "Bingo Five," he said into it, "this is Falcon Six. . . ."

I smiled groggily—did they really talk like that?—and then I must have blacked out, because the next thing I knew my eyes were closed and he was standing up, leaning over me. "They'll be along in a minute. Don't you worry, buddy, you'll be OK." ·

"Sure. Don't worry about me, I'll be fine." I was actually feeling a little better. The bleeding had stopped, and although my head hurt in a dozen places, the pain was dull and remote, as if it were in someone else's head. I couldn't breathe through my nose, but that was no surprise under the circumstances. My wrists, which had hurt so shockingly from those two crisp little blows, seemed to be all right, to my surprise; I had thought they were broken. I felt good enough, in fact, to try opening my eyes again.

I was looking directly at the shattered crate that lay at the base of the wall across from me. I forced my eyes open wider.

"Christ," I said softly.

"Yeah," the guard said, following my gaze. "You're damn lucky."

But I wasn't thinking about how it would have been if the heavy wooden container had caught me more directly. I was looking at what was inside it.

The crate itself, perhaps four feet by three, and seven or eight inches wide, leaned crazily against the wall, as ripped and twisted as if it had been glued together out of popsicle sticks. Half-in, half-out of it was an ornate gilt picture frame of the Italian Renaissance, fractured and sprung; and within this there was an age-stiffened, yellowed drawing that had buckled and cracked into several pieces. Even upside down and mangled as it was, the style of its artist was instantly recognizable.

Michelangelo, God help us. *Michelangelo*.

Such is the flinty soul of the art curator that that crumpled, broken drawing produced an icier clutch inside my chest than anything that had gone before.

I moved to it, again on my hands and knees. Michelangelo, all right; a fine, careful study for the *The Battle of Cascina*, the great fresco designed for Florence's Palazzo Vecchio but never executed. All that remained were a few of these rightly celebrated studies. This one was a pencil drawing, highlighted with white here and there, of a nude male caught bathing, twisting in surprise, every visible muscle taut and satiny, like carved, polished marble. It was Michelangelo at his most powerful, sculpting with pencil.

And yet, somehow ... I frowned, trying to focus my eyes better. What was it ... ?

With a noise like an armed invasion, two airmen came clumping excitedly down the long corridor, and then a third. Behind them scampered a slight sandy-haired man in a tweedy suit, hard-pressed to keep up.

"Oh my,". he said breathlessly. "What's happened? Oh dear Lord."

The guard explained, quickly and efficiently, calling him "sir."

"And who is this ... person?" the sandy-haired man asked, looking down at me with his nose wrinkled in distaste.

I spoke from a sitting position at his feet. "Chris Norgren. I'm—"

"Christopher Norgren? You're Dr. Norgren? Good heavens. Oh, *really*." He said it the way he might have if I'd embarrassed us both by showing up for a cocktail party on the wrong night.

Meanwhile, I was looking at the drawing again, dazedly trying to figure out what it was about it that bothered me. I twisted my head nearly upside down so I could see it right side up. That was a mistake. The blood thumped painfully at the back of my nose, and I quickly jerked upright. That didn't feel too good, either. The picture swam and blurred. I leaned back against the wall and closed my eyes again. There was a crust on my lips, and my shirt front was sodden; blood, no doubt, but I had no wish to see. My head felt as if it were pumped to bursting with Jell-O. I considered blacking out again, and I think I did.

As if they were coming from a moving echo chamber, the voices around me floated hollowly back into range.

"Yes, sir, I just had a look." That was one of the airmen. "I can't tell if they got away with anything. The guard out in back is out cold. I called for a medic. This poor bugger could use one, too."

That's me, I reflected with distant interest. This poor bugger.

"Yes, of course. Certainly." The mild voice of the small man. "I believe he's unconscious."

"Not unconscious," I mumbled, suddenly figuring out what it was about the drawing. I waved my hand vaguely toward the smashed crate. "The picture . . . there's something the matter with it."

The ensuing silence was so long that I tried opening my eyes again. Things were wavery but not too bad. The sandy-haired man, who was studying the drawing judiciously, turned his attention to me, back to the wrecked drawing, and then back to me once more. He pursed his lips.

"So it would seem."

"No, I mean the drawing itself. Look at the pencil lines. See how they glisten?"

"Glisten?" he said.

"Yes, glisten." I rubbed the back of my neck, annoyed at having to look up at him from the floor, but not about to try standing. "That means there was graphite in the pencil."

"Graphite."

"Yes, damn it, graphite."

"Ah, graphite, yes."

"Look . . . they didn't start using graphite in Europe until the end of the sixteenth century. Before then pencils were made of lead alloyed with tin."

"Tin," he said. "Of course. I see, yes. Tin."

"Listen . . ." My voice began to rise a little. I did not enjoy being humored by this irritatingly bland little man. "Don't you see? Michelangelo worked on the Cascina studies around 1500. He *died* in 1564—which means he had to have drawn this posthumously."

I thought that was pretty good for a man in my condition, but he only said in that dry, patient, maddening way: "Posthumously."

"Goddammit," I snapped with as much emphasis as I thought my nasal passages would bear, "it's a *forgery*—a *fake*!"

If he says "Forgery," I thought, I am going to bite him on the knee.

He was saved, however, by the appearance of two teams of medics hurrying down the corridor with folded stretchers on wheels. "Over here, please, you men," he called, wiggling a finger at them. Then he looked down again at me.

"Well, of course it's a fake," he said calmly. "What else would it be?"

4

I think I ought to say at this point that this kind of thing doesn't usually happen to me. I'm an art historian, as you've gathered, curator of Renaissance and Baroque painting at a major San Francisco museum. And despite what you may have read about art curators, I don't find myself habitually entangled in international theft or deceit on the grand scale, and certainly not in murder. It's not that I'm particularly unadventurous or fainthearted, you understand, but thrilling-chases-through-the-capitals-of-Europe are things I read about on long flights, not things I do.

Not until lately.

"Well, of course it's a fake. What else would it be?"

Much as I wished to pursue that laconic rejoinder, I had to let it pass. The medics, with quiet speed, did several things to my face—some hot, some cold—stuck a needle into my arm, and settled me unresisting onto the gurney. I was trundled off down the long hallway trying to focus on the questions that were already beginning to flutter off out of reach. Could I really have stumbled on Peter's forgery by having it literally thrown in my face? It seemed unlikely. And how did that tweedy little man know it was a forgery? Peter had said no one knew. Was there a second fake? If so, why hadn't Peter mentioned it? And . . . and . . .

It was too much to think about. Instead, I found myself sleepily and contentedly absorbed in the neon ceiling lights whizzing by like the lights of local train stations seen from a night express, and in the warm, lovely sensation of giving myself entirely into the competent, responsible hands of others.

I was at the air-force hospital for two days, much of it passed in a dopey haze that I barely remember, while white-coated people took X rays, stuck more needles in me, and prodded me with cheerful insistence. "Does this hurt? No? . . . Does it hurt now? . . . *Now?*" Sooner or later they got their way, and then left me to doze until the next one turned up.

At one point—sometime during the first afternoon, I think—I wafted out of a soft, drugged haze to hear someone greet me in what seemed to be Japanese.

"Dr. Norgren? Hariguchi."

"Hariguchi," I replied sleepily, and forced up leaden eyelids. A thin, bearded, somewhat shabby, and altogether occidental man was in a chair at my bedside. He looked at me quizzically for a moment, and then he spoke again.

"Harry," he said. "Gucci. My name. Like the shoes."

"Oh. Hi."

"Hi. How're you doing?"

"Not bad. Who're you?"

"Harry," he began again. "Gucci. Like the—"

"No, I mean . . . I mean . . ." I'd forgotten what I meant.

"I'm with OSI—Office of Special Investigations." He put a card in front of my eyes and held it patiently there for me to read, which I blearily pretended to do, although it could have been his Safeway check-cashing card for all I knew. Or cared.

"They said you'd be able to answer some questions. OK?"

"Sure, if they said so." For myself, I doubted it. I felt as if I were floating ten feet off the ground, bumping lazily against the ceiling like a helium-filled balloon.

"Great." From a pocket in his shapeless, shawl-collared cardigan he produced a small dog-eared notebook stuffed with protruding bits of paper and held together with a thick rubber band. He touched the tip of a mechanical pencil to his tongue. "All right. For starters, can you tell me anything about those two bozos in the storage room? The guard never got a good look at them."

"The two—"

"What'd they look like?"

"Oh. Pretty ugly."

I think he repressed a sigh. Things were going to be harder than he'd anticipated. "Anything else? Were they tall? Short? White? Black? Did they say anything? Call each other by name? Were they skinny? Fat?"

That took concentration, and it was a while before I replied. "Uh, white. Definitely white. And they didn't say anything. And ... uh ... what was the question?"

"Tall? Short?" He was very good-humored, very pleasant, not at all impatient.

"One of them was short. But husky. Strong as a gorilla. Built like a, like a ..." I was beginning to drift off again. The sheets were luscious: cool and clean and smooth.

"How short? Five feet? Five two?"

"Mm ... maybe five seven, five eight. Little guy. But strong. Mean. Dangerous." I barely knew what I was saying.

"Moderate height," Gucci said dryly, writing in his notebook and rearranging his five feet six inches or so in the metal chair.

"Sorry," I said. "No offense."

He laughed. "What about the other guy?"

"I don't know. Mean face. He had some kind of little steel whip—"

"I know." He grinned. "Smarts like hell, doesn't it?"

"It sure does. What was it?"

"It's called a sipo; a thin, flexible steel spring with a weighted knob on the end. You carry it telescoped, but it opens in a flash. Doesn't do much real damage, but if you know how to use it, it can really hurt. A single flick can make a guy helpless. So they tell me."

"You've been correctly informed."

"We found it outside on the stairs. No usable latent prints. Made here in Germany, but you can get them in the

States from those lousy paramilitary magazines. Fourteen dollars and ninety-five cents."

"Mmm."

"Hey, don't go to sleep on me. Did you notice anything else about them? Glasses, wristwatch, ring? Unusual shoes?"

"Unusual . . ." In my fuddled state, it struck me as funny, and I'm afraid I snickered. "No, I didn't see any unusual shoes." My voice seemed to be someone else's, coming from a long way off. I giggled some more, I'm sorry to say, and let my eyes close. I was floating slowly up into a gauzy, warm, welcoming mist.

"Mister . . . ?" I said, and started at the sound of my own voice. "I seem to be drifting off."

"That's OK; no problem. And make it Harry."

"OK, um, Harry . . . I wanted to ask you something."

"Sure, shoot."

But I couldn't remember. I tried halfheartedly to claw my way out of the fog, but I was sailing away, no longer bobbing against the ceiling, but far up out of reach. "Oh . . . yeah—the pictures—did they . . ." I drifted and dozed for what seemed like a long time, but when I squeezed my eyes briefly open again, he was still there, smiling patiently.

"Did they get away with anything?" I managed to ask. Whatever he answered, I never heard it.

A couple of mornings later I was pronounced fit to leave the hospital. The verdict, delivered by a birdlike, whimsical Indian doctor, was that I had gotten off lightly: an "insignificant" concussion and a fracture of the right nasal bone— "Just as well left unset, in my opinion, unless you cannot bear the idea of a small, mm, ah, kink in your nose." (I could bear it.) Also two bruised ribs and a few abrasions of little consequence (to Dr. Gupta). Thanks to a sturdy constitution and two codeine tablets every four hours, I felt remarkably fine.

I looked better than I had any right to look, too. My face, though puffy and amusingly colored around the eyes, was well on its way back to its usual appearance—which, I have been told, is nice but not unusually so.

By Bev, in fact. Right after the first time we made love, in fact. We had been lying side by side, on the floor, as it happened, and she had been relaxedly studying my face, running a finger over my lips, that sort of thing.

"Do girls generally tell you you're sexy?" she asked.

"Many times each day. It gets pretty boring."

"Well, you're not." She giggled. "Your face, I mean. It's, you know, a nice guy's face—open, pleasant . . . but not very remarkable."

"Too kind."

"No, I'm serious. You look like the kind of guy a girl feels safe with. What I mean is, you don't radiate this animal sexuality, the way some guys do. You're not insulted, are you? I'm just being honest, Chris."

So she was. I suppose I should have known then that things weren't going to work out in the end.

By 10:00 A.M. I was in my room at Columbia House. A message for me to call Corporal Jessick, the army clerk assigned to the show, had been left for me at the reception desk, and as soon as I'd made myself a cup of coffee in the electric percolator on a shelf over the bathroom sink, I dialed 2100.

"Dr. Norgren? Hey, I'm glad you're out, sir. I heard what happened. That's *awful*! How're you feeling?"

"Fine, thanks."

"That's wonderful. Listen, Colonel Robey flew in from Heidelberg this morning. He's been trying to get ahold of you at the hospital—"

"I checked out at nine."

"—but they checked you out at nine, so then he tried to call you in your room here at the O Club, but you weren't there."

"I just got here this minute."

"You must have just got there."

"This minute," I said. "Did he leave a message?"

"He wants to know if you feel able to make a meeting of senior staff at eleven o'clock."

"Sure."

"Great. It's in Room 1102, a couple of doors down from the Clipper Room."

I made another cup of coffee and wandered restlessly around the room—suite, actually: big well-furnished living room, writing area, bedroom, well-stocked minibar in the refrigerator. It was all comfortable enough, but I was at loose ends. I'd been cooped up for two days, and what I needed was a walk in the cold air, not a sit-down meeting. For a while I stood at the window, looking grumpily down on the leafless trees, the gray-green plaza, and the soaring, three-pronged monument to the airlift. An intelligent, evocative piece of work, that monument; and that is high praise from someone who sneers at abstract sculpture on principle.

There was still half an hour before the meeting, and I didn't see why I couldn't use it for a few turns around the plaza. I drained the coffee, took my second codeine dose of the day, and went downstairs.

Ten minutes in the cold was all it took to drive home the fact that I still had some mending to do. In less time than that, I was glad to take advantage of one of the benches to sit down and turn my face up into the pale sunlight, like the convalescent I was. Columbia House was directly in front of me, with the rest of the huge Tempelhof complex angling away from it, seemingly into infinity. I'd learned something about Tempelhof by now, and I knew it was one of the most extraordinary structures on earth, the entire vast warren all being under one roof and therefore making up the third-largest building in the world. (The first is the Pentagon; what the second is I don't know, but if I find out, I'll pass it along.)

It was built by Hitler in the early, heady days of the Thousand-Year Reich to look from the air like a colossal, stylized German eagle: noble head, outspread wings half a mile wide, cruel talons, and all. Columbia House—all four sizable, curving stories of it—constituted the eagle's right foot. Which was why it curved.

It had been a good idea of Robey's to choose it as the site of the exhibition's German showing. Berliners, ordinarily not sentimental folk, had never forgotten how the transports of the 1948–49 airlift, loaded with food and coal, had roared in to land on the adjacent strip every ten minutes through a vicious winter, and the place was still special to them.

The codeine had taken full hold by now, so that I was able to forget about the pain for a few minutes at a time. Sitting there in the thin, cold Berlin sunshine, in fact, I was feeling better than I had in many months. Bev, Rita Dooling, and the gloomy, silent house off Divisadero were all a long way off, on a different planet, and what was going on here was a lot more exciting than budget reallocations and management-by-objectives reviews. And at the cost of a "small kink" in my nose, I had acquired a story that would carry me through many a cocktail party to come.

This surge of well-being lasted until I walked under the blue canopy and up to the glass doors of Columbia House. The guard—a new one—sat at the entry desk coldly watching me.

"ID," he said.

With a rising sense of déjà vu, I removed the yellow card from my wallet and held it out. He wouldn't even take it, but only looked at it contemptuously and shook his head.

"Uh-uh. No banana."

"But I just walked out of here a few minutes ago—right by you. All I did was take a walk around the plaza."

"Look, mac, I don't give a shit about people going out; I watch 'em coming in. Now, you got a real ID, or just this cockamamy thing?"

Apparently I had not caught him on one of his better days. For that matter, I was not feeling overly civil myself. This ID business was wearing thin. Who was this callow twenty-year-old to deny me entrance when I had legitimate business here? Had *he* just spent two miserable days in the hospital? Had *he* broken his nose in the service of his country? Why was I being put through these continuing expressions of distrust?

"This card," I said with the quiet, telling dignity of a Peter van Cortlandt, "this goddamn card has gotten me into this goddamn building three goddamn times—"

"Not by me—" He straightened up suddenly, staring over my shoulder, and saluted stiffly.

"Sir!"

Two men carrying attaché cases approached the desk from the lobby. One of them, a civilian, looked familiar, but it wasn't until he pursed his lips in a prim but amicable little smile that I recognized him: the dry, tweedy little man whose greeting in the corridor a couple of days before had been "Who is this ... person?"

Today he was more friendly. "Good morning, Dr. Norgren. I'm very happy to see you up and about."

The other man was in an army uniform with silver eagles on the shoulders; a colonel. "So you're Norgren," he said with a slow smile.

The guard was still holding his rigid salute. "All he's got is a USAREUR privileges card, sir, and we were told—"

The colonel off-handedly returned the guard's salute. "Oh, he's OK, Newsome, you can trust me." He held a hand out to me. "I'm Robey. Happy to know you."

Colonel Mark Robey, the man in charge of The Plundered Past, was a distinct surprise. Gifted as I am with a remarkable ability to stereotype at the drop of a hat, I had conjured up someone lean and silver-templed, with something of the Lincolnesque about him: craggy, taciturn, and clothed with authority—your average army colonel, in other words, with maybe a little bit of art curator thrown in. But the hand that was thrust out to me belonged to a drowsy, soft-voiced man, comfortably overweight, with a pleasant, easygoing face, a dreamy gaze, and nothing at all of the flinty-eyed warrior about him.

"How are you feeling?" he asked. "Pretty much recovered?"

There is a distinctive and endearing V-shaped smile that

can be found on Archaic Greek and Etruscan figures—
gentle, lethargic, and (in a nice way) not quite all there. Art
people refer to it as the Archaic smile. Mark Robey had the
first live Archaic smile I'd ever seen.

"Pretty much, thanks, Colonel."

"Mark," he said. "Call me Mark, Chris. Let's see, I think
you've already met Edgar Gadney, although from what he
told me I'm not sure you'd remember. He's responsible for
logistics and day-to-day administration. We'd be lost without him."

Gadney nodded briefly. He was holding my ID card between thumb and forefinger, like a fussy matron sipping tea
in a drawing-room comedy. Around his neck was a thin,
silvery lanyard attached to a pair of glasses through which
he was examining the card with meticulous care. Mild
though he appeared, he was unmistakably vexed. He wag-
gled the offending card and frowned.

"This is very bad, very bad. It will have to go." He was
as solemn as a surgeon telling me my original-equipment
heart would need to be replaced with a Jarvik. "Form one
seventy-four is not by any stretch of the imagination an appropriate card. You *should* have one-dash-ten-eighteen."

"Sorry." I spread my hands apologetically.

"Lack of proper identification," he said severely, "can
lead to no end—"

Robey, whose attention had wandered off somewhere,
now rejoined us. "I think Chris gets the message," he said
pleasantly. "Do you suppose you could fix him up with a
one-dash-whatever?"

Gadney compressed his lips to consider the wide-ranging
implications of this question. "Well, I don't see why not."

"Thanks, Mr. Gadney," I said, "I'll appreciate that. So
will the guards."

Gadney took his eyes from the card and lifted them to
mine. "Egad," he said.

I waited, but only silence followed. "Pardon?"

"Call me Egad," he said improbably. He removed the
glasses and let them hang from his neck, continuing to re-

gard me somewhat uncertainly. "You're rather young to be a curator, aren't you?"

People say that to me a lot. I'm not that young, really; thirty-four isn't an unheard-of age for the job. What surprises them, I think, is that I just don't have a very curatorial look. Art curators, they think—and they're generally right—look and sound like Peter van Cortlandt or Anthony Whitehead: urbane, suave, aristocratic. Many are second- or third-generation collectors or curators. I guess I look like what I am, which is a second-generation hodge-podge of Swedish, German, Russian, and Irish. My father was a machinist with a night-school diploma, fingertips that had black grease permanently ground into the whorls, and an objet-d'art collection consisting of eighteen Indian-head pennies and a dozen dubious fossils from a 1949 trip to Arizona. I got my degrees at San Jose State (night classes, like Dad) and Berkeley, not at Yale (as Peter did) or Harvard (Tony), or even Stanford.

In museum circles I had often seen and quailed under that doubtful look when I was introduced as San Francisco's curator of Renaissance and baroque. And even under Gadney's inoffensive scrutiny, I confess to a small stab of insecurity. Way down deep, you see, I'm not so sure that I really am a bona-fide art curator, not just a fraud who's picked up the jargon. Art, after all, doesn't have a lot you can hang your hat on, and there are times when I *know* I don't know what the hell I'm talking about. (I'm still waiting for someone to explain neoplastic constructivism to me, for example, and I've lectured on the damn thing!) Never have I heard my self-assured colleagues confess such uncertainties, and in my dark hours I sometimes wonder if they—the Peters, the Tonys—were simply born to the field and I was not.

I murmured something noncommittal to Gadney as we walked through the lobby, and then asked Robey the question I'd asked Harry Gucci in the hospital.

"Did they get away with anything from the storage room?"

"Nope, everything's accounted for, thanks to you. You

broke in on them before they got properly started. The only thing damaged was that picture they heaved through the door. Aside from your nose, of course. But we can repair that." He smiled sympathetically. "The picture, I mean."

I nodded ruefully. "That's good, anyway. But about that drawing . . ." I turned to Gadney. "Something has been bothering the hell out of me. Down there, in the basement, when I said that Michelangelo was a forgery, you said—I thought you said—that of course it was."

"Of course I did."

"I don't understand. Why 'of course'? And how did you know about it?"

"How did I—" He stared at me in bland astonishment. "You don't know? I put the entire episode down to your understandably confused state of mind at the time. I assumed you knew all about the copies."

There was a discreet hint of reproach, as if I'd failed to do my homework. "Along with the twenty genuine works of art, signor Bolzano has lent us twelve copies of pieces that were looted from his collection by the Nazis but never recovered. The idea is to publicize them, you see, in hopes that they might be recognized, and that information on where they really are might turn up. The Michelangelo sketch is one of them."

I had, as a matter of fact, done my homework, and I knew about the copies. But that didn't explain it. Anyway, I didn't like abandoning the idea that I'd already solved Peter's mysterious puzzle.

"Yes," I said, "but this wasn't just a copy; this was a forgery—an original pencil drawing, with the paper smoked and crisped to look old—all very expertly done." I shook my head firmly. "No, this was a painstaking fake, a forgery—done to mislead."

It was Robey, with his disconcerting tendency to wander abstractedly in and out of conversations, who replied as we turned left down a curving corridor. "I don't know about all that, but I think we can be pretty sure it's not in the show to mislead anyone. Don't you know about Bolzano, Chris?"

I did, of course; quite a bit, although I'd never met him.
The venerable Claudio Bolzano was a celebrated art con-
noisseur, a welcome buyer at Sotheby and Christie's, with
a vast collection of old masters and moderns on the walls
of his villa in Florence and on loan to the great public galleries of Europe. Why he should have anything to do with
a forged Michelangelo I had no idea, and I said so.

"Because," Gadney said, "after the war he began to de-
spair of ever recovering all that the Nazis had taken, and he
replaced many of them with copies. In some cases he bought
existing copies, some of them several hundred years old—"

"And very probably painted as forgeries," I persisted.

"Originally, possibly so, but now openly acknowledged as
copies. He also commissioned a number of modern copies, I
believe. There were photographs available, of course, so it
wasn't difficult. What he wanted, naturally, were *good* copies, as near to the originals as possible. And that's just what
he has."

"All right, but I still don't get the point."

"Neither do I," murmured Robey, ambling along beside
us, "when it comes right down to it."

"You don't?" Gadney said to both of us. He lifted his
tweedy shoulders in a faint shrug as we stopped before a
closed door. "I believe I do. It's simply that he wanted to
be surrounded by his beloved art pieces. If he couldn't have
the real ones, he wanted to have the next best thing. I think
I can understand his motivation."

I wasn't sure that I did. Knowledgeable art collectors do
not generally go out and buy copies of *The Night Watch* or
View of Toledo, no matter how much they covet the originals.
For a serious collector to surround himself with copies would
be like a serious dog lover surrounding himself with the
stuffed carcases of his pets. Superficially they might look the
same, but they aren't very satisfying in the long run.

"Well, Chris," Robey said, reaching for the door handle,
"time for you to meet the rest of the team."

"Gird thy loins," I thought I heard Gadney mutter as we
went in.

5

Whatever else he might be, Mark Robey was a calm and orderly man who took things as they came.

"I know the break-in is on everyone's mind," he announced dreamily, seated at the head of a folding table and gazing through the tall French doors at the bare trees and wintry courtyard behind Columbia House, "but let's just start with our agenda as Egad prepared it. Someone from OSI should be along in a while and we can talk about the break-in then. What's the first item, Egad?"

"Reception protocol," Gadney said promptly.

And so, under Robey's equable, absentminded leadership, we spent an hour on who should and who shouldn't be invited to the preview reception two weeks away, much as we might have done at the San Francisco County Museum under similar circumstances. There was little for me to contribute, so I spent the time sipping strong, fragrant German coffee and learning about my new colleagues.

There were two of them besides Robey and Gadney, and I would be lying if I didn't admit that one of them got most of my attention. This was a vibrant, extremely attractive woman of twenty-eight or twenty-nine who had something cogent or interesting—usually both—to say whenever she opened her mouth, which is not easy when the subject is reception protocol. She also had lovely, intelligent eyes that were as close to violet as eyes can be, glorious honey-colored hair, a healthy toothpaste-ad smile, and a pair of silver captain's bars on each blue-clad shoulder.

I had no ready stereotype for female air-force captains,

but if I had, it wouldn't have been anything like Anne Greene. Robey had introduced her as having been lent by the air force to serve as "my adjutant and our intra-command liaison," and I had said, "Ah," as if I'd known what it meant.

The other person was Earl Flittner, a large, untidy civilian who was the show's technical director. With a small staff to assist him, he was responsible for physical details—exhibition layout, lighting, temperature and humidity, and so on—and for packing and unpacking. This may sound like semiskilled labor, but it isn't. It's esoteric, highly technical work. Crating and shipping thirty-five million dollars' worth of fragile, irreplaceable works of art is not the same thing as wrapping a box of brownies to send to Aunt Vivian. Moreover, the skill and taste of the technical director have made or broken many a show.

Flittner was one of the best, on loan from the National Gallery. I had met him a couple of years before when he had accompanied a show of High Renaissance wood sculpture to San Francisco, but he'd been surly and contentious from the start, and I had stayed out of his way. Now, when Robey introduced us, he said bluntly that he didn't remember me at all (which didn't make me like him a whole lot more), and he sat restlessly through the meeting, smoking cigarette after cigarette, not saying much, merely twisting his long mouth from time to time in a sour expression that sometimes seemed to indicate impatience with Robey's running of the meeting, sometimes dissatisfaction with the exhibition as a whole, and sometimes a universal and undiscriminating misanthropy.

We were still deep in the intricacies of protocol when the door opened and closed, snapping me out of a near-doze.

"Ah," Robey said, looking up from some woolgathering of his own, "come in. Let's see, I think some of you have met Major, uh . . ."

"Gucci. Like the shoes."

"Did you say, er, 'Major'?" Gadney asked.

"That's right," Harry said with a smile. "I'm just lucky. They don't make me wear a monkey suit."

Gadney's surprise was understandable. Harry looked about as much like a major as I did a curator. He was wearing the same baggy, gray, shawl-collared cardigan he'd had on at the hospital, shapeless brown pants, and loafers that had never seen polish. With pennies in them. The bulky sweater made him look not bigger but smaller than he was, and shabby besides; and a slight stoop made him seem frail and scholarly. His short, gray-splotched beard was neatly trimmed at the neck but grew unchecked up his cheeks, giving him a gaunt, vaguely rabbinical air.

"I never knew you could have a beard in the army," Flittner muttered rudely to the tabletop.

"Sure," Harry said pleasantly, "if it's for medical reasons. I got shot in the face a couple of years ago in Athens and I couldn't shave for a while. I forgot to tell 'em when it healed, and they forgot to tell me to shave."

There was a thick silence as he shambled across the room. Even Flittner had the decency to look embarrassed.

Harry flopped down in the chair next to Robey. "No thanks," he replied to the offer of coffee. "I don't drink it. Wouldn't mind some of that mineral water, though."

Robey passed him a small green bottle of Appolinaris. Harry poured it into a glass and took a long drink while he looked from face to face around the table with sharp, smiling eyes.

"Hey, Chris, glad to see you up. How's the old schnozz?"

"The old schnozz is fine, thanks. The old head's still a little fuzzy."

He laughed, emptied the rest of the bottle into his glass, and wiped a drop of moisture from his beard with the back of a finger. "Well, let me set your minds at ease. First, as some of you know, we found the truck they used. It was on base, in the pool lot behind the education center. The four missing crates were all in it." His eyes lit on me again. "What's so surprising, Chris?"

"I didn't realize they'd gotten away with anything."

"Oh yeah. None of the originals; only four of the copies." He took out his bulging little notebook and snapped the rubber band off it, letting it roll up around his wrist. "Let's see . . ." He began to read aloud: "One van Gogh—"

A corner of Flittner's unkempt mustache lifted in a faint sneer. *"Van Gukh."*

"Really?" Harry said.

"V'n *Khakh*," Gadney corrected mildly, eliciting a glare from Flittner. "I believe that's closer to the Dutch." With a finger, he delicately brushed at his own tidy, pale mustache.

"Well, thanks," Harry said brightly. "Thanks a lot. I'll remember that. Van Hah."

"Also a Cranach, a Vermeer, and a Poussin," Gadney said, pronouncing carefully, no doubt for Flittner's benefit. "All of them having considerable value, copies or not. Are any of them damaged?"

"We haven't looked at them yet, but the crates are all OK."

"Then don't worry about the paintings," Flittner said.

"What about the two men?" Anne Greene asked. "Have they been caught?"

"No," Harry said, "and to be honest we don't have a clue. Obviously, they got on base without any problem, so it looks like they had forged IDs."

Robey smiled. "Maybe that's what you ought to try, Chris."

"Not at all," Gadney said primly. "I'll have a proper card for him before the day is out."

"Why did they want to get on the base in the first place?" I asked Harry. "And why leave the truck there? Why didn't they just drive away with it?"

It was Anne who answered. "Maybe you don't understand the layout here yet, Dr. Norgren. Columbia House fronts on the street, but it forms part of the perimeter of Tempelhof. The only way to get a truck around to the back of the building, where the storage room is, is to drive onto the base."

"That's exactly right," Harry said, "and that's exactly what they did. They got hold of a beer truck authorized to deliver on base, drove it around to the courtyard behind this building, knocked out the outside guard with what we think was an electronic stun gun, then chloroformed him, and finally cut through the door with some kind of laser tool. The back door's down in the stairwell, so there wasn't anybody to see."

"Stun gun, laser tool," Robey said in his vague, musing way. "Seems like pretty up-to-date technology. They must be professionals."

"Oh yeah, for sure." Harry drank some more mineral water, tossing it into his mouth like a slug of whiskey. "When Chris scared them off, they didn't dare go tearing back out through the gate in a Schultheiss beer truck. So they left it in a protected corner of the lot, with the paintings, and as far as we know they just walked out the gate." He held out his hands, palms up. "That's all we know."

"You have no idea who might be behind this?" Gadney asked.

Harry shook his head. "As my British pals like to say, we're pursuing our inquiries. We're in touch with Interpol—they keep a file of international art thieves: MOs, connections, and so on. So far, nothing."

Flittner, slumped gracelessly in his chair, sighed gustily, shaking out a match he'd used to light still another cigarette. The first two fingers of his left hand were the color of tobacco. "You don't need Interpol," he mumbled into his chest. "It was an inside job."

The rest of us looked at him.

"It stands to reason, doesn't it?" he growled, as if we were arguing with him. "They knew just where the paintings were stored, didn't they? They were scheduled to be in the storage room for less than twenty-four hours, but they knew anyway. And they knew exactly where the storage room was, and that it had a back door, and how to *get* to the back door. That's not exactly public knowledge. It's somebody in the damn army."

Gadney shook his head. "No, I'm afraid I can't agree with that, Earl. If it was, er, an inside job, they'd never have bothered with the copies."

Robey, staring at the ceiling, hands clasped behind his neck, drifted back into the conversation. "That's an interesting point, Earl. They couldn't very well have been insiders, could they?" He turned thoughtful eyes on Harry. "Or professionals either. Pros wouldn't fool around with the fakes, would they? Not with the real things sitting right there."

Anne shook her head. "That isn't necessarily so. Everything was still packed up. How could they tell what was in each crate? And," she said, turning to Flittner, "the copies were all at the back of the room near the outside door, isn't that right?"

"So?"

"Well, then, they probably just started nearest the back door; that would be the easiest way. I imagine they were going to take everything. There weren't that many crates."

"That could very well be," Gadney said approvingly. "In any case, it strongly supports my position that inside knowledge was not involved. After all, the acquisition number of each painting is clearly stenciled on its crate. Surely anyone connected with the show would be familiar with the numbering system, and would never have touched the reproductions."

I put in my two cents' worth. "I don't think *that's* necessarily true, either. From what I saw of the storage room, it was stuffed to bursting with crates. Even if those guys understood the numbering, there wasn't enough room to walk around looking for the right stencils. If I'd been stealing them, I'd have done what Anne said—start near the back door and keep going till I had them all. It would have been faster than trying to pick and choose."

This not only made sense to me but gave me the chance to agree with Anne.

"I still say it was an inside job," grumbled Flittner through a dense cloud of smoke pouring from mouth, nostrils, and—so it seemed—ears.

"And I," Gadney said, seizing the gauntlet, "say it was not."

To display the depth of his conviction, he placed his cup in its saucer with an audaciously audible clink. He and Flittner, I had noticed earlier, rarely missed an opportunity to differ. This was one of the few times Gadney had held his own.

Harry had been listening alertly, his hand tugging at his beard or sometimes at his hair, his black eyes jumping from speaker to speaker. "Well, well," he said, "that's really interesting. I'm glad to have your ideas."

"Ha, ha," Flittner commented.

"No, I mean it," Harry said.

"I have another idea," Gadney ventured.

Predictably, Flittner sneered. Or maybe he didn't. Some people have smile lines permanently implanted on their faces, and some have frown lines. Flittner had sneer lines, as if he'd done it too often and now his mouth was permanently set.

"Yeah?" Harry said to Gadney with interest. "What?"

"I wonder if it's occurred to anyone that the Heinrich-Schliemann-Gründung might have had a hand in this?"

I leaned inquisitively toward him. "The . . ."

He didn't hear me, but Anne, sitting next to me, did. She leaned over, close enough so that I smelled her scent: citrus and citrus blossoms, faint but ravishing. "Die Heinrich-Schliemann-Gründung. It means—"

"Ich spreche deutsch," I said crisply, cutting her off in midsentence and midsmile. Her clear eyes widened momentarily, but she wasn't any more surprised than I was. What, I wondered, did I have to be curt about? And why would I want to put off a sensational-looking, single female (no ring, anyway) who was trying to be friendly? I had no idea.

Anyway, die Heinrich-Schliemann-Gründung obviously meant the Heinrich Schliemann Foundation—whatever that meant.

"Heinrich Schliemann?" I asked Gadney.

Anne had another try. "He was a German archaeologist—"

Incredibly, I did it again. "I know who Heinrich Schliemann was," I snapped, regretting it instantly; and I'm sorry to say that it sounded as snotty as it looks.

This time she drew stiffly back. "Of course you'd know, Dr. Norgren," she said, coolly polite. "Forgive me; that was silly of me."

"No," I said, "not at all." I meant to be contrite, but it's hard to say "Not at all" without a touch of the regal. Hard for me, anyway. It was the sort of thing Peter said frequently. "That is," I bumbled on, "I know who Schliemann was, but I don't have the foggiest" —I sounded more like Peter with every word— "idea what he could have to do with . . ."

I hesitated invitingly, but she had been twice burned, and she wasn't having any more, and who could blame her? It was Robey who responded.

"Hm?" he said. "What? Schliemann?" He slowly tamped tobacco into a blackened pipe. "Well, you know how he had all that trouble with the Turkish government, a hundred years back or so, about his excavations at Troy? How they wouldn't let him take his finds out of Turkey and back to Germany?"

I nodded.

"Well, this group named themselves after him because they don't want to see Germany 'cheated' again. They say that whatever the Nazis took during the war shouldn't have been given back, and they're talking about a formal claim—a suit on behalf of the German people—on the three paintings from the Hallstatt cave. They don't see why Bolzano should get them back."

"Incredible," I said, the first sensible comment I'd made in a while.

"What's so incredible about it?" Flittner said abruptly. "The rules of war. How much art would be in the Louvre if Napoleon hadn't raped the rest of Europe? To the victors belong the spoils. What's the difference in this case?"

Gadney lifted his eyes and tossed his head minutely, as if he had borne this sort of thing more times than any human being should have to. But he sat in stoic silence.

"I think there is a difference," I began, ready to have my first real say, and arranging my thoughts on this venerable issue, but Anne got there before me, and much more pithily.

"They weren't the victors," she said simply.

"True," Flittner said, as bitterly as if he'd signed the surrender himself. "We're the victors, so we make the rules."

"Well," Robey said, his Archaic smile shining gently forth, "let's enjoy it while we can. How often do the good guys get to make the rules?"

That appeared to be a reasonable end to an unpromising avenue, and while Robey went through the pipe smoker's slow voluptuous, lighting-up ritual, the rest of us held our peace.

"Anyway, Chris," he finally said behind a slowly twisting web of blue smoke, "this Schliemann group spends its time writing nasty letters to us and to the press—'The Plundered Past is an insult to the German people, nothing but American propaganda'—that kind of thing. They don't get any support, thank God."

"I have to disagree," Flittner said. "There are a *lot* of people who see this show as nothing more than self-serving propaganda. Which we all know it is, even if we don't have the guts to admit it."

Robey dug peacefully at his pipe with a gimmicky tool while his mind drifted elsewhere. Anne listened impassively. Gadney rolled up his eyes again and made a put-upon face. I kept waiting for him to say, "Oh ... *really*!" but he restrained himself. All three, it was clear, had heard Flittner on this subject before. Only Harry was attentive and interested, his forefinger curled in his beard.

Seeking a fresh audience, Flittner swung his long, somber face back and forth from Harry to me as he spoke. "Even in the Bundestag—a couple of weeks ago Katzenhaven got up and demanded to know how much this show is costing the German government."

He was not a careful shaver, I noticed; stubble glinted like shards of mica here and there along his jawline. A spattering of ash was on his jacket, and while he spoke he dropped some more from the cigarette in his hand.

"But it isn't costing them anything, Earl," Anne said. "You know that."

"I know, of course I know." Impatiently, he flicked more ash on himself. "I'm using it as an illustration. The—oh, the hell with it." He slumped back in his chair.

"Listen, let me say something at this point," Harry said. We've asked the *Polizei* to look into this Schliemann gang—"

"They're not a *gang*," Flittner interrupted. "They're a political foundation. Jesus Christ."

"Excuse me, this Schliemann Foundation. Except that they're not a bona-fide foundation. They're not on record, they don't have an address, they don't sign their letters with their real names. For all anybody knows, they could be one old Nazi crank sitting home alone grinding out crackpot letters." He winced as Flittner reared up to protest, but stuck to his guns. "Excuse me, Dr. Flittner, but that's the way they look to me. They've got no support, even from the anti-American lunatic fringe."

"Now look here, Major," Flittner said angrily, "it seems to me you're being damned free with your—"

"What I think Harry's saying, Earl," Robey cut in smoothly, "is that they wouldn't have the expertise to get into the storage room the way those two men did."

"Right," Harry said amiably, "that's all I'm saying. Or the money to buy somebody else's expertise." He smiled winningly at Flittner, who subsided, detonating another gush of smoke from his facial orifices.

An airman entered with a message. Robey read it and stood up. "Telephone," he said. "Why don't you take over, Harry?"

"You bet, Colonel. Well, I think we better get on to talking about what we do to prevent a repeat of what happened. Now, Captain Romero of my staff is an expert in this stuff, and he's been working with Captain Greene here on a new ... what's he call it, Anne?"

"An intrusion-detection system."

"Right, an intrusion-detection system. Now, these things are pretty complicated, but I want to try to explain, because it means procedures are going to be a little different starting in a few days."

"Uh, Harry?" Robey had come back as far as the doorway. "Harry, I think you better sit in on this call. Anne, you can fill them in on the security system, can't you?"

"I'll do my best, sir." She pulled some notes out of a pocket in her attaché case and glanced uncomfortably at me as Harry left with an oddly subdued Robey. "I'm sure Dr. Norgren will see very quickly that I'm out of my element."

Terrific, Norgren, I thought; the most attractive female you've met in months, obviously predisposed to be friends, and you've managed in little over an hour, with just a couple of succinct and impeccably chosen sentences, to convince her you're a boorish, arrogant ass.

"Out of mine too," I said with what I hoped was modest charm. "I've yet to meet a wiring diagram I could understand."

It was true enough. Her enthusiastic and apparently expert description of infrared beams, entry-reporting networks, pressure alarms, and photo-electric barriers quickly left me behind. I could almost feel my eyes glaze over. Gadney participated vigorously, however, and Flittner participated after his fashion.

Within twenty minutes I was once again almost asleep. It was, of course, not merely the soporific topic but the accumulated impact of many grams of codeine on a system not much used to drugs. More than that, although I didn't admit it willingly, my body hadn't altogether recovered from the knocking-around it had gotten two days before.

The expression on the two men when they returned brought me awake with a chill. Harry was grim, and

Robey's entire face had sagged; the corners of his mouth now pointed down instead of up. Neither man sat. Robey stared through the French doors with his eyes unfocused and let out a long, close-mouthed sigh.

"What?" Gadney asked nervously. "What is it? What's wrong?"

Robey exhaled again and turned slowly to face us. "Peter's dead."

6

"He's *dead*?" I asked, after a long silence.

Robey nodded. "Uh, yes. Wednesday night."

"*Wednesday!* But that's impossible! I had lunch with him Wednesday—at the Kranzler ..." The odd, irrational way one's mind twists and skitters to reject what it doesn't want to know.

"It's true, Chris." He began to say more, then shook his head back and forth. "My God."

The others at the table stared as if hypnotized while his slowly oscillating head rocked gradually to a stop.

"How well did you know him, Chris?" Harry asked abruptly.

"Not very. Better than most people did, but that isn't saying much." Why had he asked me that? "He was a good man," I added, obscurely driven to defend him. "I *liked* him."

"I did too," Robey said. Then, reflectively: "I guess I didn't know him very well either. It looks like none of us did."

An uneasy shiver trickled down my neck and settled icily between my shoulder blades. "Mark—what the hell has happened?"

Robey looked down at the table and concentrated on stroking the cold pipe in the ashtray. "That was Frankfurt Military Police on the phone. They said he—" His eyes came up and flickered apprehensively in Anne's direction. He shook his head again, this time roughly. "Damn!"

Harry quietly interceded. "You think maybe I ought to

explain? I'm kind of used to these things." He smiled gently at us. "I'm afraid it's like the colonel says: pretty bad."

It was. Peter van Cortlandt, genteel, standoffish, the ultimate patrician, had been found dead in the gutter in Frankfurt's raunchy sex district, a few blocks from the railroad station, at 3:30 A.M. He was lying in front of the Hotel Paradies, a ratty little place with a "sex-kino" on the ground floor and rooms that were rented by the half hour above. He was wearing only a shirt and a pair of socks, and had apparently been killed in a fall. The rest of his clothing—but not his watch, wallet, or Yale class ring—was found in a third-floor room of the Paradies, the window of which was immediately above his body.

The desk clerk had told the police that he thought he remembered Peter coming in a little after midnight with a blond he had seen around, but he wasn't sure; there were so many. ("So many blonds or so many gray-haired gentlemen?" the *Polizei* had asked. "Take your pick," the clerk had answered with a shrug.)

An autopsy had already been performed, the conclusions being that Peter had been killed by a fall from Room 303 of the Hotel Paradies, and that there were drugs and alcohol in his system. It was not possible to determine whether his death had been accidental or if he had been thrown from the window. A search had been instituted for a tall husky blond called Utelinde, or Linda, who was reputed to have the word *amour* tattooed on her left buttock.

"I hate to say it," Harry said, "but the *Polizei* have about as much chance of finding her as . . ." He lifted his shoulders resignedly. "This is a pretty common occurrence around the Kaiserstrasse. There's not a night goes by but some soldier or some businessman on the prowl doesn't wind up like this."

"Now, wait a minute!" I said, my throat tight. "This wasn't some bum, this was Peter van Cortlandt!" Disconcertedly, I shook my head, tried to regroup my muddled thoughts. "It's got to be a mistake."

"I'm afraid not," Robey said. "It's Peter all right."

There was more. An unopened package of condoms had been found in his trousers pocket; a few of the hairs on the tousled bed in Room 303 had been analyzed as his ("Some of them extracranial," Harry said delicately); and he had been seen blind-drunk in two nearby bars earlier that night.

As these unsavory details came out, the ends of Robey's mouth buried themselves in dry little grooves that hadn't been there before. He was angry, I thought, less at Peter's killer, if there was a killer, than at Peter himself, for the shabby, squalid way he'd permitted himself to die. Not quite angry, maybe, but let down; disappointed in the wretchedly common end of a distinguished man; shamed by proxy.

Me, I didn't feel that way, but what I did feel wasn't any more commendable. I wish I could say that I had refused to believe any of it, and insisted from the beginning that Peter had been set up, but I didn't. I was astonished, of course, because what I knew of him was as contrary to the notion of drunken whoring on Frankfurt's Kaiserstrasse as anything could be.

But you have to remember where I was myself at the time. I had been married for a decade, contentedly and (I thought) securely. I had been faithful to Bev, and, generally speaking, happy to be faithful. And then I was suddenly alone, betrayed, confused, aching for solace, and bursting with healthy young hormones. During the ensuing year I had found myself, sometimes to my considerable surprise, in a few places in which, as it now was for Peter, it would have been damned embarrassing to be found dead.

How did I know what stresses he'd been under? He was aging. Was the job getting to be too much? Was his marriage breaking up? Was he estranged from his children? I had no idea. Who was I to say it was inconceivable or reprehensible that he should lay himself down on a foul bed, rented for half an hour, in the Hotel Paradies.

And so I accepted it as simply one more proof that we never really know anyone else, regretting Peter's death but absorbed in my own life, my own problems. When the meeting drew to a low-spirited close, I went up to my room and called Tony in San Francisco, forgetting that it was four in the morning there, to tell him about Peter. I also asked him what he knew about the forgery.

"Only that Peter thought there was one," Tony said, his voice shocked and dull, "and that it was something in your line. I thought he was having a little private joke." There was a long silence. I heard him breathe twice. "You mean there is one?"

This depressing and unhelpful exchange completed, I was downhearted and headachy. I took another couple of codeine, dropped onto the bed, and slept heavily until 7:00 P.M. Down for a groggy bowl of soup, and back to sleep.

The next day was more of the same: codeine, soup, and sleep. But Monday I was better, managing to work for a few hours at learning the ropes with Corporal Jessick, and spending the rest of the morning with Harry, tediously trying to construct pictures of No-neck and Skull-face with Photofit, a jigsaw-puzzle-like set of thousands of photographs of eyebrows, noses, and chins. None of them seemed ugly enough.

The afternoon brought a setback of sorts. While I was dozing after lunch the telephone rang.

"Chris, I've been calling you for *days*!"

Rita Dooling. Calling with more offers and counteroffers and counter-counteroffers. My head started aching again the moment I heard her voice.

"I know, Rita," I lied, with sinking heart. "I've been trying to get through to you." What traitor had given her my number at Columbia House?

"Sure, I just bet you have. You probably went all the way to Europe just to get away from me. Well, what do you say?"

"To what?"

"To nine-and-three-quarters percent of your book," Rita said mildly. She was used to dealing with me.

"Oh yeah, that's right." I lay down on my back with the

telephone cradled against my ear. "Well, I've given it a lot of thought, a lot of thought, and I can't see it. In the first place, I just don't want to be bothered with figuring out nine-and-three-quarters percent on every royalty check—"

"Uh, it's not just the royalty checks. She figures she ought to get nine-and-three-quarters percent of your advance too—the one you got last April. Five hundred, she says it was, so that comes to forty-eight dollars and seventy-five cents."

"Jesus Christ, Rita."

"Look, I'm just passing on what her attorney told me. You know I'm on your side, Chris."

"I know."

"Still, if it was me, I'd give it to her," she said, generous as ever. "And if you don't want to do the figuring, why don't you ask your publisher to send the nine and three quarters directly to her?"

Because I'd be embarrassed to, that's why. "I'll tell you what," I said. "Let's put that aside for the moment—"

"I've been hearing that for a year and a half. If you want my honest opinion, Christopher, you're treading water. You don't want Bev back, but you can't face letting go and admitting ten years of marriage are just time down the drain. You've got mixed-up feelings of loyalty and guilt, and your self-concept has been so traumatized—"

"Rita, I'm going to have to introduce you to my friend Louis one of these days."

"I know your friend Louis. We talk about you a lot."

"Wonderful. Now, I was going to say: About this business of her getting the car and me getting poor old Murphy—"

"Oh, that's past history, forget that. She's mellowed on that one. She says she's happy to see you keep them both."

"If."

"Well, of course 'if.' What she suggests—and I'll tell you honestly, if I were you, I'd go for it—is that you sell the house—"

"Sell the house," I echoed hollowly.

"—and split the proceeds fifty-fifty with her, but with a guaranteed fifteen thou up front in cash. Do that and she'll forget about the car."

"And Murph, no doubt."

"Well, no. That is, not exactly. She says that if you want Murphy—"

"Uh, Rita, I have to go now. My beeper just buzzed; I mean beeped."

"You have a beeper?"

"Right. Yes. Can't talk now. Emergency. Gotta run. Call you soon. 'Bye."

I left the telephone off the hook, pulled the blinds, took two more codeine, and went numbly back to bed for the rest of the day.

On Tuesday I woke up late, feeling good again, my trusty subconscious having wedged Rita's call into the furthest, dimmest corner of my mind. Plenty of time to deal with that later. With great pleasure I tossed the remaining codeine tablets into the wastepaper basket and went downstairs for a hefty lunch of hamburger and fries. After that I took care of a few chores in the office and then went to the Clipper Room to see what headway I could make on the "minor problem" of Peter's forgery.

While I'd been on my back, Earl Flittner and crew had been busy. The Plundered Past was very nearly ready for public viewing. Most of the partitions, smelling of glue and freshly sawed wood, were in place, and some of the pictures were already hung. The others were leaning against the walls. Flittner was up on a ladder doing something with the lights, and two men I didn't know—Harry's people, I supposed—were on their knees by the entrance, installing what must have been an intrusion-detection system.

Before I got down to thinking about forgeries, I wandered around the exhibit simply for the pleasure of looking at the paintings. I respectfully admired some I hadn't seen before: a swirling, vertiginous *Wind and Snow* of Turner's; a serene, early self-portrait by Dürer, the first major artist to be fascinated with his own image.

Others I greeted happily, like the old acquaintances they were, either from photographs or from seeing them in museums to which Bolzano had lent them: Piero della Francesca's softly glowing *Madonna and Child*, with a lively dwarf of a *bambino* as charmingly repulsive as only a fifteenth-century artist could make an infant; and Gainsborough's sedate *Henry Colchester and His Family*, who peered coolly out of their frame at me, complacent and incurious, as if they never doubted that they were solid flesh and blood, and blue blood at that, but they weren't quite sure what I might be.

The show wasn't big enough for the conventional arrangement into little bays and rooms (Mannerism and the High Renaissance, Seventeenth-Century Minor Dutch Masters, etc.). Instead they were simply hung chronologically, well separated, each painting with an informational plaque at its side. The only exceptions to this staid progression were an inconspicuous alcove near the exit, where the copies of the twelve still-missing paintings were modestly hung (with the sad exception of the "Michelangelo"), and a dramatic three-sided bay, draped with green silk brocade, which was the centerpiece of the room and of the exhibition. Here three paintings were dramatically displayed: the newly discovered cache from Hallstatt. I had kept this for last on purpose, saving it the way a kid puts off the best part of dinner.

They were superb. A florid, frenzied *Rape of the Sabines* by Rubens, one of many versions, looked less like a rape than a good party that had gotten a little out of hand, but the composition was awesome, and the flesh tones, with liberal applications of his brightest, blushingest rapine pink, were marvelous. The Titian was sensual and robust too—a sexy *Venus and the Lute Player*. There are also several versions of this painting, and this was one of the best, broadly painted with a grand and sure-handed disregard for detail.

And then, seemingly from a different universe, the Vermeer. Of all painters, with the possible exception of Rembrandt, it is Vermeer who strikes the deepest chord in me. But Rembrandts are plentiful; there are hundreds of paintings, etchings, drawings. In all the world, however, there are only thirty undisputed Vermeers, with another dozen arguables—forty-two at the outside—and this, of course, was one I had never seen before. Bolzano had actually owned two Vermeers, the only private collector who did. Both had been taken for Hitler's museum in Linz by the discriminating Einsatzstab Reichsleiter Rosenberg, but the other, *A Woman Peeling Apples*, had never been recovered. A fine copy hung with the rest of the copies in the cheerless corner by the exit.

But this one, thank God, was back in this world, and I stood in front of it for a long time. When you look at a Vermeer, even after a Dürer or a Piero, it's as if you've been seeing things through badly focused binoculars and someone just turned the knob; everything is gemlike, focused, sharper than reality itself.

I knew the painting from photographs, and I'd even devoted several pages to it in my book on Vermeer. *Young Woman at the Clavichord*, done in Delft in 1665 or 1666. The remarkable, transparent light came, as usual, from a window on the left. The woman was, as always, static, cool, sweetly remote, arranged like a still life with her clavichord in front of simple furniture on a black-and-white-tiled floor.

I checked to make sure Flittner was looking the other way, then stretched out a forefinger, as gently as God reaching to Adam on the Sistine ceiling, and touched her wrist. It was an offense for which I would have mercilessly put before a firing squad any hapless visitor caught doing it in the San Francisco County Museum of Art. I did it judgmentally, thoughtfully, as if I were making an arcane assessment of texture or brushstroke, but this was only in case Flittner should look around. Actually, my reasons were the same as any gawking tourist's: the awed desire to "connect" across the centuries with the great Vermeer. Here, where his brush, possibly his very fingers, touched, I now touched, so that our paths crossed in space if not in time.

I don't do this very often. I don't think it's the sort of thing a curator *ought* to do, and I never heard another curator confess even to the desire (of course, neither have I), but it gives me a deep, soul-filling pleasure, never more than when it's Vermeer to whom I reach out. I touched the pearls around her throat, like droplets of pure light—

"How's it going, Chris?"

To say I almost jumped out of my skin would be overstating it, so let's just say I gave a guilty start.

"Harry! Whew! Is that why you wear those rubber soles? So you can sneak up on innocent people?"

He cackled delightedly. "What were you doing, anyway?"

"Doing? What was I doing? Well, I was just, uh, moistening my finger and, uh, clearing things up a little." When he didn't laugh in my face, I took courage and went on.

"Wetting old varnish lets you see through it more clearly, and when you're checking the authenticity of the painting, the first thing you want to do is get a good look at the signature. Most of the decent fakes floating around are old, you see, and they weren't painted as forgeries in the first place; they got to be forgeries when someone changed the original signature of some competent but unknown artist and substituted a more famous one; Vermeer's, for example. Sometimes a close look can show you the signs of doctoring."

That was a long answer to a simple question and Harry looked quizzically up at me, a finger curled in the hair behind his ear. "Is that right? That's interesting. But you were rubbing the middle, weren't you? Artists don't sign in the middle of a picture. Or do they?"

"I wasn't *rubbing* it," I said, to set the record straight. "I was touching it. Very lightly. Anyway, painters sign anywhere: on an arch, on a piece of furniture, over a doorway, on a bracelet, on a blank wall. Vermeer frequently signed in the middle of a picture." All true enough, generally speaking, but where was the signature on *Young Woman at the Clavichord*? I hadn't found the damn thing yet.

"Oh, I see. So tell me, did you find anything suspicious?"

Was I being interrogated, or was he just curious? I couldn't tell. He had a self-effacing way of asking questions that was meek but insistent, and a way of listening that was both intense and amicable, as if he might be probing for something but also happened to find what you were saying of genuine and extraordinary interest. A handy manner for a cop.

"No," I said, still trying to find Vermeer's name, "nothing that's caught my eye so far."

Harry studied the painting and chewed on the inside of his cheek. "You know, I don't know much about art—I mean, I know what I like, but that's about it—but now that I look at it, I think I might have been just a little suspicious about this signature."

"Oh? Really?" By now I wished dearly that I'd had the nerve in the first place to admit that I had been pawing the Vermeer for the love of it, but I was in too deep. "Why is that?" I asked. I still didn't even know where the hell the signature was.

"Because," he said blandly, "somebody else signed it."

Fortunately, I located the signature just as he mentioned it. It was roughly in the middle, all right, on the rim of an oval mirror. And Harry was right. It was not the usual "IV Meer," or any of the monograms with which Vermeer sometimes signed his work. It read, quite clearly, "Pieter de Hoogh."

Harry was grinning at me, pleased with himself. "Now how about telling me what the hell is going on around here?"

"Going on? Nothing. And as a matter of fact, that signature confirms its being a genuine Vermeer. In a paradoxical way, of course."

"It does?" The tone wasn't so much one of skepticism as of pleasurable anticipation: Now how the heck is this fast-talking Ph.D. going to con his way through this?

But I was telling the truth. "Well, it's only in the last

century or so that Vermeer's been considered one of the great painters. A hundred years ago his name would have been the one you scraped off a painting and replaced with a better-known one if you wanted to get a good price: Peter de Hooch's, for example. Or Terborch's, or Metsu's."

"Is that right? I never heard of those guys."

"Tastes change. As a matter of fact, Vermeer's most famous painting—*The Artist in His Studio*, in Vienna—still has a faked de Hooch signature on it. Even so, it brought only about ten dollars in the early 1800s."

"No kidding," he said with every indication of authentic interest. "Boy, there's a lot to learn, isn't there?" He had come in wearing a huge quilted parka that engulfed him like a great puffy tent. Now he took it off and tossed it onto a chair. Underneath was the familiar worn cardigan. "You almost made me forget what I came in to ask. What's your impression of Earl Flittner?"

"My impression?"

"You think he could be involved with the break-in?"

I had continued to look absently at the painting. Now I turned slowly to face him. "You're kidding."

"Well, I was just thinking about all those things he said at the meeting the other day—how the show is all propaganda, that stuff. You think the guy is anti-American, a Communist, maybe?"

Well-conditioned liberal that I am, I bristled at this evidence of the narrow, chauvinistic military mind at work. I had come to expect more of Harry. "Just because he expressed some honest opinions doesn't make the guy an enemy of the republic, you know. Why ask me, anyway?"

"Well, I understand you knew him in the States. What about pro-Nazi feelings?"

"*Nazi* feelings? I can't believe you're serious."

"Well, I'm not, exactly," he said, unoffended. "I'm just, you know, exploring avenues." He smiled. Under the heavy wool of the sweater his thin shoulders moved in a faint shrug. "So you don't think he has any leanings like that?"

"All I know about him," I said hotly, "is that he's the

best—" I stopped. Why in the world was I standing up so righteously for Earl Flittner? I relaxed and laughed. "What he has," I said, "are curmudgeonly leanings. The guy just naturally likes to go against the grain. He's sent in some crank letters to *The Artist* and *Artforum* that are classics."

Harry smiled. "But not curmudgeonly enough to steal paintings?"

"Not as far as I know."

"Well, I had a little more than that to go on." His shrewd eyes watched me to see if I had any idea of what he meant.

I didn't. "Like what?"

But I wasn't in his confidence yet. "Things. You know." He turned briskly to the Vermeer. "Chris, what made you think this wasn't authentic in the first place?"

"Peter told me; that is, he said *one* of them is a fake." I told him about the conversation at Kranzler's. Harry listened intently, then made me repeat it while he made desultory notes in his little spiral-bound notebook.

"Son of a gun," he said finally. "And he wouldn't tell you which one it is?"

I shook my head.

"So now what? And Chris—" He held up his hands, warning me off. "Don't tell me it takes an art expert to know. Art experts are like psychiatrists; you can't get two of them to agree on anything."

"Well," I said, having no quarrel with him on that point, "I usually start by looking for three things: Are the materials as old as they're supposed to be? Do they come from the place they're supposed to? And are the techniques the ones that were really in use when the painting's supposed to have been done? If those check out, I get down to individual styles, but that's a lot trickier."

He stood looking at the Vermeer, scrunched up in the bulky sweater, his hands in the pockets. "So take this one, for example. One of the things you'd want to find out is whether the paint on it was really available in Delft in the 1650s or 1660s—are my dates right?"

"On the button."

He shrugged modestly. "Well, I figured if I was going to get involved with this show, I better do some reading. Anyway, am I right?"

"You sure are. Most of the paint formulas used by the old masters have been chemically analyzed by now, so it's not hard to check and see if a particular painting has the right pigments—mixed in the right proportions."

"Yeah, but if *you* can get the formulas, why can't the crooks?"

"They can, but we've still got the edge. *They* have to be sure every single substance they use is right, but if we can find even one that wasn't available till later, it's got to be a fake. And that goes for everything, not just the paints. If you're looking at what's supposed to be a fifteenth-century Flemish painting, and the stretcher bars turn out to be made of wood that's found only in America . . . well, you'd better look a little closer."

"Sure, I see that. But—" He glanced around and pointed to *Venus and the Lute Player*. "Titian, right? So when was that painted—1540, 1550?"

I nodded.

"Okay, so tell me: Does the frame look authentic to you?"

We walked up to the painting, and I ran my eyes over the curlicues and rosettes of the heavy gilded Renaissance frame.

"Yes."

"Meaning it's from about the right time?"

"Uh-huh."

"All right, say I wanted to push a fake Titian. Why couldn't I go into some little old out-of-the way church and steal some three- or four-hundred-year-old picture of a saint or something—there are millions of them—and then use the frame? Or even buy some old picture that wasn't worth that much, toss the painting, and put in the Titian instead?"

"It's not that easy. It's got to be from the right place, not just the right time. You'd need a frame that was made in Venice. One from Germany or Spain—or even Rome or

Florence—wouldn't get you past an expert. And I'm not just talking about style; I'm talking about the right joinery techniques, the right nails—"

"OK, OK, but still . . ." Harry scowled and chewed his cheek, taking this as a personal challenge. "OK, then, how about this? What's to stop me from finding some old piece of wood—say, a beam from a house built at the right time, or maybe a piece of furniture—and carving the damn frame myself?"

"First of all—"

"I know, I know. I'd have to be some kind of master carpenter, wouldn't I? And I'd need to make the right kind of glue, forge some handmade nails—"

"That'd be the easy part. The hard part would be figuring out how to carve an old piece of wood without making a new skin."

"A new what?"

"When you cut into old wood, you can't help creating a fresh surface—a skin—that's 'young' to someone who knows what to look for."

Harry blew out his lips. "That's interesting." He used "interesting" a lot, drawing it out into four slow, respectful syllables: *IN-ter-est-ing*. "Look, let me know what you find out. I guess it won't take very long, right?"

When I didn't say anything, he turned his head to look at me. "Not right?"

"I don't know. A modern fake I could certainly spot. But I don't think that's what we have, and the older it gets, the harder it is to be sure."

"Like, the new skin gets to be an old skin?"

"Right. And the scientific techniques get less reliable. And if what we have is one that's so old it's contemporary with the original and done by a first-rate artist to boot—say, a Terborch that's been converted into a 'Vermeer'—we've got problems."

"Huh." Musing, he picked up his coat. "Hey, this has really been IN-ter-est-ing; I learned a lot. Listen, I want to ask you something. How come you didn't mention this forgery stuff before?"

"I didn't think of it."

"You didn't think of it?" He chewed over the words slowly.

"No. It didn't seem pertinent. It still doesn't, really. That is, I suppose it could wind up being a police matter, but—"

"It didn't seem pertinent to the break-in?"

"To the break-in?" I looked at him stupidly. "No. How could it—"

"Or van Cortlandt's death?"

"To Peter's *death*? What could it have to do with his death? Harry, if you're driving at something, you've left me way behind."

"Well, I don't know, but doesn't it seem to you like there are an awful lot of weird things going on?"

"There sure are, but that doesn't mean they're connected, does it?"

"In my line of work, yeah, it usually does. I gotta go." He worked his thin shoulders into the coat and suddenly laughed. "Hey, don't look so worried." He clapped me lightly on the arm and turned to the door. "I'm just thinking like a cop; I can't help it. Forget it."

7

I forgot it.

As much as I'd love to say that I didn't, that I mulled over his words, turned them over in my mind, realized at last how dense I'd been not to put things together myself, that isn't what happened. I forgot it. Almost the minute he was gone.

Flittner had finished up the lighting and came over to me as Harry left.

"The exhibition looks great, Earl," I said honestly. "The lighting's magnificent."

He grunted. "Something I can do for you?" The implication was that this was his domain, not mine.

"No thanks."

"Just want to look at the pretty pictures?"

"Yes." I'm not sure why it didn't seem like a good idea to tell him about the forgery. Mainly, I think, I just didn't want to explain again. But perhaps something in me felt it was better if he didn't know. Or maybe I just didn't want to talk to him any longer than I had to.

He grunted again, shrugged, and headed morosely for the door, already reaching for one of the Camels that he deprived himself of while working around the paintings.

Alone, I got on with my reason for coming to the Clipper Room in the first place, not that I had much of an idea of what I was looking for. Peter had told me that the forgery was down my alley, which might mean something as specific as the Vermeer, or possibly anything from the Renaissance through the Baroque; let's say from the fifteenth century to 1750—Piero through Luca Giordano. Seven pictures, all told. Not so bad, really.

But it was also possible that "down your alley" might have meant something else entirely—Peter had been in a whimsical frame of mind—so to be on the safe side I went through the entire collection.

I began by looking for the technical inconsistencies of place and time that I'd mentioned to Harry. You might think that an odd place to start; if, after all, I am the expert on Baroque and Renaissance art that I keep (ever so subtly) hinting I am, why would I not immediately get down to examining each painting from a stylistic perspective? Did the *Venus and the Lute Player* show Titian's characteristic use of fingers more than brush in the final painting stages? Did the Hals demonstrate his singular ability to fool the viewer into thinking he is looking at a dazzling bravura display of reckless spontaneity when in fact each stroke had been laid on with slowest, most meticulous care? Was the Vermeer illuminated with *pointillés,* those tiny, mysterious dabs of paint that seem to drench the canvas with light?

Intuitively, those are the kinds of judgments I trust the most, but they are matters of degree, subjective and therefore arguable—and, in any case, tricky to make. Easier to begin with a simpler yes/no question: Did any of the materials show outward signs of having come from some time or some place other than they should have?

They didn't. That didn't mean they weren't faked, only that there weren't any obvious signs. Later, I'd want to turn them around, to see what the backs had to say for themselves. (At the moment I didn't care to challenge our formidable new intrusion-detection system.) In the meantime there was more I could do right now. I could haul out my ten-power battery-lit lens and have a good, hard look at the craquelure.

Craquelure means "crackling"—the network of fine, black lines that covers the surface of any old oil painting as a result of shrinkages in the paint film and varnish. There is almost no such thing as an old painting without craquelure, so forgers must create it, and they have come up with a lot of clever ways to do it, from wrapping the painted canvas around a roller (which has been done by fakers since the 1600s) to putting it in a 120-degree oven for a couple of days, to using a special "restorer's varnish" that contracts while it dries and is guaranteed thus to crackle the surface of any painting to which it's applied.

But fooling a knowledgeable eye is difficult. There are all sorts of esoterica for a crook to worry about: Paint on canvas shrinks differently from paint on panels (the former cracks in a spiderweb pattern, the latter along the grain of the wood); the extent of craquelure varies less with age than with media (the deepest cracks are found in early-nineteenth-century pictures that were painted with crack-prone materials); and there is a big difference between a painting that cracks from the surface down and one that cracks from the ground up (both occur naturally, but under different circumstances).

All very handy to know, but of course, high-class forgers know it at least as well as anyone else and have devised ways of meeting the challenge. At this point, however, I was still hoping—with diminishing confidence—that I was dealing with something less than a first-class forgery, and so might find something quickly. I looked at them all, not just the seven likely ones, and found nothing. Round one to the forger.

That had taken two hours. I went out, had a couple of cups of coffee, and returned to begin again with the Piero della Francesca and work my way through to the 1881 Manet, this time concentrating on the signatures. By now I was relatively sure that I wasn't dealing with a modern fake but an old one. And as I'd told Harry, most of the old forgeries still around had begun as honest works of art by honest artists, which were later transformed into other things. Sometimes the original painting was left pretty much as it was; sometimes it was altered in one way or another to make the fraud more credible. One change, however, was mandatory: A counterfeit signature had to be added. Not all genuine paintings are signed, but all forgeries are, for obvious reasons.

What I was searching for was some sign of signature-tampering. Sometimes a forger will paint out an existing signature and then simply paint a new one over it. This is easy to detect, and more clever crooks will erase the signature down to the ground, then reprime the damaged spot, build up the paint layer by layer, and install a new signature with a new coat of varnish (appropriately crackled) over it. There are other techniques too, and to my pleasure I spotted one, but it didn't bring me any closer to what I was looking for.

It was on the Vermeer, of course; the one with the fake de Hooch signature. The false signature itself was beautifully done. I have to admit that I probably wouldn't have recognized the few signs of overpainting if I hadn't known that they had to be there. What *did* catch my eye, however, was an inconspicuous low cabinet in the background, seen through the triangle formed by the clavichord, the woman's extended left arm, and her side.

On the face of the cabinet was an odd crownlike design, vaguely oriental, which closer examination very satisfyingly revealed to be the original Vermeer monogram—IVM—deftly transformed with only four curving strokes into a meaningless geometrical decoration. Naturally, this resoundingly confirmed *Young Woman at the Clavichord* as an authentic Vermeer.

Or did it? There was always the possibility that some particularly cunning forger had done this so that I, or somebody like me, would come proudly to the conclusion I'd just reached. It wouldn't have been the first time.

It was starting to look as if I might need some scientific help before I was done. Fortunately, I was sure it would be available from Berlin's Technische Universität, where Max Kohler ran one of the world's major art laboratories. Kohler and I had worked together before, and he could do what I couldn't—chemically analyze the material in the craquelure, for example. All forgers must fill in their artificial cracks with black or gray matter—ink, paint, soot—or they won't look real. But three centuries of accumulated dust and grime are impossible to duplicate chemically. Fooling my eye was one thing; fooling Max's mass spectrometer was another.

Why, then, didn't I ship the whole batch over to Kohler's lab right off instead of messing with my Neanderthal techniques? First, because you just don't send thirty-five million dollars' worth of art treasures across the city to your nearest lab; it doesn't work that way. It creates insurance problems and logistics problems, it's risky for the paintings, it overloads the lab, and it makes everybody nervous. It's also wildly expensive.

Second, even good laboratories often produce ambiguous results. Psychiatrists and art experts aren't the only ones who sometimes disagree; chemists looking at the same computerized pigment analysis will reach different conclusions more often than they'd like laymen to know. Besides that, legitimate underpainting, overpainting, and a lot of technicalities too boring to go into confuse things enough to give any competent and resourceful forger a decent chance of getting by.

And third, I wanted the satisfaction of finding it myself, or at least the excitement of looking for it. Matching wits against a really fine forger, even if he's been dead a few hundred years, is pure pleasure, an engrossing detective game, and it promised more fun than I'd had in months.

Which gives you a pretty good idea of the state of my live.

But another hour produced nothing, not even much in the way of fun, and I decided to quit for the day. Tomorrow, fresher and stronger after another good night's sleep, I'd start again.

On my way through the lobby I saw a message in my box at the reception desk: *Pls call Capt. Greene, 4141.*

I used the desk telephone. "Anne? This is Chris Norgren."

"Oh, thank you for calling, Dr. Norgren." The formality was not lost on me. "Can I talk to you about something? Colonel Robey would have discussed it with you, but he's had to go to Heidelberg. He specifically asked me to see to it instead."

Why the meticulous explanation? Did she think I might suspect her intentions? Would that I had reason. "Fine," I said.

"Good. Can we meet in the lobby in twenty minutes?"

"I was just going down to the bar for a drink. How about there?"

A fractional pause. "All right. Twenty minutes."

The Keller-Bar of Columbia House is, as the name suggests, in the basement, not far from the infamous storage room, though entered by its own flight of steps. To me it made a colorful and exotic scene: crowded and noisy, mostly with fliers, self-consciously casual in their flight suits and satiny flight jackets, their captain's bars prominent on their shoulders. Small men, most of them. Handsome and extremely young, lithe and fit-looking; like a gathering of jockeys or lightweight boxers. There were a few senior officers, too, portly and convivial, with individual audiences of respectfully attentive juniors. It might almost have been a scene from the Battle of Britain—many of the fliers were wearing white scarfs tucked into the throats of their jackets.

There were eight or ten scattered tables, and along one wall a row of slot machines, all of them engaged and, from the steady clanking and jingling, all paying off handsomely. Not, of course, that you could tell from the players, who pumped the handles with de-rigueur expressions of joyless drudgery.

Tonight's Special, read a hand-lettered sign propped on the bar; Beefeater Martinis, 75 cents. A long way from San Francisco prices and too good to pass up. The barman poured my drink and nodded his thanks when I dropped a quarter into one of the champagne glasses placed every few feet along the bar. "Snacks over there," he said, recognizing me for a newcomer. "Help yourself."

"Over there" was a table around which pilots were congregated elbow to elbow, chattering and munching. Instantly hungry at the mention of food, I steered my way through, hoping at least for chips or nuts. They were there, all right, but so were a platter of halved, thick-sliced ham-and-cheese sandwiches; a heaped tray of cold cuts; half a wheel of cheddar cheese; hot German sausages and rolls; and more—the free lunch of yore, alive and thriving in the officers-club bar in Berlin. This much-maligned military life, I was learning, had more going for it than was generally supposed.

I snaked out a plateful of the heartier items and found a table at the back. I meant to wait for Anne before gobbling up the food, but I'd had only one meal in the last two days, and in fifteen minutes I'd wolfed down most of the plateful, along with half the martini. I was so absorbed in the process that I didn't see her come up.

"Hi," she said.

"Hi."

She sat down. "It's so horrible about Peter. I haven't been able to think about anything else."

"Is that what you want to talk about?"

"Indirectly, yes. Colonel Robey's counting on you now to carry Peter's share of the load, you know."

"Of course. Would you like something to drink?"

She shook her head gloomily.

"Well, you can tell Mark I'll do my best. Peter's already done all the hard work, so I think I can cope."

I was bothered by our formality and distance, and not just for personal reasons. The dynamics of art shows lend themselves to personality problems (something I figured out for myself without Louis's help), and one of my jobs was to defuse them, not create them.

I set down my martini. "Look, Anne—I apologize for cutting you off like that in the meeting."

"Cutting me off?"

"I was acting like a creep."

"No, you weren't." But her lips tipped upward and those clear violet eyes warmed slightly. "You sure were."

"All right. Now that we agree on something, how about calling me Chris?"

"All right, Chris," she said, and smiled a little less tentatively.

Pleased with this small victory, I sipped my martini and smiled back. Anne, however, quickly drifted unflatteringly off into her private thoughts and sat there looking unhappy and remote.

"What did you want to talk about, exactly?" I asked.

"Oh . . . sorry—I keep thinking about Peter. Look, maybe I will have a drink after all. Could I have a glass of white wine, please?"

When I returned with it, she took one gulp and was all business. "Colonel Robey's had a call from Florence. Apparently, signor Bolzano went to pieces when he heard about what happened in the storage room."

"Hardly surprising."

"No, but he's having another one of his episodes. He's threatening to pull out again. It's the sort of thing Peter would ordinarily deal with, but now, what with . . . with . . ."

I said gently, "Mark would like me to go to Florence and talk to him."

"Yes. He says you may really have to put on the pressure." She smiled slightly. "He said to tell you it's arm-twisting time."

"Oh," I said, finishing the martini and putting the glass down.

"Is something wrong?"

"No, it's just that . . . the thing is—"

The thing was that whatever my forte is, it isn't twisting arms. No doubt it was among my "other duties as required," and certainly it is something art curators must do from time to time. But back home, Tony Whitehead, resigned to my deficiencies, usually assigned it to others more temperamentally suited. Of whom there were many.

Someone turned on the television set above the bar. *"Urghah!"* it said. *"Bdao! Ooghah!"* A martial-arts movie.

"What I'm wondering about," I went on dishonestly, "is just what it is that's worrying Balzano so much. His paintings are OK, after all, and he must know that the chance of another theft attempt is infinitesimal."

"There's also that little matter of the ruined Michelangelo reproduction, which I understand was a valuable drawing on its own."

"Yes, but he was making things difficult before that happened, wasn't he?"

"From the beginning. The consensus—Earl, Egad, Colonel Robey, even Peter—is that he's just a difficult, contrary kind of person who likes making waves to flaunt his power."

"But you don't think that."

"No, I think . . ." She rotated her wineglass slowly on the table, studying the dregs like a fortune-teller reading tea leaves. "Well, they say he's a sick old man now, and he's getting feeble, and I believe he's just . . . fearful, apprehensive, you know? Afraid that something will happen to his things, afraid that maybe he won't live to see them back in his villa now that they've turned up again after so long— the ones from the cache, I mean. It doesn't seem so hard to understand. I think he went along with the show in a burst of gratitude, but now he's having second thoughts."

I nodded. Feeble or not, how would I feel about parting, even temporarily, with a Vermeer I hadn't seen in forty years? I sympathized, although as problems went, I could imagine worse.

"Ee-ya-AOH!" yawped the movie. *"HAIIEEE!"* It had been going loquaciously along for a couple of minutes and I still didn't know what language it was in.

"Refill?" I asked, pointing to her glass.

"No. . . . Yes, please."

I got another glass of wine for her and switched to it myself. I wasn't yet up to coping with two martinis.

"Anne," I said as I sat down, "did Peter ever say anything to you about a forgery?"

"In the show? No." The violet eyes widened. "*Is* there one?"

"I think so, yes."

"But—which one?" She leaned forward excitedly. "It's that Corot, isn't it? I *knew* it!"

I shook my head, smiling. I knew what she meant. *Quai at Honfleur* was the usually estimable Corot at his gauzy worst; a soft-focus panorama of muzzy fishing boats and gray-green trees done in the "poetical" Salon manner that had made him one of the most popular artists of the late nineteenth century.

"You know what they say about Corot?" I said. "That he has the most prolific posthumous production of any artist in history. That he painted one thousand pictures, of which twenty-five hundred are in Europe, five thousand in America, and the rest unaccounted for. No, Peter wouldn't have been so pleased with himself over just another fake Corot. I think it's another one."

"You *think*? You don't know which one it is?"

I sat back and told her about the conversation at Kranzler's.

"A forgery . . ." She turned it over in her mind, then looked sharply up at me, her eyes snapping. "Chris! You don't suppose it has anything to do with his death! Of course it does! It must!"

I looked blankly at her.

"The forgery!" she cried. "Peter discovered a forgery, and they killed him to keep him quiet!"

I looked blankly at her some more. Where was everyone getting these ideas? "Who's 'they'?"

"I don't know who it is—are." She made an impatient little noise. "But it's a *clue*! What else is there to go on? I *told* Colonel Robey Peter couldn't have been killed that way."

I put my wineglass down. "Are you saying," I said very

slowly, "that you don't accept the police version of how Peter was killed?"

"I don't know what the police think, but I certainly don't believe Peter van Cortlandt was crawling around Frankfurt's red-light district last Wednesday night or any other night—" She stopped. "Well, do *you*?"

I did, but I wasn't going to say so. She obviously wanted very much to believe—did believe—that Peter was above anything so sordid, and I had no great desire to disenchant her. Or to differ with her, for that matter. Actually, I was grateful to her for wanting to think the best of Peter. I wanted to think the best of him, too, but the difference between us was that she was an innocent, happily unaware of the essential baseness of men, while I, more seasoned and more tolerant, knew that all men were pretty much alike when it got down to essential baseness.

So I thought, in the full radiance of my ignorance and condescension. Anne was a naive young female, Harry was a typically paranoid cop, and I alone was worldly-wise enough to accept things for what they were.

"I'm not sure what I believe," I temporized cleverly. "What did Mark say when you talked to him?"

"You know Colonel Robey," she said wryly. "You're never sure what wavelength he's on. He listened, nodded very gravely, said 'Hmm, yes, well, I can see where you're coming from,' but his mind was somewhere else. I could tell he thought the same thing you do: that Peter was out—playing around—and got mixed up with a rough crowd, and . . . that's what happened."

"Anne, I didn't say I believed that."

"But you do." She shook her head, a jerk of frustration. "You do, don't you?"

"Well, I don't rule it out."

"But how can you think that? Peter was so decent, so *clean*. You knew him better than any of us; do you really believe he could . . . a prostitute with a tattoo on her behind . . . a horrible, filthy hotel room?" She shivered.

"Anne, listen. I really liked Peter, and I respected him.

But deep down I didn't know him any better than you did. Look, just because a man seems to be decent—*is* decent— doesn't mean that there aren't some pretty dark things going on below the surface. It's not something a man can help, you know—"

Understandably, she laughed at this vapid pedantry. "That's what Colonel Robey said, and that's just the way he said it. Chris, do you really think I'm that wet behind the ears?" She laughed again, this time with exasperation. "I've been in the U.S. Air Force for six years, you know."

As a matter of fact, it was exactly what I thought, but I warmed to her on account of it; because she liked Peter, because she thought more of him than I did. Nevertheless, it seemed like a good time to change the subject.

"Well, maybe you're right," I said. "Anyway, will you let Mark know I'll get a plane to Florence as early as I can tomorrow?"

"Sure. And thanks again." She glanced at the Dortmunder Beer wall clock above us. "Seven o'clock. No wonder my stomach's growling."

Invite her to dinner, dope, I told myself. She practically asked you to. Instead I said, "I've stuffed myself with hors d'oeuvres from the bar, so I think I'll pass up dinner tonight. I'm still catching up on my sleep."

"Oh."

"Maybe we can have dinner one night when I get back."

"Mm-hm," she said noncommittally. Which was all the answer I deserved. She pushed her chair back from the table. "Good luck with Bolzano. And thank you for the wine."

I watched her go with conflicting feelings. One part of me wanted to chase after her and tell her I really wasn't the jerk I seemed to be, that jet lag, concussion, and codeine had combined to throw me off form, and would she like to go to Kranzler's, or the Café Wintergarten, or the nearest Wienerwald after all?

The other part of me won. I sat awhile in morbid solitude, finished my wine, and got up to leave. I really wasn't hungry, and I really was tired. And thinking again about Peter's wretched ending had gotten me down; no question about that. On my way out I passed directly beneath the television set.

"But what can it awr mean, mahstah?" a sloe-eyed young man was asking earnestly. So it was English. Of a sort, anyway; the mushily orientalized version dear to the dubbers of Oriental films. I paused to hear the response.

"It means, my impetuous young flen," a sagacious robed figure replied, "that you may be heading for gleat . . . tlubble."

I took the elevator up and went to bed.

8

I called Florence from my room the next morning and spoke with Lorenzo Bolzano, the collector's son. The elder Bolzano, Claudio, was in the hospital for a twenty-four-hour checkup, so I arranged with Lorenzo to come the following day. Thus, with a free day I flew to Frankfurt to talk to the Kunstmuseum's director for administration, to see if I could resolve the insurance question that had come up on the El Greco. That was the matter that had taken Peter to Frankfurt in the first place, but of course he hadn't lived to make his appointment.

Emanuel Traben was a quiet, worried-looking man of fifty with a sparse little gray goatee, a round red spot on each sallow cheek so unnaturally bright it might have been rouged, and digestive difficulties that kept his fingertips hovering discreetly near his mouth during most of the time we talked.

"You understand," he said apologetically, "that we're most anxious to cooperate, but signor Bolzano has entrusted the care of his magnificent painting to us and"—there was a pause while he winced and belched gently behind his hand—"excuse me—we feel we cannot release it to another party, even at signor Bolzano's request, unless we are fully protected against liability."

I nodded. The Kunstmuseum was insisting that we reimburse them for taking out an extraordinary policy on the painting, one that would cover them in case of any conceivable (or inconceivable) damage to it—natural disaster, act of God, act of war, anything. Such policies come very high, and this one would cost thirty cents per hundred dollars' valued worth per month. On the two-million-dollar El Greco, that would be six thousand dollars a month for the four remaining months of the exhibition, a substantial chunk of the insurance budget.

Peter had resisted. The standard museum policy insures against theft, fire, and the like, at a cost of about three cents per hundred dollars, and he'd felt that ought to be sufficient. Herr Traben, however, was terrified by the possibility of the Kunstmuseum's having to come up with the two million dollars to repay Bolzano if something happened to the painting while it was sub-lent to us. There was a simple way out, of course, and that was to call Bolzano and ask him to formally approve a standard policy—which he would certainly do, because it was the same coverage we had on the rest of The Plundered Past, which had come directly from his personal collection in Florence.

Nobody, however, had wanted to bring it up with the touchy, sick Bolzano, so Peter and Traben had been negotiating for months. But I had new instructions from the open-handed Robey.

"I understand," I said, "and I agree. We'll reimburse you."

He was so astonished he forgot to cover his mouth, and a soft burp bellied his cheeks and emerged unrestrained. "You—excuse me—you're empowered to authorize this?"

I assured him I was, to his obvious relief, but that was only the beginning. Herr Traben was a very conscientious man, and there were other delicate questions. At what point would the museum formally relinquish responsibility for the painting to the U.S. Defense Department? When it was picked up at the museum? When it reached Rhein-Main Air Base, the American compound outside of Frankfurt from which it would be flown to Berlin? Who would be responsible for it during transit through Frankfurt? What exact mode of transportation to the air base would be used? Who would provide it? How would . . . ?

I told him we would be happy to agree to anything reasonable, as long as we had the painting in time for the Berlin opening. Much soothed, he promised to call me in Florence as soon as he had thoroughly discussed matters with the museum's counsel. He was sure things could be worked out.

And that was as resolved as things were going to get. I left the museum with almost three hours before my Lufthansa flight to Florence, and took a bus to the central railroad station, from which I could catch one of the gleaming subway trains that ran out to the airport. I alighted at the train station at noon and immediately realized I was hungry.

In Germany it is hard to be hungry for long without realizing it. The Germans are surely the munchingest people in the world. It is rare to pass three pedestrians in a row without noticing that at least one of them is chewing on something that looks, sounds, and smells delicious. If they have to walk more than 150 feet without sight of a bakery or a *Schnell Imbiss*—a hot-snack stand—they become perceptibly anxious, even panicky. As a result, railroad stations, airports, and other public places are lined with tiny stand-up bars selling sausages, beer, cakes, and other restoratives, generally of high quality.

The Frankfurt *Hauptbahnhof* was no exception, and the first thing I did when I got there was to order a chunk of warm *Leberkäse* and a roll, served with a dab of sweet German mustard on a paper plate, along with a half-liter of beer. I stood with two other men at a table made from a big barrel and downed the meal happily, wondering, not for the first time, how this pulpy, slippery, delicious sausage is made. (I've never dared to ask. There are some things . . .)

The Frankfurt *Hauptbahnhof* was typical of big-city Germany in other ways too, being cavernous, bustling, clean, and pleasantly located, fronting a lively square from which a mall led a few blocks into the heart of the city.

But in Frankfurt's case something has gone wrong. When you head down the pedestrian shopping mall, the Kaiserstrasse, you quickly see that although the pavement is clean, the architecture generally handsome, and the lamp standards charming, a sleazy urban rot has taken hold. It is as if the office-supply stores and flower shops are there on sufferance, and their clients and personnel had better be gone before dark if they know what's good for them.

Obviously, Peter hadn't known. It was here, within a few blocks of the *Hauptbahnhof*, that he had died in the gutter. I hadn't come to Frankfurt with that on my mind, except in a general sense, but now that I was there with two hours before my flight took off, it seemed a natural thing to want to see the place where he'd been killed. Whether a sort of veneration was operating, or simply an unwholesome curiosity, I didn't ask myself. I left my shoulder bag in a locker and walked east from the station, buttoning my coat collar against the dreary gray snow flurries.

It was about as much fun as starting from Market and Turk in San Francisco and strolling into the Tenderloin. The scenery was different, but the cast of characters was the same.

Men with faces as leathery and corrugated as old valises, many with crusty sores on cheeks or foreheads, stood hunched in shivering, unsteady groups of three or four, or leaned shakily against the walls of buildings, staring with bleary hostility at well-dressed passersby who kept their own eyes straight ahead, their expressions judiciously nonobservant. Younger men, earringed and leather-jacketed, stared more openly and aggressively.

Every other storefront was whitewashed or curtained, with a sign that said Sex-Shop or Sex-Kino—or, in one enterprising case, *Sex-Supermarkt*—and near their doorways, and other doorways as well, there were miniskirted, fat-thighed hookers, red-splotched from the cold, with grubby hands and mean, pinched faces. A respectable-looking man in shirtsleeves and tie came out of a photographic-equipment store to shoo one of them away from his entrance. He did it with a vigorous slap on the rear. The woman moved on with a silent grimace and a disgusted flap of her hand at him; he went back into his store flushed and laughing, hooting something to a customer.

There were no big, blond Utelindes. The wigs were all jet black or copper-wire red.

It took me a while to locate the Hotel Paradies, because I didn't know where it was and it wasn't listed in the telephone book. I found it finally in a forlorn alley between Kaiserstrasse and Taunusstrasse. It looked the way I had expected it to. Had it been in America, there would have been sad torn window shades and a red neon sign. Here, those windows that weren't covered by drab metal blinds had grimy, ancient gauze curtains in them, and *Hotel Paradies* was painted directly on the gray stucco wall in rusty, faded brown.

It took only one look to convince me of what I should have known days before; that Anne had been right in her conviction, that Harry had been right in his conjecture, and that the *Polizei*, Robey, and I had gotten it all wrong. Peter van Cortlandt, with his taintless French cuffs and clean, slender hands, would never have gone near the place; not willingly. The man, as Anne had said, was just too fastidious. And if that doesn't sound like a cogent reason, all I can say is that if you'd known him, you'd have thought so, too.

And that meant, of course, what Anne had said it did: that his death had not been a straightforward, squalid little affair but a more complex matter trumped up to look like something it wasn't. Unexpectedly, I felt a whooshing rush of relief. Funny to be relieved when you realize that someone you liked hadn't died in an accident after all but had been murdered. But that's what I felt. Regardless of what I'd been telling myself, I'd been troubled by the sordidness of the thing, and finding out I'd been wrong made a big difference.

I had stood too long staring at the Hotel Paradies; long enough for the wet snow to collect on my eyebrows, long enough for a puffy-faced woman with copper hair to open the front door and call out across the street to me.

I turned and walked back to the *Hauptbahnhof*, reflecting. What about motive? Was there really any reason to think, as Anne did, and Harry seemed to, that it was anything more complicated than a robbery? Peter did carry a lot of cash on him; once I saw him ask a waiter if he could change a thousand-dollar bill at the Thanh Longh, a tiny Vietnamese restaurant on Geary, not far from the museum. (I wound up paying the $9.80 lunch check for the two of us, although Peter had repaid me by 2:00 P.M.)

More than that, Peter *looked* rich—the way he talked, lit his cigarette, crossed one slim leg over the other. As considerate and polite as he was to anyone who came his way, he moved in an aura of self-assured complacence that would probably make a really poor man want to kill him on sight.

So the obvious motive was robbery, especially since the valuables he'd carried with him were missing. And yet, by the time I took my seat on the smooth, silent airport train, I knew I didn't buy it. It was too elaborate for so ordinary a theft: watch, ring, wallet. Peter's killer—or killers—had gone to a great deal of trouble throwing up a smoke screen to befuddle the police. They must have drugged him, put him into a walking trance so that witnesses would remember seeing him "blind-drunk" in a couple of bars, dragged him into that awful hotel, arranged for the tattooed Utelinde . . . but why go through all that when a blow on the head and a quick toss into the Main would have sufficed? Why kill him at all?

And if it wasn't robbery, then I could think of only one reasonable alternative: Anne's hypothesis that "they" had killed him to keep him quiet about the forgery he'd found, the forgery he'd been so quietly jocular about. The idea no longer seemed absurd. One week he discovers a forgery in The Plundered Past, and the next he's murdered in a well-planned setup; set up to have no apparent connection with the show, set up to make his friends, his associates, his family only too happy to see the resulting inquiry get as little publicity as possible. Given the circumstances, "they" must have reasoned, there was hardly likely to be an outcry for an exhaustive investigation. The sooner he was buried, the sooner his miserable end could be forgotten.

It made sense, but it was all conjecture. No, not all. He was murdered; of that I was sure beyond doubt, and his murder was not what it seemed. It had been natural enough for Harry to think along those lines, but why, I wondered irritably, had Anne been able to see it from the beginning, while I, with all my smug condescension, had not? Well, I would tell her that she was right and I was wrong when I saw her next, and I would try to say a few more things too.

As the Lufthansa jet, predictably punctual, rose from the runway, bound for Italy, I was turning a hundred questions over in my mind, and two in particular: Who were "they"? And what was the forgery Peter had found? The first I couldn't do anything about, other than put it in the hands of the police. The second, I could. And would.

I began that evening. Fog and ice storms over much of northern Italy made it impossible for the jet to take off from Milan's Malpensa Airport, where it had made an intermediate stop. I checked into an Agip Motel near the airport, called Lorenzo Bolzano to tell him I'd be a day late, and then telephoned Robey's office in Heidelberg, which would not give me his telephone number but promised to give him mine.

Twenty minutes later, while I was under one of those functional, unenclosed Italian showers where the entire bathroom serves as the shower stall and the water runs down a drain in the middle of the floor, the telephone rang. I grabbed a towel and ran for it.

"Chris?" Robey's daydreamy voice asked. "Where are you—Florence? Is there a problem with Bolzano?"

"I'm in Milan. I'll see Bolzano tomorrow."

"Ah."

"That's not what I called about, though. There's another problem." I sat down on the bed, toweling my hair, and went through what Peter had told me one more time.

"A forgery in The Plundered Past," Robey mused, with all the feverish intensity he might have shown if I'd told him we needed another bottle of glue for the partitions. "Are you going to be able to find it?"

"I don't know. That's what I'm calling about. I think I may have to bring in some technical help. It's expensive. Can the budget stand it?"

"Oh, don't worry about that. If we need help, we'll get help. You let me worry about the budget."

These words were so unlike any I'd ever heard at the San Francisco County Museum of Art that I was momentarily struck dumb. "That's good," I finally managed.

"Well, that's what I'm here for." He was ready to go back to whatever else was on his mind.

"There's something else, Mark. I think Peter's death was a setup; I think he was killed because of the forgery."

"You *what*?" I had his full attention at last.

I explained as well as I could the conclusions I'd come to in Frankfurt, but my reasoning sounded pretty lame even to me, and I could feel his concentration wander as I told him about the seedy Hotel Paradies.

"Well, yes," he said. "I can certainly see why you'd think that. Hm." Back to business as usual with Robey. It was what he'd said to Anne.

"But what do *you* think?"

"Well . . . I wouldn't rule it out."

That was what *I'd* said to Anne. "I think I ought to talk to Gucci about it."

Silence.

"Do you have any objection?" I asked.

"No, no objection. Just—well, I wouldn't want to see a lot of adverse publicity about the show. It's bad enough already."

"Mark, I'm as concerned about the show as you are, but Peter's been killed, for God's sake—"

"You're right, you're right," he said soothingly. "Totally. I was just worried about the media getting a hold of it in some sensational way, that's all. I know you'll conduct yourself discreetly."

"I'll be discreet," I said, not showing my annoyance.

"Of course you will. And Chris?"

"Yes?"

"Assuming for the sake of argument that you're right about Peter's death having something to do with the forgery, then, well . . . I guess what I'm trying to say is pretty obvious."

"I don't think I—"

"Well," he said with a long, slow sigh, "you better take care of yourself." Pregnant pause. "Hadn't you?"

And that was the first time, right then, while I sat naked on the bed, with my hand still on the cradled telephone, that it belatedly dawned on me that I was in danger myself. Peter had been killed, I was now assuming, because he'd come upon a forgery. And here was I, doing everything I could to find the same forgery. I remained there, thinking that over for a while, but I never seriously considered— never considered at all—giving up the investigation.

I don't mean to imply that I'm particularly brave, because I don't think I am. (I was proud of the way I'd reacted in the storage room, but I knew very well I had charged into that fracas instinctively, without stopping to think about it, which is a different thing than bravery.) But when I get started on a problem, there is a dogged streak that surfaces—that old anal fixation, I guess—and it had most certainly surfaced now. I was not about to pull back until that forgery was identified. And until Peter's killer was found.

Resolute as all that may sound, I was glad I'd bought a small bottle of Italian brandy at the airport, and when I'd slipped into my robe, I poured myself a substantial dollop. Then I sat down at the small round table and called Harry Gucci.

It was after eight, but he was still in his office.

"Hey, Chris!" he cried happily. "What's up? Where are you, anyway—Frankfurt? Florence?"

"Milan. Harry, you were right. I think Peter was murdered, and that it had something to do with the forgery."

"What brings on this change of heart?"

"Well, I'm not sure it'll make much sense to you, but I had a look at the Hotel Paradies today."

"And?"

"And Peter van Cortlandt would never in a million years have walked into that place. Not of his own free will. It didn't really hit me until I saw it."

"That's your evidence?"

"I'm afraid so. But I know I'm right, Harry."

The earpiece whistled with a sigh. "Yeah, I think you are, too. The whole thing doesn't sit right, does it?" He was quiet for several seconds, if you don't count tooth-sucking.

"Are you going to follow up on it?" I asked.

"Yeah, I'll follow up, but technically this is the *Polizei*'s case, not the army's; all I can do is sort of work along with them. I think it'd be a good idea if you talked directly with the guy that's running the investigation in Frankfurt."

"Oh, sure, I can hear it now: 'Herr Inspektor, I know with certainty that Peter van Cortlandt would never have gone to bed with a prostitute in the Hotel Paradies.' '*Ja?* And how do you know this, Herr Doktor?' 'I know, Herr Inspektor, because it would have offended his aesthetic and hygienic sensibilities.' That'll really get them going, won't it?"

Harry laughed. "OK, leave it to me. Listen, do you have any idea at all who might have wanted to kill him?"

"No. Nobody."

"Well, somebody. What about motive?"

"All I can think of is what Anne Greene suggested to me: Somebody wanted to keep him quiet about the forgery." I stood up and looked at the sleet thrumming against the black windowpane. "It isn't much, is it?"

"I wouldn't exactly call it a watertight case, no," he said cheerfully. "But have a little faith. Hey, what about the forgery, by the way? Any luck yet?"

"No. But I'll find it."

"Right on. And Chris?"

"I know." I swallowed the rest of the brandy. "Be careful."

I have been to Florence a dozen times, first as an impoverished graduate student grinding out a dissertation, and then as an expenses-paid curator from a rich and acquisitive museum, but I have never stayed anywhere except at the Hotel Augustus. When I was a student, it was a little more than I could realistically afford; now it is a lot less. Whenever I turn in my expense account after a visit, Tony predictably fumes and tells me I ought to put up at the Excelsior Italie. ("At least think about appearances, Chris. Jesus Christ, what will the Uffizi people think?")

One reason I stay there is that it's interesting; a sixteenth-century town house that's been altered so many times you can't figure out where the original rooms were. The exterior is nothing to write home about: a plastered facade of mustard yellow—plain, peeling, and ugly—with a few touches of old stonework that are next-to-invisible under all the grime. But inside it's a clean family hotel with Florentine touches that never fail to please me: vaulted ceilings, worn stone seats tucked in corners, surprising little reading niches, handsome but transparently fake antique furniture old enough to be antique in its own right. There is a tiny bar with a domed ceiling on which is a creditable fake seventeenth-century fresco of birds and foliage.

The other reason I stay at the Augustus is that it's on the Via della Scala, just around the corner from the ancient church of Santa Maria Novella, to which I never fail to make my own personal pilgrimage as soon as I arrive. This time was no exception, even though the taxi let me off at the hotel less than half an hour before Lorenzo Bolzano, Claudio Bolzano's son, was due to pick me up.

Five minutes after I'd checked in and been effused over by Alberto like the old client I was, I was inside the church, standing before a shadowed fresco in pale browns midway down the left wall of the nave. Inconspicuous, washed-out-looking, pretty much ignored in this city crammed with fabulous art treasures, it is a landmark in the history of art.

There have been a lot of landmark artworks and a lot of landmark artists, but only once has a painter single-handedly launched with a single painting a movement that changed art forever. The painter was Masaccio, the painting was *The Holy Trinity*, and the movement, if that's a strong enough word, was the Renaissance. In painting, anyway; Donatello and Brunelleschi had already gotten the ball rolling in sculpture and architecture.

The twenty-four-year-old Masaccio's innovations were stunning. He used light as no painter before him had. Even the great Giotto's light had been flat, sourceless, an obvious necessity but no more. Masaccio illuminated with it, hid with it, molded with it. And Masaccio's figures are the first "clothed nudes"; they look as if they could get out of their robes if they wanted to, and nobody in a painting had ever looked that way before. Even more important, the chapel in *The Holy Trinity* is the first painted space that is not "on the wall" but an extension of the space in which the viewer stands. The awestruck Vasari said it was like peering into a cave in the wall. And Masaccio accomplished this not merely with an artist's cunning but with a deft, precise application of Brunelleschi's new insights into the laws of perspective.

The fresco hit Florence like a thunderbolt. Seventy-five years later young artists like Michelangelo were still coming to study it.

And another five hundred years after that, so was I. It is a hell of a feeling for an art historian to stand a few feet from it (no, not to touch it; I have my limits), just where Masaccio himself stood, and Michelangelo and Ghirlandaio and the rest, and to know that it all started right here, right on this wall, right in front of you.

A couple of elderly women, one fat and one thin, but sisters from the look of them, plodded up beside me on tourist-weary feet. They held a shiny green guidebook open between them and looked from the fresco to the book, and then back again.

"It's not much to look at," the thin one finally said in a midwestern accent. "This can't be it."

"Yes, it is," the other replied, and read aloud from the book: " 'On the wall of the third bay in the north aisle, one will find Masaccio's timeless masterpiece, the magnificent and deeply moving *Holy Trinity*.' This has to be it." But she didn't sound too convinced herself.

"Well, I don't think it's so magnificent," the thin one said, querulous, perhaps, after too many timeless masterpieces. "Anyway, it looks too new. This must be a copy. I mean, the original must be in a museum."

I wasn't unsympathetic to her reaction. The innovations that had stood fifteenth-century Florence on its ear were old hat now. To twentieth-century eyes, the *Trinity* was one more drab religious painting, not notably different from thousands of others. Its importance is historic, not aesthetic, and the average tourist mooning over it (unlike this honest woman) is only mouthing so many vaguely comprehended platitudes.

I think I just achieved a new acme of snobbery: If *I* like an old painting, it's acute perception; if *you* do, it's ignorant hypocrisy.

"Per piacere, signore," the plump one said uncertainly, turning to me and clearing her throat, *"questa pittura . . . è la Trinita . . . la Trinita Sacra?"*

"Si, signora," I said.

"La . . . la originale? De Masaccio?"

"Si, signora. Ha proprio ragione." She was so timidly pleased with being the linguist of the team that I enjoyed being able to tell her she was right in Italian.

"Grazie tante, signore," she said.

"Prego, signora."

"This gentleman says," she explained to her sister, "that this is the original."

"That much I can understand," said the other ungraciously. "Anyway, what does he know? I say it's a fake."

And off they shuffled toward the more popular Ghirlandaio frescoes in the chancel.

"It's a delicate point, don't you think so?" asked a high-pitched, Italian-accented voice behind me. "The fresco has been rather zealously restored, you must agree."

The speaker was a tall, hollow-chested man with a bald, domed head, wearing wire-rimmed glasses mounted on a long, pinched nose. He stared amiably at me with the button-eyed gaze of an alert and optimistic dog that has just heard the refrigerator door open.

Lorenzo Bolzano. Although I had never met his father, I knew Lorenzo slightly, having encountered him at art symposia now and then. Lorenzo had a reputation of his own, quite apart from being the son of the eminent collector. He was an art scholar of the more abstruse variety: adjunct professor of the philosophy of art criticism at the University of Rome. He was also European editor of the frighteningly intellectual, usually incomprehensible (to me) *Journal of Subjectivistic Art Commentary*, to which he sometimes contributed his own incoherent (to anyone) monographs ("Reality as Metaphor"; "Is Art 'Real'?").

"Hello, Christopher," he said. "I was told at your hotel that you would be here."

"Hi, Lorenzo. I'm glad to see you."

And I was. His views on art were laughable but harmless, and he himself had an agreeable daffiness that made him fun to talk to if you didn't mind pursuing learned theoretical circumbendibuses that never got you much of anywhere. I was also glad to see him because I hoped he might help when it came time to deal with his father.

That hope was short-lived.

"My father?" he said with an unmistakable stiffening of his small mouth when I asked about Claudio Bolzano's health. "Much better, thank you."

"That's good, Lorenzo. And is he really serious about taking the paintings back?"

"With my father, who knows?" he said curtly. "Anything is possible."

"But what about you, Lorenzo? How do you feel about it? Surely you've got some say in it, too."

"How do I feel about it?" He laughed shortly. "What difference would that make? Perhaps we should go now?"

Lorenzo was not one to stay grumpy for long. As we began to walk over the vast, echoing tiled floor of the church, his mood lightened perceptibly. "All right, then, tell me," he said. "What do you think about the *Trinity*?"

"What do I think about it?"

"Real or fake?"

"*The Holy Trinity*? Real, of course. There's never been any doubt about it."

"Ah, I think you miss my point, you miss my point."

"I think maybe I do," I said, looking forward to some Lorenzian hairsplitting.

"My point is, Christopher, that the question involves far more than a distinction between 'authentic' and 'inauthentic,' you know? There are many gradations. *Trinity* has been restored more than once over the centuries, true? Parts have been removed, parts have been too thoroughly cleaned, parts have been, shall we say, amplified, parts have been completely redone—"

"As with any old painting."

"Yes, exactly, exactly. And so the question is, how much of an old painting must be the work of the original *maestro* for it still to be authentic—that is, in this case, still to be a genuine Masaccio? Or let me put it another way: What percentage must be the work of restorers before you would call it *in*authentic?"

"Well, I don't think it's a question of percentages. The *Trinity*—"

"Ah, ah, but, as you suggest, the issue is broader than the *Trinity*, broader than restoration. Consider Rubens, for example, with his vast student workshop, all right? Well, is a portrait in which the head and hands were done by Rubens and the rest by his students a genuine Rubens or merely a school project? What if Rubens signs it?"

"Well—"

"What if the head alone was painted by the *maestro*? What if only the mouth? What if only the signature is his entirely?

"Well—"

"For that matter, who can distinguish with certainty how many square millimeters of a painting are by Rubens, and how many by his pupils? Can I? Can you? Ah-ha-ha."

"Well—?"

"Or consider a thoroughly authentic Piero della Francesca that was 'improved' in the nineteenth century, as so many fine paintings were, to make it more salable? How would you classify that? Eh?"

As interesting and important as these questions are, they're unresolvable. They have to be handled case by case; there aren't any generic answers. But Lorenzo was attacking them with all his usual relish for abstract and insoluble problems.

I laughed, cheered as always by his enthusiasm. "Well ..." I paused automatically, but this time I was allowed to go on. "In the first place, there aren't any 'authentic' Pieros in that sense. We're talking about the mid–fifteenth century. In those days, you know, an artist's signature was more or less a trademark for the products of a sort of mass-production workshop. It wasn't until da Vinci that the idea of artistic individuality—"

This descent into the concrete did not keep his interest. "But!" he cut me off excitedly. "But! Take the case of an artist undervalued in his own time—Vermeer, Manet, Degas—to which a more famous, more marketable signature has been added. What then? How do we classify that? Art or fake? Eh?"

"Well—" I began, and this time I interrupted myself with a start. Was this merely Lorenzo's usual academic babbling, or was there a point to it? It had just occurred to me that every artist he'd mentioned was represented in The Plundered Past. Did he know something I didn't know? Was this his roundabout way of getting to it?

"It's both," I replied. "A work of art and a fake. And a forgery. Like the de Hooch signature on your Vermeer."

I said this as meaningfully as I could, but all I got in return was a continuation of his wacky smile and an absent-minded nod of the kind that tells you you didn't get through.

I tried again as we stopped before the door of the church. "Lorenzo, are you trying to tell me something?"

"Tell you something?"

"About art forgery? About one particular forgery?"

"I'm not talking about particularity at all, Christopher, but about universality—the universal absurdity of objectivist definition, with specific relevance to authenticity in art."

What could I say to that?

What could anyone say?

Outside, in the welcome winter sunlight, we strode over the ancient, uneven paving stones of the Piazza Santa Novella, scattering the grumbling pigeons before us. Lorenzo was waving his bony arms and ranting about synthetico-functional intuitions of reality, but my mind was going back over what he'd said. Whether he had intended to or not, he had me thinking about forgeries from a highly particular perspective indeed.

Was it possible that what I was hunting for wasn't a forgery in the ordinary sense at all, but something else? A legitimate if "overzealous" restoration, for example, perhaps centuries old, that had obscured the work beneath and could now be cleaned away with modern techniques? A painting that had gotten by until now as a Rubens or a Reynolds, but that Peter had spotted as a student project? Was that why he'd been so ambiguous when I'd tried to pin him down?

"As to defining forgery from a historico-contextual perspective," Lorenzo raved on, "you have to remember that the *lex Cornelia de falsis* wasn't formulated until the last century B.C., so forgery as such didn't—*Urp!*"

He yelped as I grabbed him by the arm and yanked him back onto the curb of the piazza. Without even glancing at the murderous Florentine traffic, he had started across the Via della Scala.

"—become a criminal act until quite late in the development of Roman law," he continued, unshaken. Was he aware that three drivers were screaming obscenities at him? Had he noticed that I had saved his life? That I still had him firmly by the arm? I doubted it.

When the traffic light permitted, I nudged him, and he moved trustingly into the street, still going on about forgery in ancient Rome. He stopped, however, when we came to an old red Fiat, dented (as all cars must soon be in Italy), weathered, and indifferently cared for. "Here we are," he said.

I must have looked surprised, because he said, "In Italy people of wealth are wise not to draw attention to themselves." He opened the passenger door and motioned me in. "I think you will agree," he said dryly, "that this automobile has been well chosen in that regard."

I laughed, but I was sure Lorenzo Bolzano wouldn't care—or notice—whether he were driving the old Fiat or a new Alfa-Romeo. He edged the little car out of its cramped parking spot, first crunching against the car behind, then scraping the rear fender of the one in front, muttering peevishly at them all the while.

Driving in Florence is not quite as terrifying as it is in Rome or Naples, but it is still less a matter of skill and judgment than of raw courage. Lorenzo was one of the people who made it that way, undergoing his Jekyll-to-Hyde transformation the moment he grasped the wheel. Once out on the street, he drove his little clunker with defiant bravado, zigzagging around other cars when there was no need, aggressively thrusting timid pedestrians back onto the curb, contemptuously forcing gigantic trucks to slam on their brakes to avoid pulverizing us.

We drove down the Via de Fossi toward the Lungarno, that highly civilized avenue of walled, guarded palazzos where there was reputed to be more great art than in the Uffizi and Bargello combined. It was where I had always imagined Claudio Bolzano to live, but we passed it and drove over the Ponte alla Carraia into the distinctly less tony section of the city south of the Arno. After a few blocks, we turned onto the Via Talenti, a nondescript street lined with huge square-fronted Renaissance palazzos.

If you've never been to Florence, you're wondering how anyone could call a street lined with Renaissance palazzos nondescript, right? But in Florence you'd have a hard time finding a city block without a few of them, and many blocks are made up of nothing but. Some of these old town houses are very beautiful, among the most beautiful buildings in the world; others, like those on this drab, grimy street, are not. People understandably assume that anything erected during the Renaissance was a work of art, but of course that isn't so, any more than it is so that something built in the twentieth century is necessarily ugly, although there you'd have a better case.

With a final unnecessary lurch around and in front of the car ahead of us, resulting in a quick, expert exchange of raised fists, Lorenzo jerked the car to a stop half-in and half-out of the vaulted entryway to a gloomy, boxlike palazzo. This prompted one more yelp of outrage from the other driver, who swerved around us and continued on his way, one hand leaning on the horn and one fist sticking out the window, raised and quivering. It didn't occur to me to wonder who was steering.

"Maniac," Lorenzo muttered happily. Then he sat quietly for a few moments while the fur on the back of his hands faded away and his fanglike canines receded.

The only way into the building was this old carriage entrance, an arched passage fifteen feet high and ten wide, firmly blocked by great wooden double doors—the original ones, I thought, studded with iron, and with two great, rusty door-knockers at head height, shaped like lions with wreaths in their mouths. As eye-catching as all this may sound, it wasn't. The neighboring old buildings had similar entrances, and all of them were dusty and black with age, like the buildings themselves. The impression the street gave was of a back alley running between the rear entrances of two rows of dilapidated warehouses; not the kind of places anyone would want to live in.

On the left door of this one, just below the knocker, was a plaque that read *DIVIETO DI SOSTA*—No parking—and on the door opposite was the sign beloved by privacy-seeking Italians since Pompeii: a picture of a snarling dog above the words *ATTENTI AL CANE*. (*CAVE CANEM*, it would have said in Pompeii, but the sentiment was the same.)

Lorenzo reached a gangly arm out of the car window and pressed a button on a brass plate attached to the wall of the passageway. There were five other buttons on it, each with a neatly engraved name next to it, as if each of the three stories of the palazzo had two tenants. That I doubted, although there was certainly more than room enough. The buzzer he had pressed was labeled Uffici Tacca: Studio di Architettura e Grafica; not the sort of sign likely to bring drop-in visitors. In addition, the square ceramic address-tile above the plate was artfully broken so that nothing but a fragment of the last number—a 3—was visible. Or was it a 5? Whatever else they might be, the Bolzanos were masters at not calling attention to themselves.

The heavy doors swung inward, scraping along deep curving ruts in the cobblestones, and we drove into the vestibule, stopping before another tall gate, this one of steel. At our left was the old gatekeeper's lodge, its window cut like a ticket-taker's box into the wall. In it was a man in a dark blue uniform sitting before a rack of four television monitors.

He nodded at Lorenzo and inserted a key into a slot beside him. The wooden door behind us creaked closed, the inner gate swung smoothly open, and the Fiat chugged slowly out of the vestibule, away from the grungy Via Talenti, and into the golden world of the Florentine Cinquecento.

10

Not every sixteenth-century Florentine's world, of course, but the world as it might have looked to you if you'd been a Medici or a Pazzi.

To start with, everything was clean. The flooring of the courtyard was made of square pink paving stones, the walls of rough-textured almond-colored blocks. Around the four sides, stuccoed, intricately figured columns supported the vaulted roof of a hollow-square loggia, the sides of which were decorated with enormous frescoes of sixteenth-century Austria and Hungary.

In the center was an atrium, open to the sky, with a mellow, musical old fountain topped by spouting bronze dolphins of the sixteenth-century variety. Marble and bronze statues stood on pedestals, and urns were everywhere—Roman, Etruscan, Greek, Minoan—all of them overflowing with out-of-season flowers.

All at the same time I admired it, I envied it, and I thought it a ridiculous, affected, and offensively ostentatious way to live in the 1980s. No, not ostentatious; I don't imagine many people got a chance to see it.

"This is beautiful," I said to Lorenzo as we walked through the incredible loggia to a discreetly disguised elevator.

"Oh," he said. "Yes."

I motioned at the battle scences. "Vasari?"

"Mostly. That one over the door is a Signorelli," he pointed out with little interest. "Shall we go up now?"

We rode to the second floor in silence, and then went

through a set of double doors into the reception room, a modest little salon with sixteenth-century Spanish leather wall paneling, seventeenth-century Florentine tapestries, and a colossal French Renaissance marble fireplace hacked from some French chateau, bearded, grim caryatids and all. Lorenzo glanced at his watch.

"My father's getting his afternoon shave now. We can wait here if you like, or there's time to see the collection. I meant the collection per se, not these." He waved carelessly at the Tuscan and Venetian mannerist paintings on the leather walls.

The Bolzano art collection "per se" took up the entire floor above, which we reached by walking up an oppressively grand staircase under a domed ceiling covered with an exuberant allegorical fresco—*Courage, Prudence, and Destiny Carrying the Globe of the Florentine Republic Into Immortality;* something like that. It seemed impossible that the grubby Via Talenti ran by below, but there it was, darkly visible through the grimy (only on the outside) hallway windows.

Knowing my tastes, Lorenzo took me directly to the Dutch baroque wing. Not surprisingly, he wanted to talk about the conflict between symbolistic and phenomenological world views in Flemish genre painting, but when he saw that I just wanted to look, and appreciate, and say nothing, he showed mercy and walked silently along beside me.

We moved past rollicking low-life scenes by Jan Steen, a glowering landscape of van Ruisdael, an antiseptic church interior by Saenredam—

I stopped suddenly. "Wait!" I was staring at a painting on the wall at the far end of the room: a Vermeer—a girl, cool and reflective, standing at a clavichord. . . .

Lorenzo looked inquiringly at me.

"That painting—" I said confusedly. "It's the one from the cache. I was just looking at it in Berlin. How . . ." My mind raced while I nattered on. Could I have been wrong? Was the Vermeer I'd examined so closely in Berlin a copy after all? If *this* one was the original—

Lorenzo tittered. "It's a copy, Christopher."

"A copy?"

"Didn't you know? My father had copies made of most of the pieces stolen by the Nazis."

Yes, of course I knew that; I nearly got killed by one. "But this one—that is, the original of it—it's been recovered now. Why—"

"Ah, recovered, but not yet returned to its home. While it's in your exhibition, we keep the copy in its place. Why not?"

When we got nearer, I saw that it was extraordinarily well done, but definitely not the real thing. And yes, I would have known it even if no one had told me.

"Quite a piece of work," I said.

"Ah-ha-ha. What do I detect in your tone, Christopher? You don't approve? You think it déclassé to hang copies alongside authentic masterpieces?"

"No, not déclassé, but puzzling. If you're going to have genuine art—"

"'Genuine'? 'Art'?" He crowed with pleasure at having snared me. "Define your terms! What do you mean by 'art'?"

Oh boy, I thought, here we go again.

He gestured at the Vermeer copy. "Will you admit this is an object of beauty?"

"Yes, it's beautiful—"

"But not art?"

"No, not in the sense I mean; not with a capital A. It's an imitation. The person who did it was trying to reproduce something already done, not to make something new. It was a mechanical operation, not a creative one; craft, not art."

I was speaking quickly, hoping to head him off, but a startling new idea had burst in on me, one that I should have thought of a long time ago.

"Not art?" Lorenzo repeated archly. "Not art? Do you so completely accept the contextualist position, then, that—"

But I had other fish to fry. "Lorenzo," I interrupted, "tell me something. A copy like this—or the copies in the show—they're extremely fine, good enough to fool almost anyone. Isn't there a danger of their accidentally getting out into the market sometime as originals?"

Or into The Plundered Past itself as originals, accidentally or otherwise. With dozens of fine Bolzano copies around, a little mix-up—a small confusion of false with real—was far from impossible.

Happily, Lorenzo was willing to be diverted. "No," he said, "impossible. We've taken precautions. I'll show you." He went to a wall telephone. "Giulio? Will you turn off the alarms in Room Nine, please?" he asked in Italian.

He came back to the painting. "First, my father has kept the most careful records of the reproductions, both the old ones he's bought and the new ones he's commissioned. There are copies of the records, and photographs of the reproductions themselves in our vaults and in our attorney's hands. And on the pictures themselves—"

The telephone rang and he picked it up. *"Bene."*

"Will you help me take it down and turn it around?" he said to me.

We removed the cumbersome painting carefully—its heavy gilt frame was authentically seventeenth-century Dutch, I was sure—and turned it to the wall. "See?" he said. "The provenance is there, right on the back."

So it was. A neatly hand-lettered statement concisely explaining that this was the work of one Rodolfo Venturi, commissioned in 1948 by Claudio Bolzano for an unspecified price and executed that same year in imitation of *Young Woman at the Clavichord* by Jan Vermeer, taken from the Bolzano collection by the Nazis in 1944.

"All the copies have such a statement, inscribed in indelible ink on the backs of the canvases or etched into the backs of the panels."

"Indelible ink can be removed; etching can be smoothed."

"But there's more. On the face of every reproduction is a tiny pattern, almost microscopic, of drilled holes. Even our old copies—and we have a false Raphael almost three-hundred years old—have this. It's certain proof, you see, that a painting is not an original."

"Holes can be filled in."

He whinnied with laughter. "How distrustful you are! When did you become so cynical, Christopher? But no; they can't be filled in—not if they can't be found. And they're impossible to see with the naked eye; next to impossible with a lens, if one doesn't know precisely what to look for and where to look for it. And if they *were* to be filled in, the foreign material would be easily identifiable. No, this can never be confused with an authentic Vermeer."

We turned the painting around and rehung it.

"Well," I said, studying it, "if there's a design punched into this one, I can't find it."

Lorenzo's mild brow furrowed. "Er ... Christopher ... you understand that I can't show it to you. I would if it were up to me, but my father's adamant about keeping it confidential." He shuffled his long legs uncomfortably. "I probably shouldn't even have mentioned it. You're not offended? It's only to prevent the sort of possibility you mention."

I told him I wasn't offended but thought that as director of the show it might be a good thing for me to know.

He continued to frown. "Why?"

Why I hadn't told him before, I wasn't sure, except that, knowing as little as I did, it seemed sensible to play it as close to the vest as possible. But the paintings in the show were his, after all, his and his father's, and I had no reason to suspect either of them.

I was blunt. "Peter van Cortlandt told me just before he died that he thought there was a forgery in the exhibition, but he didn't tell me which one. I've been trying to find it."

"A ... a ..." Lorenzo had one of those prominent, pointy Adam's apples that seemed to have a life of their own, and now it ratcheted up and down his throat three times before he could speak. "That's impossible—you don't know what you're saying. You ..." His plastic-button eyes bulged even more. "Surely you don't mean to suggest that my father, that

I, would knowingly . . ." His voice petered out and then
came back in an outraged squeak: *"Christopher!"*

"No, Lorenzo," I said hurriedly, "I wouldn't think that;
neither did Peter. But isn't it possible that one of the copies
might accidentally have—"

"But no!" he cried with scandalized dignity. "We know
art, Christopher; it's our life, as it is yours. It's inconceivable that I—let alone my father—could be . . . be fooled in
the way you suggest. Really . . ."

He was only partly right. As wackily erudite as he might
be about art criticism, when it came to assessing individual
works of art, I wouldn't have trusted him to tell the difference between a Rembrandt and a Rauschenberg. But his father was another matter; one of the world's most discerning
collectors.

"And," he continued, "we know our limitations well
enough to call in scientific assistance when we're in doubt."

"I know you do," I said.

"Peter was . . . was joking, perhaps?"

"Could be," I said. Or it could be that the substitution of
a fake painting for a real one had been made after the last
time Claudio Bolzano had seen them. This more likely possibility I kept to myself, not seeing much point in suggesting that one of the family masterpieces had disappeared
since it had been placed in the care of the United States
Army. "I guess you're right."

"No, you don't," Lorenzo said with surprising perception. Then, doubtfully: "Christoper, you're not going to
raise this with my father, are you?"

"Well, I wouldn't want to excite him. His health—"

"Yes, certainly, that, of course. But, in addition, it would
hardly be a way to win him over to your side."

"To my side?"

"I thought you were here to try to convince him to per-
mit The Plundered Past to go on." He smiled. "Or did you
come to discuss subjectivist art criticism with me?"

I laughed. Strange to have to be brought down to earth
by Lorenzo Bolzano.

11

Bullet-headed, small, intense, Claudio Bolzano was everything his son was not. Where Lorenzo was professorial, Bolzano was down to earth; where Lorenzo was wandering and abstract, Bolzano was direct; where Lorenzo's intelligence was amiably eccentric, Bolzano's was incisive and focused.

He was also irritable, restless, and cranky; a man very much used to power, but now forced into a convalescent's feeble routine. He received us with his arms folded, seated erectly in the corner of an immense sofa, not at all the decrepit invalid at death's door I'd been expecting. He was wearing a cashmere sport coat with the collar of his open-throated shirt flattened out over the lapels, so that he looked like a member of the Israeli Knesset about to take his turn pitching hay at a kibbutz.

He was far younger than I'd imagined, in his sixties, with a thick gray fringe of close-cropped hair at the back of his neck, and lively black Italian eyes. There were a few signs of illness—a shadowing around the eyes, a hint of pallor—but he seemed very much a man on the mend, energetic and impatient, and more than capable of snapping the gravely fawning Lorenzo over one knee.

If the man was a surprise, the room was a shocker. The study of the famous collector of old masters was relentlessly modernistic, its walls hung with plainly mounted abstracts by Rauschenberg, Rothko, Bazaine, Nay, Twombly, and others that I didn't know and didn't want to know. The huge desk along one wall was a weird combination of copper and glass; almost everything else was white—the walls, the big couch and armchairs, the rectangular plastic tables, the floor, the rugs, the track lighting. And everything seemed to be made of right angles and straight lines, including the compact, squarish Bolzano himself.

He waved us into two cuboid armchairs while Lorenzo was still introducing us. "We'll speak English," he announced. "I speak it fluently." He patted a quiet dog—also white—who sat on the floor at his side, and waited for me to say something.

"I hope I'm not disturbing you, signor Bolzano. I've wanted to meet you for a long time."

A negligent wave of the hand, and then a shrugged afterthought. "I've heard of you too."

Another lengthy silence while Lorenzo, looking uncomfortable, grinned encouragingly from one of us to the other.

"And I hope you're feeling well, signore," I said.

"Not bad for someone my age." He indicated that one must accept life on its own terms, that one takes the good with the bad, that one doesn't know what the future holds, and that on the whole we were better off not knowing. All this accomplished with a small movement of one hand, a lift of a shoulder, and a slight downward turn of his mouth. (The Italians can do these things.) "Everyone gets old."

"True," I said penetratingly.

A bowed old man in gray, who never once raised his eyes from the carpet, came in with a bottle of Acqua Minerale Panna for Bolzano, and brandies, espressos, and dry biscuits for Lorenzo and me.

When we'd each taken a ceremonial sip, Bolzano put his glass down heavily. "I was very sorry to hear about Peter van Cortlandt. He was a fine man. I thought extremely highly of him."

"Thank you. He thought a great deal of you too. I had lunch with him the day he died, and I know he was looking forward to talking with you that night."

Bolzano's brows knit. "He was coming to Florence?"

"No, but he said he was going to call you from Frank-fort."

"He was? About what?"

That, unfortunately, answered that. Peter had not fol-lowed up on his idea of telephoning Bolzano with some "pertinent, subtle" questions. So one more possible line of inquiry on the forgery was closed to me. I tried not to show my disappointment.

"About what?" Bolzano said again.

"I don't know."

While Bolzano looked queerly at me, Lorenzo said, "Fa-ther, signor Norgren is here on behalf of The Plundered Past—"

"Signor Norgren should speak for himself," Bolzano said, looking steadily at me.

"You're right, signore. I *am* here to speak on behalf of The Plundered Past. It's a magnificent show and a great tribute to your taste and your generosity—"

"And a magnificent tribute to the American army; don't forget that." For the first time he smiled. "But I don't be-grudge them that. I appreciate very much what they've done for me. But, frankly, I worry about my paintings, sig-nore; I don't want to lose them. What happened in Berlin is a disgrace."

"Father, please. You shouldn't excite yourself," Lorenzo put in.

Bolzano made a face. "I'm not excited. But I ask you: How could it happen? Were there no alarms, no protection? Were the pictures simply left lying in the cellar?"

"No," I said uncomfortably, "there were guards at the front and back doors—"

"And both were overcome. You too, I understand."

I nodded. "I'm afraid so."

"Well, I'm sorry you got hurt," he said gruffly. "And thank you for saving my pictures." He cleared his throat and poured some more water into his glass; he was not a man used to thanking others.

"I've had a careful look at the damaged Michelangelo

copy," I said, "and I'm sure it's salvageable. We'll pay for having it restored, of course."

He shook his head roughly. "I don't give a damn about the copies; that's not the point."

"Father, please," Lorenzo murmured.

"The point is," Bolzano said, "it's only luck that it wasn't a Rubens or a Tiziano—a real one, I mean. For that matter, it's only luck that they didn't get away with all of them. What kind of security do you call that?"

"Father, please," Lorenzo said. When that earned him only an irritated look, he tried a different approach. "Please, Father."

"Please, Father; Father, please," mimicked Bolzano wearily. "Signor Norgren, I ask you: Do I seem overexcited to you? In danger of imminent death?" He held out a steady, blunt-fingered hand. Not only did he fail to seem overexcited to me, but I had the impression that he was enjoying himself very much.

"No, sir," I said, "but I want you to know that security isn't a problem any longer. We've installed the most up-to-date devices that exist."

I should have known better.

"Such as?" Bolzano asked.

I gulped and tried to remember what Anne had said at the meeting. "Well, there are infrared and ultraviolet barriers at the doors and windows, and photoelectric cells and electronic sensors that are triggered by movement or body heat." I didn't know what the hell I was talking about, and I hoped I was getting it right. "And pressure-sensitive alarms on the paintings that splatter indelible green ink on whoever sets them off." That I recall as a particularly memorable touch.

"That's extremely impressive, Christopher," Lorenzo said, doing his pathetic best to help. "Extremely. Isn't it, Father?"

"Eh," Bolzano said neutrally.

"And," I went on, "most of it runs on car batteries in case the electricity is cut."

I hoped that was it for questions. My fund of knowledge was exhausted.

Bolzano seemed to be weighing things. "And what about this group, these Nazis?"

"The Heinrich-Schliemann-Gründung?"

"Yes, them. How do I know they won't convince the German government to keep my pictures?" He smiled grimly. "They've already done it once."

"The police say they have absolutely no support. And in any case, you've lent your paintings to the United States Department of Defense, not Germany. Nobody's going to take them."

"Ahh," he said gravely, "the United States Department of Defense. That's different." He laughed, not offensively, and leaned back against the white couch, his hand kneading the loose skin at the dog's neck.

I was certain he was wavering, and pushed home my arguments: Of all the private collections looted by the Nazis, Bolzano's had benefited more from American military efforts than any other private collection except the Rothchilds'—

"So let Rothschild put on a show."

Besides that, I pointed out, months of work by many people had gone into the preparations, the catalog, the insurance, the excruciating maneuvering to secure a temporary export license from the Italian government. And the show had been extensively covered in the world press, much to the enhancement of the Bolzano reputation. If he were to pull out now, his credibility would suffer enormously.

"Ah, my credibility," he murmured.

"And of course," I said, reluctantly getting down to serious arm-twisting, "there's a signed agreement—"

His black eyes fixed mine sharply. "Would you really try to hold me to that?"

"We'd have to," I said, knowing that if it were up to me I wouldn't. "We think The Plundered Past is an extremely—"

He held up his hand. "Enough. I'm convinced. All right, the show will continue."

Lorenzo expanded his narrow chest and beamed, as if he had personally engineered this, and I sat back, relieved but not surprised. From the moment he'd grunted hello, I'd had the feeling he wasn't serious about pulling out. Anne, who'd never met him, had read him all wrong. He was no feeble, fearful old shut-in but a man who enjoyed asserting his considerable power, and getting me down to Florence had just been a way of perking up his life a little.

The white dog, which had done nothing but gaze enchantedly at Bolzano, suddenly turned its head sideways, snapped at the air, and looked astonished when it didn't come up with anything. One of its baggy ears had flopped inside-out with the effort, so that the pink interior showed.

Bolzano laughed, a gravelly rasp deep in his throat. "Hey, *cane*, you look ridiculous. Put your ear back the way it should be." He leaned over and affectionately straightened it with his hand. The dog, an ordinary mutt without visible pretensions, gazed up at him in a tongue-lolling ecstasy of admiration.

Lorenzo and I laughed, too, and we all relaxed a little.

"So, signor Norgren," Bolzano said expansively, "you like The Plundered Past? Please, have a cake."

I bit into one of the dry, anise-flavored biscuits. "I think it's superb. There are paintings in it I've wanted to see for years."

"And the copies? Tell me, what do you think of exhibiting the copies of the missing pictures?" His bright eyes darted momentarily to glare at Lorenzo, then came back to me.

Lorenzo's Adam's apple jounced, and the tip of his droopy nose turned a shade bluer. He looked beseechingly at me. I had no idea what was in the air between them, and said something safe.

"I think there's something to be said for the idea."

Lorenzo was so relieved his breath whistled, but it wasn't the answer Bolzano wanted.

"I don't!" he said, so emphatically that the dog started. "I see no purpose in it. It was a childish fancy ever to buy them. I should have disposed of them long ago."

"I must disagree, Father," Lorenzo ventured in timorous rebellion. "I say that if an object is beautiful, why shouldn't it give pleasure for its own sake? From a purely aesthetic point of view, why should it make any difference whether it was painted in 1680 in the throes of divine inspiration—ah-ha-ha—or copied three hundred years later, with every stroke faithfully reproduced?" His shiny eyes brightened. "Not more than thirty minutes ago, even the learned Christopher was deceived by our excellent copy of the young woman at her clavichord."

Bolzano looked at me with something close to disappointment. "Is this true?"

"Well, momentarily," I admitted.

"And why should he not be?" Lorenzo said, gaining momentum. "It's a wonderful painting in its own right: every line laid on razor-sharp; the pearl earring a small masterpiece of its own, portrayed with a delicate precision that might fool Vermeer himself."

"Do you agree, signore?" Bolzano asked me dryly.

"Not entirely, no." I was still unsure of where I was treading, or on whose toes.

But he wouldn't be put off. "Do you agree that the painting my son describes so eloquently might fool Vermeer himself?"

I was being tested, then, and I thought I'd better prove myself, even at the cost of some face for Lorenzo. "No," I said, "not the way he described it. Vermeer's precision is a brilliant illusion. There are no lines, no outlines. Those pearl earrings that seem so perfect and pearl-like—seen up close they're just three or four formless dabs of paint. Everything in a Vermeer is fuzzy—"

"*What?*" Lorenzo's eyebrows shot up to the vicinity of where his hairline had once been. "Fuzzy? *Vermeer?* Christopher, I cannot believe—"

"Of course fuzzy!" Bolzano snapped. "Vermeer was the

most painterly of painters—more so even than Rembrandt,
Velázquez—not some mere linear drudge like Bronzino
or—"

"Not linear?" echoed Lorenzo, who seemed stunned a lot
of the time. "Vermeer?"

"The forms themselves are anything but precise, Lorenzo," I said, heading off a less gentle response from his father. "When you look at a Vermeer, it's your mind that sorts
things out, not your eye. It's not so different from you own
subjectivist—"

"Ha," Bolzano muttered.

"But the texture," Lorenzo persisted, "the *clarity* . . ."

"But that's just what makes him so great," I said. "It's all
a magical illusion, a deceptive clarity—"

"Ah." Bolzano nodded his bullet head with approval. "A
magical, deceptive clarity. Well said, Christopher Norgren."
He looked sharply at his son and shifted to brisk, rapid
Italian.

"And this magic, Lorenzo, this magic flourishes only
with that 'divine inspiration' you sneer so superiorly at, and
which makes a work of art a living thing. An imitation is
lifeless, no matter how wonderful it seems at first, and the
longer one lives with a bogus painting the more hateful it
becomes."

"Surely, Father, you don't seriously suggest—"

"Whereas the longer one lives with a work of art con-
ceived and executed in the grip of"—a bristling glance at
poor Lorenzo—" 'divine inspiration,' the more one can
sense in it the vital flame, the genius, that created it." He
turned to me. "Do you agree, signore?"

"Yes, I do. But if you feel this way, why did you include
the copies in the show?"

"Why?" he grumbled, returning to English. "Ask the
professor of subjectivist art criticism."

Lorenzo's Adam's apple jiggled all the way up, down,
and back up his neck. "When it came time for the final arrangements, you see, my father was seriously ill—"

"A gallstone operation," Bolzano muttered petulantly,

"not a mental attack. I had my faculties; you could have consulted me."

"And I was acting for him—power of attorney, you call it? And when Colonel Robey suggested it might be an excellent idea to exhibit copies of some of the pictures that are still missing—to publicize them and perhaps lead to their recovery—I agreed with him. I still do." He looked at his father and actually managed to stare him down. "Anything is possible. Who can tell?"

"From that standpoint, I think it is a good idea," I said quietly to Bolzano. "It could very well turn up some leads."

He shrugged and then sighed good-humoredly. "It begins to look as if I am not going to win any battles today. My opposition is too unified. Signor Norgren"—he gestured at my brandy snifter—"do you know what you're drinking?"

"Cognac?" I said. "It's extremely good."

This made him clap his hands. "No, and you're not the first to be fooled. It's a good old Italian product: *Vecchia Romagna*." He tapped his thigh. "You know, I'm going to have some, too."

"Father!" Lorenzo began, but was silenced by a look.

"This battle I win."

When the bowed servant brought us all fresh brandies, Bolzano drank with pleasure, licked his lips, and looked sharply at me. "Something is on your mind?"

Something was. "Sir, you said you were ill at the time the final arrangements were made. Does that mean you weren't here when the paintings were crated?"

"I was in the hospital. Lorenzo was here to attend to it." There was one more disgusted look at his son; Lorenzo might have won the battle of the copies, but he wasn't getting much pleasure from it.

"So you oversaw the actual packing?" I asked Lorenzo.

"Of course. I was in the gallery for two entire days."

"Who did the crating? Your own workmen?"

"No, yours. Signor Flittner's."

"Then Earl was here?"

"Naturally. Also signor van Cortlandt."

"The entire time?"

"Do you mean the entire time of the packing? Yes, as he should have been." He was looking at me with a puzzled frown.

"And did you actually see the crates nailed up?"

He slowly nodded his head.

Bolzano, tucked into his corner of the couch, had been studying me for some moments. "Signore, what are all these questions?"

I had decided a while back that I was going to tell him about the forgery. Peter's idea that the revelation might be more of a shock than he could stand I dismissed. Bolzano had obviously come a long way since his operation. More than that, he was clearly not the sort of man to shock easily.

"Sir, I think there's a forgery in The Plundered Past."

"Christopher!" Lorenzo murmured reprovingly, and turned with an anxious look toward his father.

But Bolzano lived up to my expectations. He sat motionless, still studying me, his right hand slowly stroking the left side of his jaw, his dark eyes luminous and steady.

"Explain yourself," he said calmly.

"Peter told me the day he died." And for what seemed like the tenth time in the last few days I described the conversation at Kranzler's.

Bolzano listened, stone still. Then he picked up his snifter, drank once, twice, and placed it firmly on the white plastic table in front of him. "It doesn't sound like Peter," he said slowly. "Like signor van Cortlandt. Do you realize the significance of a forgery in the Bolzano collection? Why would he keep it to himself? Why not tell you which one? Why not me?"

"Father!" Lorenzo exclaimed. "You don't mean to say you give credence—"

Bolzano waved him down with a flap of the hand. "Credence? To Peter van Cortlandt? Of course I do."

"But—but how—"

"I don't know how, Lorenzo. I think that's what your

friend is trying to establish with his not-so-subtle questions."

"Yes," I said.

"And what have you established?"

"That Lorenzo and Peter were both there when the paintings were crated and neither apparently saw anything wrong at the time."

Bolzano looked at me without expression, then smiled. "Yes, I see."

"What do you see?" Lorenzo asked. "I don't understand."

"I see why signor Norgren was asking his questions. He now can assume that since no apparent forgery caught signor van Cortlandt's attention at that time, there was no apparent forgery. At that time."

"You mean," Lorenzo said, "that there was a . . . a substitution after the paintings left? Someone has . . . has stolen a picture and replaced it with another? Is that what you mean?"

The dog was half-asleep at Bolzano's feet, its head between its paws. With his toe, Bolzano rubbed its ribs. "So it would seem. Do I read your mind correctly, signor Norgren?"

"Not entirely. There are also the three paintings from Hallstatt: the Rubens, the Vermeer, and the Titian."

Lorenzo put a hand to his heart. "My God, not the Tiziano."

"Signor Bolzano, how much time have you spent with those pictures since they turned up again? Have you had a chance to really study them?"

"No," he said with some bitterness. "They've never been out of your government's hands. We went to Hallstatt when they were found—it was before my attack—but we had no time alone with them. None."

"All right, then; neither of you had seen those paintings in forty years. Lorenzo, you were a baby in 1944. How can you be certain the ones in Hallstatt were genuine?"

"I'm sure," Lorenzo proclaimed, "because when I see a Tiziano, I swoon."

"I didn't notice you swooning," Bolzano muttered. "But then, who could tell?" He drained his brandy. "So, signore, you think it may be an old forgery we are discussing, from the time of the Nazis?"

"Impossible," Lorenzo said stubbornly. "The unassailable provenances . . . the inarguable testimony of their sheer beauty—"

Bolzano cut in irritatedly. "What unassailable provenances? They've been out of sight, no one knows where, for forty years. And as to their 'sheer beauty,' haven't you already told us there's no difference between a genuine painting and a forgery?"

"No difference . . . ? *I* told you . . . ?"

While the sorely offended Lorenzo groped unsuccessfully for speech, Bolzano looked levelly at me. "Let me tell you what I think. I think you're wrong. For forty years I thought about those paintings, dreamed about them. They were never out of my mind. You think I wouldn't recognize them in an instant? Even the crates the damned Nazis packed them in I recognized. Do you know what was stenciled on them? 'A.H., Linz.'" He pressed his fingertips to his eyelids. "Adolf Hitler, Linz."

He spoke quietly, but with a raw undercurrent of emotion that made me lower my eyes. He exhaled noisily, then went on in a softer tone. "Could I be wrong? It's possible; I'm only human. But I don't think so. Isn't it possible signor van Cortlandt was having a small joke with you?"

"That's what I told him," Lorenzo said.

"And something else occurs to me," Bolzano said. "Even if I did not have time to thoroughly examine the Hallstatt paintings, signor van Cortlandt most certainly did. He spent many hours with them last summer. If something wasn't as it should have been, he would surely have noticed it then— not last week."

"It might have been something technical or complex, something that wouldn't be found right away."

"And yet he suggested that you would merely glance over the paintings and it would leap out at you? I respect your scholarship, signore, but still—without offense—are you so much more proficient than he was?"

Not by a long shot, I wasn't. Bolzano had hit on a weakness that undercut every half-baked theory I'd come up with. Why had Peter taken so long to find a forgery that he expected me to spot by simply looking at the paintings and seeing if something caught my eye? It was inconceivable that he'd found a fake months before and kept it to himself. And if, on the other hand, it were something new—if in the last couple of weeks a forgery had been slipped into the show in place of an original, then it was inconceivable that he would have made such a playful, coy production out of it. It would have been nothing to be jocose about, yet that's exactly what Peter had been.

I sighed. "You're right, signor Bolzano. Nothing seems to make sense."

He tapped his hands on his thighs. "It's easy enough to settle. I will come to Berlin and look, and in ten minutes I will tell you—"

"Father!" Lorenzo said. "Absolutely not. This time I must put my foot down. Dr. Rovere was quite adamant. You are to do no traveling for at least a month. To think of going to Germany in this weather . . ."

Bolzano quieted him with a resigned flap of the hand. "All right, calm yourself. You're right." He looked at me. "Perhaps in a month. In the meantime, tell me what you want to do."

"I'd like to check it out. Right now there's a cloud over your collection, and I'm sure you'd want."

"Not what I want; what you want."

"All right. In the first place, I think one of your own copies may somehow have turned up in place of an original."

"That's simple enough to settle. Look at the backs. And if that doesn't convince you, compare them to the certificates of guarantee."

A certificate of guarantee is one of many highly fallible methods of proving authenticity. A detailed photograph of a painting is made, and on the back of the print are the painting's dimensions, a description of any identifying details, and a signed statement by some eminent or not-so-eminent authority that the painting reproduced on the other side is most certainly the long-lost self-portrait of Michelangelo last seen in the collection of the Dukes of Burgundy in 1696.

The trouble is that art authorities, eminent or otherwise, can be wrong. They can even be bought. The trouble is also that a certificate of guarantee by a deceased authority is not very hard to fake, and many of them have been turned out to match some glorious old master that came fresh and hot from the oven the day before. Even the great museums have been bilked many times by spurious certificates, only to wind up carting their new treasures quietly and permanently down to the cellar years later, as the Metropolitan Museum did in 1973 after "reclassifying the authorship" of three hundred paintings from its European collection.

The upshot is that there is simply no way of *proving* that the art object at which you are looking is the art object it's supposed to be. When you stand before the Mona Lisa, trying to see it through the thick glass the Louvre protects it with, how do you know it is the very picture painted by da Vinci in 1503? How do you know it's the same picture that was hanging in the Louvre fifty years ago, or fifty days ago? You have faith in the integrity of the Louvre, you say? Would you bet your life that it's the same painting?

Neither would I, and certainly not on the basis of a certificate of guarantee.

"I'd like to do it more directly than that," I said. "Lorenzo told me that all your copies have a secret design drilled through the paint layers. I'd like to know what that design is, and where, so I can be sure it's not on any 'genuine' painting in the show."

Bolzano's gray eyebrows slowly climbed. "You want me to tell you . . . ?"

"I explained that was impossible, Christopher," Lorenzo said sternly.

Bolzano's dog now had its head on his knee. His blunt fingers slowly worked the loose skin of its neck. "All right," he said simply. "Lorenzo, you'll make a copy of the key and give it to signor Norgren. Signore, I know you'll treat this information with discretion."

Lorenzo stared mutely at him, his eyes popping with surprise.

"I want this settled," Bolzano said. "Signore, will that relieve your mind?"

I hesitated. There was something else, but I didn't look forward to Bolzano's reaction. "There is one more thing," I said warily. "I'd like your permission to have some of the paintings scientifically analyzed if need be." I held my breath.

So did Bolzano. I thought for a moment that it was all over, that he was going to renege on The Plundered Past and have me thrown out of the house as well. The dog's eyes popped open as his hand inadvertently tightened on its fur. Then the hand loosened and the bullet head nodded once, firmly. "You have it."

Tony Whitehead has told me that I've fouled up a lot of deals by an overinsistence on clarity, that there are a lot of things better left open to interpretation. I suppose he's right; I'm uncomfortable when things aren't out on the table. "You understand," I said, "some tests might require the removal of material: a sliver of stretcher-bar for radio-carbon dating, a tiny cylinder of pigment—no more than a few hundredths of a gram—for microscopic core analysis—"

It was too much for Lorenzo, who leaped gawkily to his feet, toppling a white plastic table lamp off a white plastic end table. "Can you be serious? Destruction of the painted surface? Of a Rubens, a Hals? A 'mere' few hundredths of a gram from a Vermeer?" He looked down at me with a choked, incredulous laugh.

Bolzano, very somber, let him finish. "If you have to make physical tests, make them," he said quietly to me.

We both stared at him, Lorenzo not much more surprised than I was. It wasn't the sort of thing a collector willingly submitted to. When Lorenzo finally got his mouth working to protest, Bolzano talked over him.

"I want this settled," he said again, more harshly. "I don't want gossip, whispers, insinuations. I trust you, signor Norgren. I know you'll treat the pictures with the respect they deserve."

"Of course I will."

"One thing I ask—I demand. Should you find something you believe to be inauthentic—"

"Father!" poor Lorenzo cried disbelievingly.

"—then I hope I will hear before anyone else."

"I promise."

He nodded, sighing. "*Bene.* Now. Would you like some more *Vecchia Romagna*? A little more coffee?"

"No thank you," I said. It was time to go. I was beginning to feel a little guilty, wondering if I'd put too much strain on him after all. I'd won all the battles, as he'd said, and over the last few minutes the energy seemed to have drained out of him.

"You've seen the gallery?" he asked as I rose.

"Yes, Lorenzo took me over it."

"You liked it?"

"It's magnificent."

"And this room?" he said. His look was slyly challenging.

I looked at the immense Rothko behind him: three fuzzy, immense, dark dabs on a red background. Next to it was an even larger Twombly, looking like nothing so much as a big blackboard covered with a child's orderly twirls in chalk.

"It's, uh, quite interesting—"

He laughed. "You don't like postpainterly abstractionism?"

I didn't even know that's what it was called. "Well—"

"Neither does Lorenzo. But let me tell you something: The paintings you saw upstairs, the objects in the other rooms—those are my reason to live. Every time I buy a work of art I train myself, I commit myself, intellectually and spiritually, to its essence. My involvement with my paintings is total, total. I converse with them, I *become* them. They are my life."

It is an indication of Bolzano's rough charisma that he could deliver even a speech like that in a credible way.

"So my days are full of intensity, full of unattainable strivings, you see. And then I come here." He gestured at the walls. "I look at a de Corolli, at a Klos, and it's wonderful; I can relax. They don't mean a damned thing."

I burst out laughing. "Guggenheim once said the same thing about his Kandinskys."

"Well, then, I'm in good company. You'll tell me what you find?"

"Definitely."

"Maybe you'll have nothing to tell."

"I hope so. Sincerely."

But I doubted it.

Later, Lorenzo drove me back to the Hotel Augustus. There were, of course, no parking spaces on the Via della Scala, so he stopped in the middle of the street in front of the hotel.

"Christopher," he said, leaning a bony elbow on the steering wheel, oblivious of the honking and shouting behind us, "do you remember all the questions you asked about the packing of the paintings? Did I oversee it? Did I actually see the crates nailed up . . . ?"

"Yes, I remember."

"Well, there's something I didn't mention. I don't see how it can be important, but still . . ." He paused to roll down the window, shake his fist and make Italian gestures at the impatient drivers behind, then roll the window back up.

"What I want to tell you is, yes, I did see them nailed up. But the next day, the day before they were shipped, someone came and had them opened."

"Someone?"

"The small man, the assistant to Colonel Robey. His name—"

"Edgar Gadney? Egad?"

"Yes, that's it."

"Egad had them opened? Why?"

"I don't know," he said sheepishly. "Some sort of paperwork. . . . I don't understand these things very well. I had to commute to Rome that morning, but I gave my permission."

I sat silently, thinking that over.

"What else was I to do?" Lorenzo asked nervously. "He's an official of the exhibition, isn't he? Was I not to trust him?"

"Was Peter with him?"

"No. He went back to Berlin as soon as the packing was done, along with the other one, Flittner."

"And your father was in the hospital. So what you're telling me is that Gadney had a day all to himself with the paintings. In open crates."

"Well . . . yes. The workmen were there, of course. Christopher, you're not suggesting . . . you don't mean to imply that—"

"Lorenzo, I just don't know," I said honestly.

12

The next morning I breakfasted in the hotel's little bar with its fake but charming rococo ceiling. The meal was brought by Luigi, the ageless, taciturn man who had worked at the Augustus ever since I'd begun coming, and whose duties seemed to consist of serving breakfast from seven to nine, manning the never-very-busy switchboard, and wandering the hotel for most of the day, sniffling, plumping cushions, and mumbling to himself. In all the seven years I'd been a client, he had never said anything more to me than *"Caffè o tè?"*

No, I take that back. In the old days, the hotel had served inexpensive fixed-priced dinners to guests, and once, reading the menu incorrectly, I had asked for *frutta e formaggio* as the final course. "No, sir," he had sternly intoned, wagging his head, and then continued in Italian, "Not fruit *and* cheese." His finger prodded the appropriate line on the dittoed menu. "Fruit . . . or . . . cheese!" This burst of prolixity had never again been equaled.

"Caffè o tè?" he said to me this morning.

"Caffè, per piacere."

Luigi grumbled off to the kitchen to get it.

Caffè, of course, was *caffè latte*, a huge pitcher of espresso and an even bigger jug of hot milk, to be mixed together in a cup large enough to bathe your head in. Along with it came hot rolls, pastry horns, zwieback, cheese, and preserves. Breakfast was another one of the reasons I kept coming back to the Augustus.

Just as I finished, Luigi returned, driven by extremity to

converse once again. There was a telephone call for me, which I could take in the lobby if I wished.

It was Herr Traben of the Kunstmuseum, joyfully calling to tell me that he had a plan that met with the approval of the insurance company and museum counsel. I would take formal possession of the El Greco, which would be crated in my presence, on the following Friday—provided that the trip through Frankfurt to Rhein-Main Air Base was made in the museum's armored truck under museum guard. Once within the limits of American military jurisdiction, the painting would be fully released to me. Did I agree to this?

I did, as laughably overcautious as it seemed. (I'd carried equally valuable masterpieces on my lap in the coach section on United; and I'd certainly never felt the need of an armored truck before.) Then I telephoned Robey to give him the good news about having the El Greco in time for the opening. It took him a moment to remember what I was talking about, and then he said he thought that was nice.

"And Mark? Can you let Harry know? He'll want to make some security arrangements for getting it from Rhein-Main to Berlin. It's going to be too heavy for me to lug."

"Fine, good idea," he said vaguely. "Will do."

I made a note to talk to Harry myself when I got back.

My flight didn't leave until ten-thirty, which gave me an hour or so to visit my favorite museum. No, not the Uffizi, which, fabulous as it is, is no one's favorite museum, being laid out in a wearying series of stuffy cubicles opening off two endless corridors. (*Uffizi* means "offices" in Italian, and that is what it was built as in 1560.)

Only a few blocks away, however, is the thirteenth-century palace-museum that is the Bargello, roomy and never crowded except in July and August. The Grand Council Chamber of the Bargello is surely one of the loveliest rooms of art in the world, and it was there I went. In it are some of Donatello's finest sculptures: the handsome Saint George, the two Saint Johns, the svelte, effeminate little bronze David with which Michelangelo's stupendous marble version would contrast so effectively seventy years later. There are some gentle, touching lunettes of della Robbia too, and other things worth looking at, but it is the room itself that is so wonderful.

The vaulted ceiling must be eighty feet high. Light pours in visible shafts through narrow windows, streaking the old red-tile floors with long, pale swatches of light. Above all there is a feeling of open space. There aren't more than thirty objects in the whole big chamber, almost all of them on pedestals—not a glass case in sight—so everything has twenty or thirty feet of open space around it. There's so much space that the floating dust motes and the cool shadows combine to make a sort of natural *sfumato*, so that you feel as if you're in the smoky, shaded, middle distance of a painting by da Vinci or del Sarto.

I had discovered a long time ago that this serene and stately room is a place to think and sort things out. Near one of the arched stone doorways is a bench that might have been made for contemplation, and it was there I sat.

What did I know? I knew, or thought I knew, that The Plundered Past had had no forgery in it when it was originally crated in Florence; Peter had had two full days with the paintings and had seen nothing suspicious. That meant one of two things: First and most probable, the forgery hadn't come from Florence at all but was one of the three from the Hallstatt cache. They had been out of sight for forty years with plenty of opportunity for skulduggery, the Bolzanos had never gotten a hard look at them, and it could be that with all the tumult and publicity surrounding them, Peter hadn't, either, until later. That would account for his taking so long to discover it.

The less likely possibility was also less attractive: The forgery was part of the collection that had been shipped from Florence, all right, but it had been slipped in *after* it was in American care; that is, one of the famous originals had been made off with, and a fake—a most excellent fake, I knew—had been put in its place.

Now, substituting a fake for a familiar painting is extraordinarily difficult and complex, over and above the problems of artistic reproduction. It requires an immense amount of detailed information, such as the weight and balance of the picture and its exact appearance, including the auction-house marks or other annotations on its back, repairs that have been made to the frame, and so on. Such information simply can't be gotten without inside help. And that meant someone on the exhibition staff would have had to be involved. (That's what made the idea so unattractive.) And that someone was very likely to be a member of the senior staff.

Gadney, for instance. What the hell had he been doing that day in Florence? I couldn't imagine what kind of paperwork would require opening the crates, but then it was the army that was doing the shipping, and I didn't doubt that they had paperwork requirements I'd never dreamed of. That wouldn't be too hard to check. In any case, Gadney had had a day alone with the opened crates, right in the palazzo, within striking distance of the copies—while Bolzano was in the hospital, Lorenzo was off to Rome, and Peter and Earl had gone on to Naples. That hardly proved him a criminal, but it did give me a suspect to start with, and that gave me a sense of making some progress.

Would that mean that Gadney had something to do with Peter's murder? I rolled that around my mind while I used my last fifteen minutes to make a lightning tour of the rest of the Bargello. (I always like to stop and look at the young Michelangelo's smarmy, godawful Bacchus downstairs because it soothes me with proof that even the best of us can make mistakes.) By the time I walked back out through the great courtyard, I had decided that wondering about Egad's role in a murder was going a long way beyond what the facts, such as they were, warranted. Anyway, that part of it would have to be Harry's job; I had the forgery to figure out.

I did a little more figuring on the Alitalia flight from Florence. There was another possibility aside from the two I'd already considered. Maybe the forgery was something that had been in the Bolzano collection all along. That would mean either that Bolzano and Lorenzo hadn't been aware of it . . . or that they had. But if the admittedly expert Bolzano and his son hadn't spotted it in years of living with it, how could Peter have found it in a few weeks—and how could he think I could find it in a cursory walk-through?

As for the idea that either of the Bolzanos had knowingly permitted a forgery to be part of the show, that made no sense at all. People with fakes in their collections don't put them on public exhibit to be scrutinized by thousands.

By the time I changed to a Lufthansa 707 in Frankfurt— only flights originating in Germany are permitted to land in Berlin—I had exhausted the subject and myself, and I let my thoughts wander to something more pleasant.

Anne Greene. Somehow, thirty thousand feet above it all, with a little plastic jug of coffee and an *Apfelstrudel* on the tray in front of me, it seemed like a good time to haul out and consider something that had been niggling away at me, buried under weightier matters: Why had I behaved to Anne at the staff meeting like such a condescending and supercilious prig? And then, a couple of days later, why did I back off so cravenly from the prospect of dinner? It certainly wasn't that I found her unattractive; on the contrary, I liked the way she looked, I liked the way she spoke, and I liked, from what I could tell, the way she thought and felt.

Was I still loyal to Bev or, rather, loyal to the idea of being married to Bev, and unwilling to risk a step that would make an end of it? Maybe, but what was left to make an end of? I knitted my brows, sipped the surprisingly good coffee, and considered. Was it simply a matter of "once burned, twice shy?" Having walked trustingly, even eagerly, into one lousy relationship, was I afraid of blundering into another? Did Anne's very attractiveness frighten me into a defensive stance that shielded me against more damage to my shaky ego?

Where was Louis when I needed him? I sighed and, as the wheels thunked down on the Tegel runway, put it all out of my mind.

For about forty-five minutes. As soon as I got to Columbia House I dialed her room.

"Well, hi," she said. "What happened in Florence?"

"It went fine. Bolzano's pacified."

"Congratulations. The colonel will put you in for a decoration."

"Oh, it wasn't too hard." I took a breath and plowed ahead before I could change my mind. "Are you free tonight? How about that dinner we talked about?"

"Tonight . . . ? Well, actually, I—"

"It's just that I wanted to talk about a few things related to the show," I said quickly. God forbid that she should think I might be attracted to her.

"I'd like to, Chris, but I've got a MAC flight to catch at six-thirty."

"Oh. Well, it's nothing that—"

"How about now? I haven't been off base all day, and I'd love a good long walk. Are you doing anything this afternoon?"

Too direct, I suppose. I almost retreated instinctively with a song and dance about having just gotten in, needing to do several things, etc., etc. What I said before about not being fainthearted still holds, but I never said I was terrifically secure, you know. Fortunately, I held firm for once.

"No, I'm not," I said. "Do you like the zoo?"

"I love it."

"Not too cold for you?"

"Cold? It's beautiful for December. You've lived in the Banana Belt too long. Meet you in the lobby in ten minutes."

She was dressed in civilian clothes this time; a trendy waist-length winter jacket and slacks, and pleasingly unsensible shoes. She was slighter than I'd realized, narrowly built in the shoulders and upper body, small-breasted and narrow-waisted, but with robust, rounded hips and curvy, athletic legs; something along the lines of a Venus of Lucas Cranach the Elder, but with longer legs. Cranach's Venuses and Lucretias, hot little numbers in their time, had never seemed very alluring to me, but quite suddenly I realized I'd been looking at things all wrong. In fact, I couldn't imagine a more attractive way for a female to be formed. Old Cranach rose considerably in my estimation.

We walked to the U-Bahn station at the other side of the plaza and caught one of the fast subway trains headed downtown. "First of all," I said as we sat down, "I owe you an apology. You were right and I was wrong about what happened to Peter. I went to look at the Hotel Paradies in Frankfurt. He never walked into that place voluntarily."

"Of course he didn't. Do you think there's some connection to the show, then?"

"Yes. So does Harry, by the way."

"Ah, that explains it. I spent an hour over a cup of coffee with him yesterday. He was being very charming and ingenuous, but I was being grilled, all right. About Peter's work, about his habits, his schedule. . . . He really enjoys being a detective, doesn't he?"

I laughed. "He loves it."

"And how's your own detective work going? Have you gotten anywhere on the forgery?"

"No, except that my best guess now is that it's one of the three from the cache. And it may not be a forgery at all, in the narrow sense. It might be one of Bolzano's copies masquerading as an original, or maybe a genuine old painting that's been restored or reworked—or resigned—so that it's not what everybody thinks it is."

"Mmm, interesting. But it still leaves a lot of possibilities, doesn't it?"

"Oh, and one more possibility: If it *isn't* from the cache—if it came out of Bolzano's Florence collection—then I'm pretty sure it was substituted after and not before it became part of the show. At least," I said, struck with something that hadn't occurred to me before, "I'm sure about it if what the Bolzanos told me is true."

"What did they tell you?"

"That Peter himself was there for the packing."

"That is true. He and Earl spent two days down there getting the pictures ready for shipping."

"What about Egad? Did he go too?"

"I think so, yes. For a day. Some sort of paperwork."

We got out at the zoo station and climbed the stairs up into the cold. "You know," she said thoughtfully, zipping up her jacket, "if the forgery did get into the collection after it left Florence, I don't see how it could have happened without one of our own people knowing about it." She frowned, thinking it over. "Isn't that so? Colonel Robey, Egad, or Earl. Or me, I guess, if you want to include eveyone. Or even Peter."

"I don't know about you and Peter, but otherwise I agree with you. It's hard to imagine anyone else having the access or the knowledge to do it. Of course, there's Jessick, or maybe one of the workmen, or some visitor—"

She shook her head. "The guards had specific orders. Only senior staff—and that doesn't include Conrad Jessick—was allowed near the paintings. Anyone else had to have a senior staff member with him. Of course, a guard might have been careless, or even bribed. . . . Chris, is this starting to sound as bizarre to you as it is to me? I feel like I'm in a movie or something."

"Me too. Let's forget it for a while." We were at the entrance to the zoo. "Still feel like going in?"

"Sure. I missed lunch, though. Can we stop for a snack?"

I was hungry, too, and we followed the signposts to the Zoo Restaurant, past indifferent antelope, gnus, and zebras. We joined a few hardy Berliners and ate outside in the pale sunshine, on the *Sud-Terrasse*: orange-checked tablecloths and rattan chairs overlooking a wintry but mostly ice-free pond with quacking ducks. Huddled in our coats, we had bratwurst and rolls, hot potato salad, and the invariably good German coffee.

"No," Anne said, dabbing mustard from her lips with a paper napkin, "it just doesn't make sense. How could any of those people be a *forger*?"

"We're not talking about a forger. Whatever the counterfeit is, it's not a copy that was dashed off in the last few months—or in the last ten or twenty years. It may have been doctored a little to match one of Bolzano's paintings, but that's all. We're talking about a crook—a big-time crook—but not a forger."

"If that was supposed to make me feel better, somehow it doesn't."

"Well, maybe this will. Remember, the most likely possibility is that the forgery is one of the ones from the Hallstatt cache. And if that's true, the crook we're dealing with is probably some sneaky *Oberleutnant* who's been dead for twenty years."

"Maybe." She looked up from a crumb she was holding out on her palm to a nervy but irresolute sparrow at the edge of the table. "But Peter wasn't killed by a sneaky *Oberleutnant* who's been dead for twenty years."

"No, not likely. You know, except for Earl, I don't know anything about the others on the staff. Who is Egad, anyway? Where did he come from?"

"Attaboy," she said to the sparrow, which had finally made its move and flown off with its prize. "Is Egad suspect number one?"

"Have to start someplace."

"All right, Egad is Edgar Franklin Gadney, a DOD civilian—"

"Department of Defense?"

"Uh-huh. He's on special assignment to this project— like me. Ordinarily he works for EDPSC as—"

"Would it be too much trouble to speak in words, please?"

"Sorry, the European Defense Personnel Support Center. He's deputy director for subsistence contracting."

I laughed. "Maybe you ought to go back to initials. I don't understand the words either."

She smiled at me. "That's the first time I've seen you laugh."

"It is?" Was it really?

"Yes, you're a very serious person." *Very Serious Person*

is the way she said it. "Terribly formidable and intimidating."

"I am?" I was genuinely surprised.

"Uh-huh, but you look almost human when you smile. It warms up your eyes. You look much better than you did a few days ago, by the way."

"I think you're absolutely fantastic-looking," I blurted out to my own surprise, and God help me, I think I blushed. I had been away from the wars too long; my courtship technique was in desperate need of polishing.

"Thank you," Anne said, and pleased me by seeming to be pleased herself, but then unnerved me by continuing to regard me and my reddening cheeks with those lovely, solemn, violet eyes. "Would you like another wurst?" I asked romantically.

"Half of one," she said, "and how about some more coffee?"

"Fine," I said, and made my escape to the cafeteria line.

By the time I returned, I was firmly back at the helm. "Now then," I said briskly, cutting the sausage in two, "what does it mean to be DDSC of the EDPSC?"

"It means Egad's the deputy purchasing agent for the commissary system."

"Am I wrong, or does that translate to 'assistant buyer for the grocery stores'?"

"No, you're right, but don't look so condescending. It's a tough job, and he's absolutely amazing with details. And he knows everything there is to know about army logistics. Ask him sometime what's involved in getting fifty thousand quarts of Belgian strawberries onto the shelves in ninety commissaries in six different countries before they spoil, if you don't believe me."

"I believe you."

"Which probably won't do you any good. You'll hear about it anyway. Everybody does. But it's worth it. Without Egad—especially since Colonel Robey tends to be a little, well—"

"Off in the clouds?"

"Immersed in thought, I was going to say. Anyway, without Egad, peculiar as he can be, The Plundered Past would be a madhouse." She shook her head firmly. "Nope, sorry. I can't see him as the bad guy."

"All right, who can you see?"

"Well, I could see Earl. Not for any special reason, I mean, just . . . What is it? Did I say something clever?"

"I was just remembering something. Harry's a little suspicious of him, too."

"He is? About what? Why?"

"I don't know. He was asking me what I knew about him."

"Oh yes, you knew him from before, didn't you?"

"A little. He's one of the most respected conservators in the States; nobody better. I grant you, though, he doesn't add much to the general hilarity level, does he?"

She laughed and pushed away her empty plate. "Are we going to look at some animals, or are we not?"

"By all means." I picked up her napkin. "Mustard," I said, and dabbed at the tip of her nose, thereby establishing a more intimate level between us, in my own mind at least.

We went from enclosure to enclosure in the handsome zoo, looking at the *Elefanten*, the *Bären*, the shaggy *Büffel*, and one grouchy, cold *Känguruh*, and when we got cold ourselves, we went inside to watch the apes get fed.

"What about Robey?" I asked, while the keeper brought out cardboard boxes of oranges, bananas, and lettuce. "How much do you know about him?"

Anne burst out laughing. She had a way of doing it with a sudden little explosion of air, as if she'd been holding her breath, that always made me want to laugh, too.

I smiled, but I didn't know what about. "What's the joke?"

"What made you ask about Colonel Robey?"

"Well, he's the only one we haven't talked about, and—"

"No, I mean, why did you ask just now? This minute?"

She was still snuffling with laughter, hardly able to talk,

and with her eyes she motioned me to look at the glass-walled, tiled cell in front of us.

"The orangutan . . . ?" And then I shouted with laughter, too. It was impossible not to. The thing was, it looked exactly like Robey. Not something like him, but just like him: soft heavy body, dreamy drowsy eyes, even a wispy cloud of orange-red hair that covered but didn't hide his scalp. While the other animals ate, the orang sat placidly, slowly rotating a banana before its face, lost in contemplation of its mysteries.

"God," I sputtered, "put a pipe in its mouth and a uniform on it, and it could chair our next staff meeting. Nobody would know the difference."

We had to move on, to a morose gorilla, before we could stop laughing.

"That's better," I said. "More like Earl."

Her hand went to her mouth. "Chris, please, don't start me off again." She pulled in a deep breath. "Whew. Now, what was the question?"

"Tell me about Mark."

"Right. He's head of HNR—darn, did it again; it's an occupational hazard—Host Nation Relations. As I understand it, The Plundered Past truly was his personal idea, and so he likes to oversee it, but Egad does all the real administration, and I help where I can."

The apes had gotten their food, and the building was getting stuffy, so we went outside again, averting our eyes from the orangutan. We stood for ten minutes in front of the cage with the famous Chinese pandas, waiting for them to do something, but they slept, snoring, the whole time, curled up in chubby balls of black and white.

Anne looked at them and laughed when they scratched their noses or turned over in their sleep with discreet little snorts. And I looked at Anne, trying to figure out what it was that was so devilishly attractive about her. She was pretty, but not that pretty. She reminded me, in fact, of the heroines in romance novels. Not quite beautiful in the usual sense (whatever that is); eyes set a little too far apart (never too close together); nose a trifle too pert, even tilted (never too long or hooked down); mouth a little too wide and generous (never narrow, and never, never ungenerous). The total effect was devastating.

She caught me looking at her, or maybe I let her catch me, and we turned away from the pandas to begin walking again. "I know a little about everyone involved with the show now, except for you," I said, cunningly shifting the conversation to a personal level. "Who's Anne Greene?"

"So I'm a suspect, too?"

"You wouldn't want me to play favorites, would you?" I was ready to kick myself for being arch. This fumbling, getting-to-know-each-other process was positively painful. It had me self-consciously chafing over almost everything I said. What had been titillating fun at eighteen or nineteen—at least that was the way I remembered it—was agony for an out-of-practice thirty-four-year-old.

But still titillating.

"Yes, I would," Anne said, "but I'll tell you anyway. I'm on special assignment to Colonel Robey. Ordinarily I work in Community Liaison Services—"

"Usually called CLS, of course."

"No; for some reason ordinarily called Community Liaison, but you're learning. I'm a sort of glorified tour guide, a contact between visiting VIPs—congressmen, foreign dignitaries, media people—and the military community. I have to make sure they get to see who they're supposed to, and don't get to see who or what they're not supposed to. And I seem to spend a lot of my time smoothing over rough spots before they become 'incidents'—not always successfully."

"You don't sound like a glorified tour guide to me. Where are you headquartered?"

"Berchtesgaden. That's where I'm taking off for tonight. The annual visit of the Congressional oversight committee on military morale starts tomorrow." She grimaced. "The big event of the social year."

"I didn't know there were any American facilities in

Berchtesgaden. Isn't that where Hilter had his mountaintop retreat—the Obersalzberg, is it called? Are you anywhere near there?"

"We're *in* it. Or on it. The whole Obersalzberg is a U.S. military R and R operation. Some of the Nazi-era buildings are still standing, and they're army hotels now. There are restaurants, a golf course, ski lift—it's a great place to show visitors, which is why I'm stationed there; lucky me."

"You like it?"

"Anybody would like it. Hilter had a great eye for scenery. The Bavarian Alps are breathtaking. It'll be like heaven after Berlin."

"I imagine so. How long will you be there?"

"Eight days. I'll be back next weekend for the reception."

Eight days? I wanted to groan with dismay. *Eight whole days?* I smiled and said, "That'll be nice for you."

We had left the zoo and turned into the Tiergarten, that elegant swath of woods and meadow in the heart of the city, green even in December. We walked up the Spreeweg, past the Schloss Belvedere, the delicate canary-yellow château that serves as the presidential residence in Berlin, and then along John-Foster-Dulles-Allee, where we watched chilled, miserable-looking scullers in sleek five-man shells gliding an ice-free quarter mile or so up and down the Spree.

For perhaps fifteen minutes we didn't talk while I moped along, and then I had an idea. "Berchtesgaden sounds great," I mused casually. "I wonder if my ID card would get me in. I'll probably be able to use a little R and R before long."

"Are you serious? Wednesday's Christmas; why don't you come down for a couple of days? I'll give you the super-duper tour usually reserved for only the most august visitors, like TV anchormen."

"Gee, that's a great idea," I said as innocently as Tony Whitehead might have done it.

"Fine," she said, and again we walked without saying

anything, but conscious of something good in the air. This boy-girl maneuvering wasn't all agony by any means.

"How did you get assigned to the exhibition?" I asked. "I suppose you got involved with all the hoopla over the cache, and then just stayed with it?"

She nodded. "That's the way it was. Hallstatt isn't that far from Berchtesgaden, and when that soldier stumbled on those crates in the *Salzbergwerke*—that's the salt mine . . . oops, I believe you *sprechen deutsch*, if I'm not mistaken."

"Anne, I really am sorry about that."

"I know you are," she said laughing. "Don't go all frowny on me again. God, you're so intense."

"Intense? Where do you get these ideas about me? That I never laugh, that I'm intense. . . . I am *not* intense. I am anything *but* intense. I am easygoing; relaxed to the point of somnolence."

"So why the puckered brow?"

I unpuckered. "I seem to get a little nervous around you, that's all. How about some chestnuts?"

We bought an aromatic bagful from a vendor who had them roasting over a brazier of charcoal, and munched them while we walked. Mostly I asked questions and Anne told me about herself. She was thirty years old; she was from Syracuse, New York; and she had an M.A. in career counseling. She'd joined the air force as an educational-services officer after they'd promised her tours of duty in the Far East and Europe. They'd kept their word on the tours, but in time-hallowed military fashion she'd been assigned to Community Liaison, and there she'd stayed. To her surprise she'd enjoyed it. She'd been a captain for two years, and a pair of major's oak leaves was in the offing if she decided to stay in the air force.

She'd been married for two years in her early twenties, she told me, getting down to important things, but had made a bad job of it, and she now saw two or three men on an intermittent basis, but they were just friends. More or less. (You can imagine how fiendishly subtle my questions

were. Nevertheless, I could get no elucidation beyond
"more or less.")

"All right," she said, tossing a steaming chestnut from
hand to hand. "Now you. I'm having a hard time figuring
you out."

"What is there to figure out? I'm not very complex."

"I don't know about that. You look like a, well, like an
average guy with not too terribly much upstairs, if you'll
forgive me for saying so, so that it's a shock when you start
talking. You're very articulate, you know, very cogent—"

"Formidable," I said. "Intimidating."

"Highly. But then when you loosen up, there's another
layer that comes peeking through, kind of wistful and
vulnerable—that's very 'in' now, you know—with a sense
of humor . . . even sexy, I suppose, if you happen to like
the type."

"Thanks, I think." On balance, it was an improvement
over Bev's evaluation. "What can't you figure out?"

"Which layer is really you?"

"Oh, the sexy one. Ask anybody."

"Well. I'm certainly glad to have that settled. Now, what
else should I know about you?"

I was glad to talk about myself, and Anne was a good
listener. In twenty minutes she knew more about me—
about my recent past—than I'd ever expected to tell anyone.

"You walked in one day and your wife wasn't there?"
she asked incredulously. "Just like that? Out of nowhere?"

"Yes." We were at the eastern edge of the Tiergarten
now, which is also the edge of West Berlin. We had walked
along quiet, pretty paths at the very foot of the ugly Wall,
past the gaunt, shell-scarred Reichstag, past the Branden-
burg Gate (visible through one of the checkpoints), past the
colossal marble soldier atop the Soviet Army Memorial (the
Grim Raper, the West Berliners call it).

"No," I said after a little more thought, as we turned
back toward the center of West Berlin and began to look
for a taxi stand. "No, not out of nowhere." And then I be-

gan telling her things that even Louis hadn't been able to nondirectively pry out of me, things I hadn't pried out of myself. How Bev and I had been drifting apart for three or four years and never faced up to it, how she had tried one thing after another to find what she needed—transcendental meditation, transactional analysis, assertiveness training— and I buried myself in work, gradually coming to spend most of my Saturdays at the museum (while Bev took glass-blowing lessons, or so I was given to understand) and pretty much left the twentieth century for the eighteenth.

"It must have been a miserable time for you," Anne said.

"But it wasn't," I answered truthfully. "I thought I was happy, and if you think you're happy, you must be happy, right?"

"You really didn't have an inkling?"

I shook my head. "I really thought everything was all right. We went out to dinner a couple of times a week, we went to concerts, to plays—"

"You know, I'm starting to think you might be that guy with not a whole lot upstairs after all."

"You know, I'm starting to think you're right."

We found a taxi stand near Potsdamer Platz and climbed into a cab, grateful to be out of the deepening late-afternoon cold. "All this time she was out finding herself while you were dreaming away in the museum archives," Anne said, "you were faithful to her? Or don't I know you well enough to ask?"

"No, you know me well enough. And yes, I was." The world's changed, I thought. Here I am feeling ashamed of having been faithful to my wife.

"Even in thought?"

"Well, not always in thought."

"I'm relieved to hear it."

"But mostly even in thought," I persisted, wanting to be honest. "Look Anne, I loved Bev, and we got along fine in bed, and I didn't feel misunderstood or anything else." I shrugged. "I just didn't need anything on the side."

She looked out the window at the quickly darkening streets. "If this is a line," she murmured, "it has its points."

"It's—"

"I know it's not. What about since you broke up? Anything important in the female line? Just curious."

"Not much. I mean, no. Not till now." Her hand was lying palm-down on the seat. I covered it with mine, and she turned it over to clasp my fingers.

OK, it was straight out of Booth Tarkington, but I couldn't have been happier. "Anne, I'm awfully glad you didn't just write me off that day at the meeting. I would have deserved it."

"Oh, I did. But later on I figured out what was going on."

"You did, huh? What was going on?"

"What was going on was that you were attracted to me—we both were, to each other—and it scared you."

"Scared me . . ." I laughed.

"Sure. You were afraid of being burned again, and you were still feeling guilty and hurt over Bev—"

"*Guilty!* What did I have—"

"—so you put up this prickly barrier. Then, when we met for that drink, you started letting your hormones call the shots again, which was very sensible. But then when the possibility of dinner came up, you backed off in a hurry."

"And why did I do that?"

"Because in the bar we were talking about the show, so you had a nice, safe role to hide behind. But dinner would have been just you and me, no business talk, and that made you nervous again."

"Anne, that's . . . Is this what they teach you in career counseling? It's ridiculous."

"Uh-huh."

"Come on, people don't behave that simplistically. You're talking pop psychology."

"Mm."

"OK, if you're right, why have I spent the afternoon with you? And enjoyed it, I should add."

She shrugged. "Hormones talking again, I guess."

"Well, you're right enough about that," I said laughing.

We got to Columbia House at four-thirty, an hour before she was due to catch a military bus to the terminal. At the desk there was a stack of messages waiting for her, and a couple for me, one of which said that Harry Gucci had telephoned. Would I call him at 3660 or look for him in the Keller-Bar at about five?

"He might already be there," Anne said.

"Yes, I guess I'll go see. It's been a good day, Anne."

"For me too, Chris."

She didn't invite me up to her suite for a warm-up cup of coffee or a drink, and I didn't suggest it. The day was right, perfect, just the way it was, and neither of us wanted to risk spoiling it. Hormones be damned.

13

I had already gotten a bottle of Löwenbräu at the bar before I saw Harry at a table near the back. Gadney was with him.

"Hiya, Chris, come on over. Egad and I are just shooting the breeze."

"So he pretends," Gadney said. "In fact, I'm suffering a merciless interrogation. I advise you to find another table if you don't want some of the same."

Harry laughed, scratching at the side of his scruffy beard, and pushed out a chair for me. He was slumped in a cardigan I hadn't seen before, with faded geometric Northwest Indian designs on it.

"I understand your mission to Florence was a great success," Gadney said.

I nodded. "Lorenzo asked me to be sure and say hello for him."

"Lorenzo?"

"Lorenzo Bolzano."

"Of course," he said impatiently. "But I don't understand. I barely know him."

"Really? He gave me the impression that you'd spent a day down there."

"Only to attend to the shipping of the paintings to Naples. I don't know why Lorenzo would remember me kindly. I'm afraid I was rather cross."

"Why?"

"Oh, Peter and Earl had left without completing the

146

paperwork. My fault, really. I shouldn't have expected them to know about it. And certainly not Lorenzo."

"Is the paperwork pretty complicated, then?"

"Complicated? Not really; it's just a matter of following procedures. It's nothing compared to the difficulties of commissary logistics, I can tell you." He finished the sherry in his glass, pressed his lips together, and allowed himself an appreciative smack. "Consider, for example," he said with a fine, dusty enthusiasm, "how you would go about getting fifty thousand quarts of fresh Belgian strawberries onto the shelves of ninety commissaries from Bremerhaven to Izmir. With a permissible lag time of four days, I might add. There's excitement for you."

"I can imagine. But what about getting all those crates open and closed again in a single day? That must have been pretty harrowing too, considering how careful you have to be."

"Crates? Do you mean the paintings? What makes you think I did?"

"Didn't you say so a moment ago?"

"No, I didn't."

"You didn't? I thought you did. Didn't you hear him say that, Harry?"

Harry, who had been listening with interest, as he listened to everything, tugged at the hair behind his ear. "Well, yeah, I thought you said that, Egad."

"No," Gadney said again, his pale blue eyes looking levelly into mine, "I didn't say that. But as a matter of fact I did have to have the crates opened. Each one had to have its own bill of lading and a copy of my travel orders from Florence to Naples, since I was the authorizing officer. And no, it was not exciting. When we move from Berlin to London," he added stiffly, "I assure you it will be done properly in the first place. You needn't concern yourself."

"I'm sure it will, Egad. I didn't mean any criticism."

"Yes. Well, I really must run. Is that all right with you, Major?"

"Me? Sure. Enjoyed talking to you."

We both watched him stalk out. "What's up, Harry?" I asked.

"I thought we ought to touch base on next week."

"What's happening next week?"

"The El Greco pickup in Frankfurt. What, did you forget about it?"

I had. Fortunately, though, it appeared that Robey had remembered to alert Harry after all.

"Here's the way it'll work," he said, and rolled the rubber band off the limp little notebook. "Eleven hundred hours, you show up at the museum to verify the picture's OK when they crate it. Twelve-fifteen, you leave on the truck with it, along with a couple of museum guards. Thirteen hundred hours, the truck arrives at the Rhein-Main MAC terminal, VIP parking area. My people will meet you there and take over. Fourteen hundred hours, you come back with them on a special MAC flight. When you get to Berlin, there'll be a truck to meet you; then straight to the back of Columbia House."

"Very impressive. Herr Traben will be pleased."

"Yeah," he said doubtfully. "Look, you've done this kind of thing before. Do you usually go through all this hassle to get a painting from one place to another?"

"That picture's worth two million dollars, Harry. And it's literally irreplaceable. All the same, Traben's overdoing it a little, if you ask me."

"Yeah," he said again. He put down his orange juice. "You want another beer?"

"No thanks."

"How about some food? You hungry?"

"A little. They've got a steak special upstairs tonight."

He made a face. "I don't eat meat."

I don't know why, but it didn't surprise me. "Health or ethical grounds?" I asked.

"Both. Why eat all that cholesterol, and why slaughter cows or pigs or sheep when there are a lot of other ways to get protein?" He gave me the kind of look civilized beings reserve for carnivores, then said abruptly, "Hey, how about some fried chicken? There's a Wienerwald a couple of blocks from here."

I laughed. "Sure, but what have you got against chickens?"

He looked at me as if he couldn't believe I'd ask so self-evident a question.

"They're *ugly*."

In a corner booth at Germany's answer to Colonel Sanders, he grimaced at the menu. "Jesus, isn't that awful?"

I looked down at my own and saw nothing objectionable. "What?"

"The picture, the picture. Uch."

I still didn't know what was bothering him. The only picture I could see was a cartoon of a friendly and inoffensive chicken in a chef's hat, with a checkered kerchief around it's neck. "What's wrong with it?"

"Are you kidding? I hate this kind of picture. Look at it. He's holding a knife and fork, he's got an apron on. . . . I mean, the implication is that he's gonna eat himself—or at least another chicken—and he's laughing like crazy. It's horrible. You're telling me that doesn't bother you?"

"Harry," I said, "you're weird."

But not so weird that he didn't order half a sautéed chicken.

I wasn't very hungry, and asked for a small chicken salad.

"Oh, by the way," he said, when the waitress had brought apple juice for him and a glass of Mosel for me, "speaking of pictures . . ." He unfolded a poorly photocopied sheet with four photographs on it: two men, each photographed from front and side, with names and numbers beneath. "Would these possibly be friends of yours?"

They were like faces from a nightmare. No-neck the gorilla-man and his sidekick Skull-face. "You got them!" I cried. "The guys from the storage room! Harry—"

"Ah," he said with satisfaction, "good. But don't get too

excited. We don't have them yet; we just know who they are."

"Who?"

He took back the sheet and spread it out on the table in front of him, smoothing down the creases. "Just a couple of particularly nasty rent-a-thugs. The *Polizei* has records a mile long on them. They call the one with the forty-inch neck the Beast."

"Gee, I wonder why that is," I said, remembering with a shudder how it felt to be lobbed six feet into a concrete wall.

"Got a little more news for you, Chris," he said, watching me over the rim of his glass. "We also know the guys who killed van Cortlandt—that is, the ones who walked him through those bars that night."

I slowly put down my wine. "Why didn't you tell me that before? Who are they?"

He smiled and tapped the sheet.

My eyes widened. "The same ones? How did you find all this out?"

"Wasn't too hard. I got a dozen possible matches to your Photofit and took them to Frankfurt yesterday. Then I spent last night with a couple of *Polizei*, showing the pictures to people in the bars around the Paradies. Three people positively identified them as the guys who were hauling him around from bar to bar, more or less holding him up between them."

I turned the sheet around and looked hard at the pictures. The men who'd killed Peter. "Why did they do it?" I asked dully.

"Well, how the hell am I supposed to know that? Somebody hired them, I guess."

"And somebody hired them to rob the storage room?"

"I think so."

"And that's all you know?"

"Hey, look, Chris, I'm not Superman," he said testily. "Don't worry, we'll find these guys."

"Of course you will," I said quickly. "I'm sorry, Harry;

you've done a terrific job. It's just . . . well, even if we know who they are, we don't really know anything more than we did before, do we?"

"Oh, I wouldn't say that. We know the murder and the break-in are connected now. We didn't know that before."

"That's true. You don't suppose—you don't think Peter somehow found out that the robbery was planned, and they killed him to keep him quiet?"

He didn't seem impressed with the idea. "Possible, but what happened to your forgery theory?"

I shook my head. "I don't know."

We sipped our drinks thoughtfully until the waitress came back with our dinners.

"Aahh," Harry breathed, "that smells great. He tore off a wing and went to work on it—quite carnivorously, I thought. "Now," he said, licking at his thumb, "you want to tell me what that was about with Gadney?"

"What what was about?"

"Your burning interest in logistics."

"I wanted to see if he'd admit to being alone with the open crates," I said, and went over the conclusions I'd reached in Florence, while Harry nodded and made steady progress on his chicken.

"OK," he said, "so you're saying, (a) either the forgery is one of the three paintings from Hallstatt—in which case probably nobody connected with the show had anything to do with it—or (b) it's from Bolzano's Florence collection—in which case somebody in the show *has* to be involved. And you figure it's *b*?"

"No, I figure it's *a*, but I didn't think it would hurt to talk to Egad. Did what he said sound right to you, by the way? About the bills of lading and the travel orders?"

"It sounds possible."

"Well, I'll check around and see."

"*I'll* check around." He wiped his fingers on a napkin and reached for another. "You really think that little guy's mixed up in this thing?" "That little guy" was an inch taller and at least ten pounds heavier than Harry.

"No, but if the fake is from Florence—which I doubt—and not from Hallstatt, either he's involved with it, or Flittner is, or Robey is. One of them has to be."

"No, I don't see it that way."

"There's Jessick, you mean? I don't think so. He wasn't cleared to get near the paintings. Flittner, Robey, and Gadney are the only ones with the access and the knowledge. It's got to be one of them."

"No, it could have been *all* of them. Or any two."

I put down the Mosel and thought about that. "A conspiracy? That's pretty—"

"Or van Cortlandt."

"*Peter?* Are you serious? My God, Harry, he was murdered!"

"Yeah, well," he mumbled into his beard, "I was figuring that any involvement would have been before he died, you know?"

"That's not what I meant. There's no way Peter would have had anything to do with something crooked. And if he did, why would he tell me about it?"

"Hey, calm down, Chris; don't get excited. Eat your salad."

"I *am* calm, damn it!"

"All I'm doing," he said, searching sadly in the debris on his plate for any shreds he might have missed, "is thinking out loud, building possibilities from what you told me, you know? And it's possible—*possible*—that van Cortlandt was involved in something shady, and that he wound up getting killed on account of it."

"Yes, I know, but—"

"There are some other possibilities too. Anne Greene, for instance."

"Anne? You're out of your mind! She didn't know anything about it. And she's the one who kept trying to tell everybody Peter was murdered right from the beginning."

"Look, you said—and it's a good point—that the people who had access and knowledge are our best bets. Now, she's got both, right? Stop being so subjective, for Christ's sake. *Whoever's* guilty, you can bet there's someone, some-where, who thinks he's a wonderful person." He cocked his head and scratched raspily at the hair on his cheek. "Well, maybe not Flittner."

"I understand what you're saying, and you're right. But Anne Greene—well, hell, *I* had access and knowledge, too, for that matter. What about me?"

Harry licked grease from his pinky and nodded thought-fully. "Yeah, then there's you."

"Not likely," I said, in a tone implying that of course he was being playful. "I just got here last week."

"And how do I know this forgery business didn't get set up last week?"

"Because Peter told me about it the very first day I was here, for one thing."

"Yeah, so you say."

"So I . . . Why the hell would—"

Harry threw back his head and chortled. "Hey, relax, will you? You're not on my list of suspects, OK? Neither is Anne. I just enjoy seeing the veins stand out on your neck, that's all, but I don't want you to have a stroke. Loosen up; don't be so intense. I'm on your side, you know."

What was this? When did I get so intense? "That's nice to know, but how come you're being generous enough to exclude me?"

"Intuition. Also the fact that you almost got yourself killed in the storage room. But mostly intuition."

"Thanks for the vote of confidence." I took a long sip of the Mosel. "I'd like to help any way I can, Harry."

"Good; find that fake. And there's one thing you can tell me that might help a lot. Do you have van Cortlandt's ap-pointment calendar?"

"It isn't on the desk in Room twenty-one hundred?"

"No, but Jessick's sure he had one. Blue, he thinks."

"I haven't seen it, but I'll have a look. I have a few of Peter's files in my room."

"That's fine. Well, I don't know about you, but I'm

bushed. Let's figure out how we split the check. Your salad was ten marks, right? My chicken was only nine, so . . ."

The night had turned a dry, bitter cold, and on the walk back to Tempelhof Harry humped along with hunched shoulders, buried in his parka like a turtle, so that nothing below his eyes showed over his collar. And everything above was hidden by a thick knit cap, so he seemed to be peering warily out of the slit of a big, soft tank.

"Oh, by the way, Chris," he said from deep in the coat as we waited to cross the eight-lane Tempelhofer Damm, "did Flittner ever come up in your conversations with van Cortlandt?"

"No."

"How he got along with him, that kind of thing?"

"Harry, maybe if you'd just trust me and come out and tell me why you're so interested in Flittner I'd be able to help you. Since we're on the same side, it'd be nice to know just what the hell is going on."

He had to swivel the whole thickly encased upper half of his body to look at me. I think I heard him laugh, or he might have grunted; the sound was lost somewhere in the depths of his coat. "You know, you've got a point. All right, did you know that he's not on leave from the National Gallery—that he was canned?"

"Canned? Why?"

"Bad PR, lousy attitude, uncooperative behavior—all those curmudgeonly leanings you told me about. Come on, the light's changed."

Berlin traffic lights do not encourage dawdling. We jogged quickly across the broad street and onto the Platz der Luftbrücke, dark except for the spotlit monument. "I suppose," Harry sent on, "you didn't know that Robey's dumping him too, effective the end of the month, for pretty much the same reasons."

"I didn't have any idea. Poor guy. Does he know?"

"Yeah, Robey told him a couple of weeks ago."

"Hm. So why did you want to know if Peter—"

"Because he's the one who talked Robey into getting rid

of him—according to Robey. Let me ask you: Would van Cortlandt do something like that? Go to Robey and ask him to get rid of somebody else?"

"If he thought the paintings were being endangered or the show was being compromised, yes. Definitely. He'd consider it a matter of honor." I turned to look at him. "Are you saying you think Earl might have killed him—arranged to have him killed—out of revenge?"

"I don't think anything yet. I'm trying to get my facts in order. Here's the funny part: Robey says van Cortlandt told him he'd had a couple of tough talks with Flittner about it."

"That sounds like Peter. He'd want to be aboveboard. What's funny about it?"

"What's funny is that when I asked Flittner about it, he said he didn't know what I was talking about; Peter never talked to him about his behavior or anything else."

"So somebody is lying?"

"Right. And Flittner's got a pretty good reason. With me prying around asking questions, he's probably scared to admit he had any reason for hating van Cortlandt."

"Which makes him worried, but not necessarily guilty. Earl's pretty paranoid at the best of times."

"That's right," Harry said approvingly. "I never said he was guilty."

Once in the lobby at Columbia House, Harry woofed and stamped his feet as if we'd been trudging in three feet of snow. "Sheesh, it's freezing outside! Brr." He began unraveling himself from gloves, hat, scarf, and coat, emerging like an undersize moth from its cocoon. "I gotta get some wool socks."

"Harry, I was thinking. It's pretty natural for people's guard to be up with you questioning them—"

"I don't *question* them; I'm pretty subtle."

"Yeah, you really had Egad fooled."

He laughed. "You didn't do any better. He's madder at you than at me."

"That's true, but with me, anything about the show is a legitimate concern. I might get them mad, but I'm not going to make them suspicious. I thought maybe I might do a little . . . well, talking to people—"

"Forget it," he said firmly. "Here's the deal: You leave the investigation to me, and I'll leave the forgery to you."

"Look, I didn't mean I was going to confront Earl about Peter. I could do it indirectly. Maybe if I got a little more information from Robey—"

He sighed. "Let's go sit down for a couple of minutes."

We went to the same grouping of chairs that Peter and I had sat in when I'd first arrived in Berlin. Harry heaped his peeled-off garments on the chair next to him, and sighed again. "Flittner's not the only one I've got questions about."

"Who else? Not Mark?"

"Yeah, Mark."

"What questions?"

"Two of them. Why he went to Frankfurt with van Cortlandt the day van Cortlandt got killed—"

"What?" I exclaimed, then lowered my voice at Harry's wince. "But—Peter would have mentioned it. He went alone; I'm sure of it."

"Not exactly. Robey was in the same plane, sitting twenty rows behind him, in the smoking section."

"Well . . . why? What did he say?"

"That's my other question: Why won't he admit he went?"

"He out-and-out denied it?"

"No, I wouldn't say that. Didn't I tell you I'm subtle? I just gave him about ten different chances to mention it— you know, 'Been to Frankfurt lately?'—that kind of stuff. He wouldn't bite."

"Then how do you know he went?"

"High-class police work. I checked the passenger list of van Cortlandt's plane to see if anything turned up. Robey's name did."

"Wow, I don't have any idea what to make of that. When did he come back, do you know?"

"Not till just before that staff meeting. Two days and

three nights in Frankfurt, right when van Cortlandt bought it, and it slipped his mind. Funny, huh?"

I sagged back against the soft chair and thought about all this. "Yes, it's funny. Earl's such a miserable character I don't have any trouble imagining him as a murderer. But I like Mark. I don't like to think . . . Hey, that gives him a reason for lying, doesn't it? About whether Peter really talked to Earl, I mean. He could have been trying to throw you off, to invent a motive for Earl's killing him." I suddenly knew what Anne had meant about feeling as if she were in a movie.

"It's conceivable. But let me find out what's what in my own simpleminded way, OK? I mean, as much as I value your help—"

"All right," I said, smiling, "I won't get in your way."

"And don't look so gloomy. One of the things you learn in this business is that people spend a hell of a lot of time sneaking around and lying, and if you assume that the particular lie you just found out about has something to do with the case you're working on, you're going to be wrong ninety-five percent of the time. People just act that way out of habit."

He stood up and began the lengthy process of gathering up his clothes. "So don't assume anybody killed anybody until we know a lot more."

"I'll remember that," I said, and got up too. "But you know, on second thought I think I was happier not knowing what was going on."

"So next time don't ask. See you in a couple of days; I'm gonna spend some time in Frankfurt." He shambled off to the elevator, engulfed by a mountain of clothing and trailing a six-foot-long striped scarf.

Upstairs in my living room I sat by the telephone looking glumly at the other message that had been in the box with Harry's. It was from Rita Dooling. *Pls. call,* it said. *Bev will take 40% on house. You keep Murphy. Other devels.*

I sighed. It was 9:30 P.M.; 1:30 in the afternoon in San

Francisco. Little chance of getting Rita, who took late and leisurely lunches. Ah well, too bad, maybe tomorrow. No, that was Saturday. Well, next week sometime.

Whistling, thinking about the afternoon at the zoo, I went to bed.

14

I woke up at a little after six the next morning, itching to get back into my forgery-hunting. Because it was Saturday, I would very probably have two days entirely to myself in the Clipper Room, which suited me fine. When the restaurant opened at seven I was there, already missing the Augustas's *caffè latte*, but willing to console myself with ham and eggs, potatoes, toast, grapefruit juice, and American coffee. And at ten to eight I was at the door of the Clipper Room, Bolzano's certificates of guarantee under my arm, eager to dig into The Plundered Past.

This was easier said than done. I got through the two-man guard outside the Clipper Room all right, but getting the alarms turned off so that I could have the pictures taken down required the written approval of a grumpy, sleepy Harry, and the detailing of two more guards to help with the tricky attachment system. Still, by ten o'clock the paintings were off the walls, and a long ten hours later I had completed the first phase of the investigation: I had satisfied myself that each picture matched the description and photograph on its certificate in every particular.

If any of them hadn't, that would have been it right there, but the lack of variance didn't prove a thing. I already knew, after all, that Bolzano had scores of exact copies that would also match the "certificates of guarantee" of the originals—except for two differences: the provenances on their backs and the micropatterns on their fronts. By now I knew that none of the backs proclaimed themselves as fakes, but that was hardly a surprise; altering the backs would be no problem for a competent forger or, for that matter, a competent restorer or conservator.

Such as Flittner, for example. But that was getting off the track. My concern was *what*. *Who* and *why* were Harry's affair.

After a late dinner I got on to the next step—an examination of each painting with the ten-power lens and a penlight, to see if I could find a tiny, shield-shaped design in the upper left corner of the canvas, eighty-two millimeters from the top and sixty-six millimeters from the left edge, the entire design tilted clockwise one millimeter from the vertical: Bolzano's delicate micropattern of fifty-one tiny holes, which no one else connected with the show was even aware of. Find it and I would find a masterpiece of a reproduction masquerading as a masterpiece of an old master.

I began with the Vermeer, which was an act of bravery. Not long before, right there in Berlin, neutron photography had proved that *The Man With the Golden Helmet*, among the most beloved of Rembrandt's paintings, wasn't a Rembrandt at all. When asked to comment at the time, my statement to the *San Francisco Examiner* had been to the effect that it was no less a masterpiece than ever, and who had or hadn't painted it didn't affect its power or its intrinsic worth.

I had lied. It mattered a lot to me that Rembrandt had never stood before that lovely portrait, considering, adding a touch of red ocher to deepen the shadows of the sad face, a tiny blob of stiff impasto to highlight the glowing helmet. A lot of the magic was gone, and even some of its power and intrinsic worth, whatever I had meant by that.

And now, as anxious as I was to find the forgery, I didn't want to lose this "new" Vermeer too; I wanted the beautiful young woman standing at her clavichord to be genuine, and I believed she was—and yet Peter's "Right down your alley" kept bringing me back to her. I leaned over the canvas almost holding my breath, the lens close to the surface, and the penlight a few inches off to the side, to highlight the texture. Ten careful minutes later I straightened up with a creak.

No pattern, thank God. And none on the Rubens or the Titian. Or the Piero or the Dürer or the Hals. There wasn't any on the Giordano either, and at that point it occurred to me that I might not be recognizing the micropattern when I saw it, since I'd never seen it on an actual painting. I went to the alcove where the reproductions hung and, without taking it down, had a close look at the "Cranach" (not one of those flirty little Venuses but one of his ugly, bloat-bellied Eves, painted to please his friend Martin Luther).

The painting, like the other copies, was beautifully executed, but it took only a few seconds to find the telltale pinholes. It was just as easy on the copy of Vermeer's *Woman Peeling Apples* and on the "Poussin." So at least I knew that I knew what I was looking for. I went back to the originals, but without much hope of success. I had already examined the older paintings without finding a micropattern, and Reynolds, Géricault, Monet, Corot, and the rest were simply not "down my alley" by any criterion I could imagine. Nevertheless, I looked.

And found nothing. I called it a day. It was almost two in the morning now, and the guards who helped me put the paintings up again were the same ones who'd taken them down eighteen hours before on their previous shift. They were grumpy about it, and so was I; grumpy, grubby, and bone-tired.

But not disappointed. To find nothing, after all, was to learn something: Whatever I was looking for, it was not a legitimate Bolzano fake that had found its way into the authentic collection. The dull, mechanical search for secret markings was over; it was time for some serious, scholarly analysis, to which I looked hungrily forward. But not until I'd gotten some sleep.

Late Sunday morning, strengthened by Columbia House's colossal weekend brunch, I got down to business, with particular attention to the down-my-alley paintings. In addition to the Titian, Vermeer, and Rubens from Hallstatt, there were the Dürer self-portrait; the Piero Madonna; an extremely beautiful *Portrait of the Officers of the Saint George Militia Company* by Frans Hals; and *The Four Apostles*, a pair of matching panels by Luca Giordano. Again I worked until nearly 2:00 A.M., but for a change I came to some real conclusions.

The Dürer and the Hals were genuine. They were just too dazzlingly perfect. Hals is one of the most frequently forged painters, often successfully so, but it is always the seemingly careless Hals of *The Jolly Toper* or *The Laughing Peasant*. No faker in his right mind would try to ape the brilliant and exacting group portraits.

The Giordano I spent a lot of time on, although on the surface it was an unlikely candidate. Giordano was an excellent craftsman, quite difficult to imitate well. And although he was the leading Neapolitan painter of the late seventeenth century, he has never become popular with collectors. The result is that forgers stay away from him. Why bother, when there are so many less daunting painters whose works, or reasonable approximations of them, bring so much more money?

But there was another side to it. Giordano himself was a celebrated forger. In an age when artists were expected to borrow each other's ideas freely, he had been in a class of his own, figuring in one of art's earliest lawsuits. He was hauled into court over his *Christ Healing the Lame Man,* which he had painted very much in the style of Dürer—so faithfully, in fact, that it included Dürer's monogram. When the angry buyer learned what he'd really bought (the prideful Giordano had put his own name at the edge of the canvas, where it was covered by the frame), he sued the artist. The town council's verdict: Not guilty; no one can blame our Luca for painting as well as the great Dürer. Which goes to prove what I'd tried to tell Lorenzo Bolzano: Attitudes change.

The reason all this is pertinent is that in my wondering about Peter's uncharacteristic playfulness that day in

Kranzler's, I had begun to think I might know what his little joke was. And, artistically speaking, it would have been worth smiling about—a forgery of a painting of one of history's great forgers. But there wasn't any joke. In technique and style, it was pure Giordano. The real thing, without question.

That left four paintings, including the ones from the cache, and I had doubts about them all. Under ordinary circumstances they wouldn't have been very grave, but circumstances being what they were, I wasn't quite ready to give any of them a clean bill of health. One of them, I was sure, had to be a forgery.

The Madonna of Piero, our earliest painting, was the best bet, at least on technical grounds. It was a canvas, and that was extremely unusual for 1460, when frescoes and panels were the norm. Canvases didn't become popular until Titian's time, almost half a century later, when it was learned that they would hold up better in moist air. The artists of the day, who were given to sudden departures, also found it quite an advantage that they could quickly be rolled up and stuffed in a trunk. Try that with a wooden triptych or a ceiling fresco.

And there was something else. In 1460, tempera was still the primary binding medium, although people were beginning to experiment with oils. For the Madonna to be painted in either medium would have raised no suspicions, but it was painted in both, and that was unusual.

Unusual, but not unknown. Piero himself had used the two media in another painting, *The Baptism of Christ*. And as for the use of canvas, Uccello, painting at about the same time, had used it for his *Saint George and the Dragon*, the famous painting now in London's National Gallery. So what I had were two unlikely features in the same piece, and they were enough to make me wonder. The tempera-oils issue was more complicated than it might seem on the surface: the Madonna had probably been restored a dozen times, and for all I knew Piero had done it completely in tempera, only to have it retouched in oils three or four hundred years later.

Fortunately, old paint fluoresces differently from newer paint, so this was an issue with which Max Kohler of the Technische Universität could help me. Max tends toward the hysterical, and when I telephoned him, he practically wept. It was impossible, his lab was overflowing with work, he was laboring twenty hours a day. But finally he agreed to come the following Tuesday and to bring his portable ultraviolet lamp and some other equipment with him. This was on my solemn promise to ask nothing else of him for at least a month. That didn't present a problem; my questions about the remaining three paintings weren't technical, and they were for me to answer, not Dr. Max and his mysterious machines.

First, the Titian: *Venus and the Lute Player*, a lush, reclining nude being serenaded by a black lutenist, the earliest of several versions. It wasn't that it was a bad painting by any means. And it wasn't that it was uncharacteristic of Titian; it wasn't—but it was the wrong Titian, the Titian of his seventies or eighties, done with quick, slashing thrusts of color, intuitive and unrestrained.

It is a piece of conventional wisdom that you can't verify a late Titian by comparing it with early ones, or vice versa, because his approach changed so radically. *Venus* was supposed to have been painted in 1538, when he was in his late forties, still using a careful, linear style. (Some authorities think that his later approach was less a matter of artistic growth than of an old man's farsightedness.) But perhaps the painting had been misdated some time in the last 450 years. Or perhaps he was experimenting with the style he would later adopt. Either could easily be true. Still, it was something to think about.

And then there was the Vermeer. The more I looked at it, the more I liked it. I could find nothing questionable— nothing except Peter's "down-your-alley" remark. On that basis alone, I held off final judgment. I had some research

I wanted to do, and I was probably going to have to go to London to do it.

Finally, the last of the three from the cache, Rubens's fleshy *Rape of the Sabines*. Once again, there was nothing particularly wrong with it. But any sensible curator is queasy about giving his unqualified blessing to a Rubens. Lorenzo had remarked that Rubens ran a workshop. "Factory" was more like it. Not only did he sign works that had been painted mainly by his students, but he (or they) executed signed copies to order, and the number of canvases and panels issuing from the great house just off Antwerp's Meir was prodigious.

What this adds up to is that telling a mostly real Rubens from a hardly real Rubens from a good fake Rubens isn't easy. On this one too, there was some research I would have to do.

So, for the first time, I felt as if I were really getting someplace; not twenty possibles anymore, but four: Rubens, Vermeer, Titian, and Piero. That was fine. But what was taking me so long to pin it down to one? Peter had clearly expected it to jump out at me as soon as I had a casual look at the paintings. Well, I'd had a lot more than a casual look, and nothing was jumping. What was I missing?

Monday I spent catching up on "other duties as required." Yes, I actually did have some duties, although in this case they were no more than calling the luminaries of the Berlin art scene to ask them to the spiffy preview reception at Columbia House on the following Saturday. They had already received printed invitations, as had civic and military dignitaries, but Robey had thought, laughably, that my personal touch would add some *ton*.

At about two o'clock I hung up the telephone, made my final check mark on the list, and stretched, very nearly tipping over the old straight-backed wooden chair at my desk. Carrying my empty coffee mug, I left the bedroom-converted-to-office that had been Peter's and was now mine, and walked into the living room of Suite 2100, which was Corporal Jessick's permanent domain, and also offered workspace for any senior staff members who needed it.

The coffeepot was on a cleared corner of a table otherwise overflowing with lighting plans, flow charts, and critical-path diagrams.

"Conrad—" I said, pouring the dingy fluid.

A respectful sort, he jerked upright. *"Sir!"*

"There's going to be a Dr. Kohler from the Technical University here tomorrow to look at a painting in the Clipper Room. I won't be here; I'm going to Berchtesgaden and then London for a couple of days. Does he need a pass or something?"

"You know, he'll need a pass, sir. That's going to be hard to get."

"Well, who do I talk to, Harry Gucci?"

"You know who you ought to see about that, sir?"

Let me guess.

"I'd recommend you talk to Major Gucci about it." He smiled, happy to be of service. "He's in Frankfurt. You want me to try to get a hold of him?"

"Please." I stirred some powdered creamer into the coffee and frowned down at it while it coagulated into a gummy clump. "Conrad, I think you forgot to turn on the pot again."

"I did? Gosh, I'm sorry." Jessick was actually a pretty good clerk, but it made him nervous to leave electrical appliances on while he was at lunch, so he turned the coffee off when he left, and since he didn't drink it himself in the afternoon, he was likely to forget about it. He leaped up to turn on the switch.

"That's OK," I said quickly—the same pot had been on since 8:00 A.M. "Never mind. Kohler's going to have to be paid. What do I do about that?"

"Requisition for consultive services."

"Do I need Robey's signature?"

"You'll have to get Robey's signature, though" was the predictable reply. "He's probably back by now. He was supposed to fly in from Heidelberg this morning."

"That's fine." I went back through my office to the bathroom and dumped the cold coffee into the sink. While I was holding the mug under the tap and swabbing it out with two fingers, I remembered something. I walked quickly back to the outer office.

"Conrad—"

"*Sir!*"

"Do you remember, a couple of weeks ago, right after I got out of the hospital, you talked to me on the telephone to tell me about the staff meeting that Robey'd called? You said he'd just flown in from somewhere. . . . Where was it?"

If he found anything unusual about the question, he didn't show it. "Heidelberg."

That's what I'd remembered. "Are you sure?"

"Well, sure. I mean, that's where he said he was. Why would he lie?" He laughed at the idea.

That was the question, all right, and I wasn't sure whether or not I'd just learned something that might bear on it. Harry had already told me that Robey had flown to Frankfurt the day Peter was killed, and had returned just before the meeting several days later. He'd also told me that Robey hadn't admitted it. But that was after Peter's murder, when he might have been afraid of being implicated in something he didn't do. Now I'd found out he'd lied about it even before the telephone call that brought the shocking news from Frankfurt. Why?

Well, there wasn't anything for me to do about it except pass that on to Harry. His affair, not mine, right?

I ran into Robey himself a few minutes later when I was coming back from the dining-room kitchen with a mug of fresh coffee I'd managed to beg even though it was between mealtimes. The moment I saw that muzzy, amiable countenance, my suspicions evaporated. Surely murderers didn't look like that.

"Why, hello, Chris. Congratulations on your session with Bolzano."

"Thanks, Mark. It wasn't too tough."

"Oh, now, now," he said vaguely. "Everything going along all right?"

"Yes. I've asked Max Kohler to look at one of the paintings, though, and I guess I'll need your signature."

"OK, sure. Have Conrad type up the req and I'll sign it."

"Kohler's kind of expensive, but he's the best—"

"No problem. Don't worry about it."

"Great. And there's one other thing. I still have some questions about a few of the paintings, and the only place I'm going to find the answers is the Witt Library, and that's in London. I'd like to spend a day or two in their stacks."

He was nodding in rhythm with my words, his eyes cloudy, Archaic smile comfortably in place. "Fine, sure."

"I know it doesn't really have anything to do with the show, so if the budget can't afford the trip, I'll be glad to—"

"No, no, fine. Whatever you need. I'll take care of it."

"Thanks, Mark." Would life at the San Francisco County Museum of Art ever be the same?

"You'll be back in time for Saturday's reception?"

"Definitely. I thought I'd go down to Berchtesgaden for Christmas Eve"—he was paying more attention than it appeared; I got a surprising, avuncularly lecherous look out of the corner of his eye—"and head to London from there. Then I'll stop off in Frankfurt for the El Greco, and be back with it late Friday." This meant only a single day with Anne in Berchtesgaden, but there was no help for it.

"Good, fine. So how are you doing on the forgery? Are you getting anywhere?"

"Sort of, but no final answers. Maybe after I've been to the Witt."

"Mm." He nodded, and went on nodding, and I watched his customary aura of vague impenetrability resettle about him like a warm, dense cloak. "Well," he said, looking slowly around (wondering where he'd been headed?), "let me know how it goes."

* * *

When I got back to Suite 2100, Flittner was in the outer room, at one of the tables near Jessick's desk, writing up some forms of his own.

"Hi, Earl. Keeping you busy?"

I was pleased with the way the talk with Robey had gone. I'd managed to bury my lurking suspicions and treat him like the pleasant, sweet-natured man he no doubt was—but at the same time I'd kept to myself the specifics of my progress on the forgery. That was the way I wanted to treat Flittner too, allowing for the obvious and repellent differences in personality.

"Busier than you," he mumbled around a cigarette, not bothering to look up.

"You're probably right," I said with a smile, and went into my office.

"I goddamn well know I'm right," I heard him mutter to Jessick, or to himself, or maybe to me.

He did have a point; as Tony had predicted, I was not overloaded with responsibility. Mildly stung, I decided to save the harried Jessick some work by typing up the consultive-services form myself on the venerable Remington beside my desk. I got out the folder labeled *Administrative Forms and Procedures,* and while I searched through it for a blank form I found something else.

The moment I saw it, I knew what it was, and I took it out with growing excitement: a slim blue leather booklet with the initials *PVC* in gold in the lower right corner of the cover.

Peter's appointment calendar, the one Harry had been looking for. Of course it was Harry's concern, but of course I went through it anyway. For December 11, the day he was killed, there were two notations: *Lv Fkft 2:15* and *CN arr.* In his simple shorthand they referred to his flight to Frankfurt and to my arrival in Berlin. No surprises there.

No surprises elsewhere either, and only one entry that got me to thinking. It wasn't in the square for any particular date, but in the lower margin of the two pages allowed for November.

Tk F re HS! it read. I thought for a moment.

"Talk to Flittner about HS," I said aloud. "Exclamation point." Who or what was HS? And why the emphasis?

"HS," I repeated. "HS." After five minutes of that I could come up with only one possibility: the Heinrich-Schleimann-Gründung, the organization that was so hostile to the show. I walked thoughtfully to the outer office. Flittner was still there.

"Earl, could I talk to you?"

Having just given Jessick some things to type, he was on his way out. He turned to look at me over his shoulder and was, I think, about to inform me that he didn't work for me (which he didn't), when he appeared to read something in my face that made him change his mind. He followed me back into my office and sat down heavily in the chair beside the desk.

"What do you want to talk about?" he demanded, relentlessly surly. He glanced around for someplace to put the remaining half-inch of his cigarette.

I found a small aluminum-foil pie plate I'd remembered seeing in a bottom drawer and placed it at his elbow. "I want to talk to you about the Heinrich-Schliemann-Gründung."

He looked sharply up from grinding the butt into a stale-smelling mess. "So talk."

Belatedly, it occurred to me that I might have given this conversation a little more thought before starting. "No," I said, fishing blindly, "you talk. What's it all about?"

He stared at me, his hand still over the ashtray, his long gray face not more than two feet from mine.

"Peter told me everything," I said when he didn't speak.

He snorted. "Peter didn't know everything." I could see he wanted to take it back as soon as he'd said it.

"But he did, Earl," I said, wondering what the hell we were talking about. "And what little he didn't, I figured out."

"What did you figure out?" He said it with a sneer that didn't quite come off. I was onto something.

"About the Schliemann group . . . about where they're located . . ." I watched his face to see if I was getting closer, but he merely reached for his pack of cigarettes with no expression other than his usual resigned disdain.

"What they're after . . . who's behind them—who they really are . . ."

Bingo. The pack spurted from his hands. He fumbled with it convulsively and managed to catch it, but one cigarette fell out onto the table like a sign of guilt in some primitive trial by ordeal.

I'd hit it, but what had I hit? "Yes," I said quietly, "I know." And then I had the good sense to shut up and wait.

It didn't take him long to recover. He picked up the cigarette, lit it, sucked in, and noisily blew out twin ropes of smoke through his nostrils. "What does it matter anymore? All right, what the hell, so I wrote those letters."

If I'd had a pack of cigarettes to drop, I'd have done it.

"So," he went on, "the horrible, bloodcurdling gang that makes Egad piss in his pants was just poor old harmless Earl Flittner stating a few painful truths." He laughed, or sneered. "It was damn salutary, if you ask me. What harm did it do?"

"For one thing, it got Harry Gucci off on a false lead on the storage-room break-in—or was it a false lead? I don't suppose your one-man *Gründung* had anything to do with that?"

He sat straight up, spilling ash into the files in my open bottom drawer. "Are you out of your fucking mind?"

"Egad thought it was a possibility."

"Egad! Jesus Christ . . . now you listen to me. I stopped writing those letters a week before that ever happened, and that was that. I figured the point was made." He gestured at me with the cigarette. "Don't try to hang any of this other crap on me."

"But what *was* the point, Earl?"

"The point? The point?" He jumped up from the chair, a ponderous, pear-shaped man with wide hips and a long torso that tapered to sloping, fleshy shoulders. "The point is that everybody was so goddamn smug and self-satisfied they needed a boot in the ass, that was the point. This show was supposed to be God's gift to the human race. I just wanted them to know that not everyone saw it that way."

He had gone to the window to look down onto the plaza, and now strode back to the desk. "You don't need to look at me like that. I did my job, didn't I?"

"Yes, extremely well."

"All right, then. As long as nobody can complain about my work, I'm entitled to my personal opinions." He slumped back into the chair. "I suppose you're going to run to your pal with this earthshaking information?"

"My pal?"

"Gucci."

I nodded, and then on second thought I said, "I've already told him." On the one hand, I was inclined to accept what he'd told me as nothing more sinister than another example of his nasty quirkiness. On the other, he just might be a killer, and I didn't want to put myself in the precarious situation of those people in novels and movies who blithely announce to the villain that they will shortly go to the police with the damning evidence of which they and they alone are aware.

"I figured as much," he said with a shrug. "Big deal. Tell me something, will you?" He pulled in another of his ferocious drags and let the smoke dribble out as he spoke. "I know van Cortlandt thought I was helping the *Gründung*, but he never figured out I was *it*, and don't tell me he did. How the hell did you?"

"I'm afraid I can't tell you that," I answered mysteriously.

15

Somebody once said that when World War II ended, the British were in control of Germany's industry, the Russians had the agriculture, the French the fortresses, and the Americans the scenery.

If Berchtesgaden is any example, he was right. What's more, the Americans still have it. Not Berchtesgaden per se, which is a lovely old Alpine village with winding streets, quaint shops, and a picturesque sixteenth-century square complete with an elegant little royal palace. That Berchtesgaden is as German as ever. What the Americans have is the Berchtesgaden of Hitler and Göring and Bormann and Speer. The Berchtesgaden to which Lloyd George, Daladier, Mussolini, and the Duke of Windsor trekked. And of course the Berchtesgaden at which Neville Chamberlain found peace in his time.

This more notorious Berchtesgaden is actually a forested plateau more than half a mile above the town and properly called the Obersalzberg, sitting as it does on top of the Salzberg, or Salt Mountain. By the war's end, Anne had told me, almost all the buildings on the Obersalzberg had been bombed. Those that hadn't were razed during the next few years, except for a few that were ambitiously restored to make a vacation complex for American servicemen, and that's what it's been for forty years: R and R at Hitler's playground in the Bavarian Alps.

I had arrived at ten after a flight to Munich the night before, a pleasant morning train journey, and a ride on the military shuttle bus that regularly drives up the mountain road from the village center. Anne was waiting at the bus stop, laughing, rosy and fresh from the cold, and convincingly and satisfyingly glad to see me. We hugged like old friends, which was just right for that time of the morning.

"It's a work day for me," she said, "but they've given me a couple of hours off for you. I told them you were a bigwig art expert with government connections."

"Damn right."

She laughed. "I'm glad you're here. Any new, exciting developments?"

"Not since yesterday," I smiled. I'd called her from Munich the evening before and told her about the last couple of days.

"Well, you know, I've been thinking. We've been assuming that the forgery—"

I held up a hand. "Please. Could we talk about something else for a while? I've been up to my eyeballs in forgery. Right now it'd be great just to get my head clear in this fantastic air."

"OK," she said amicably. "I'll save my brilliant deductions. How'd you like that tour I promised? It's all open-air."

And so we spent an intriguing couple of hours poking around the snow-dusted rubble that had been Göring's house, probing with our toes at the dismal frozen marsh that had been his tiled swimming pool, clambering over the nearly nonexistent remains of Bormann's extravagant home, wandering through the burned-out skeleton of Hitler's guest house.

The Eagle's Nest, which I asked to see (as did everyone, Anne said) was now a restaurant, open to the public, but closed in winter. It was visible another two thousand feet above us, not much more than a speck on the very tip of Kehlstein Mountain, and the amazing road to it that had been blasted from the granite by slave labor wasn't drivable for seven months of the year.

"It was a birthday present from Bormann to Hitler on behalf of the German people," Anne explained, slipping into her standard lecture. "It was just a tea house, not any kind of special headquarters, and it cost ten million dollars by the time the road was completed. Hitler never liked it much; he preferred it down here. He went there exactly five times, which comes to two million dollars per cup of tea. Obligatory laughter, please."

To get to the site of Hitler's celebrated home, the Berghof, we had to fight our way through tangled brush and small trees, and ignore an *Eintritt Verboten* sign that was there to ward off the random tourist who found his way up the unrestricted road to the Obersalzberg. Nothing was left but the massively walled garage, and most of that was below ground, impossible to find unless you knew exactly what you were looking for. The house, Anne explained, had been damaged by wartime bombing, but it had been the Bavarian government that had leveled it a few years later, for fear that it might become a shrine.

Even now, it felt enough like a shrine—of sorts—to exude a dank, evil aura that made me want to get out of there. And, believe me, I'm not the kind of person given to making dopey statements like that.

"Let's go," I said almost as soon as we'd found it.

She shivered sympathetically. "It does the same thing to me. Usually I tell people we don't know where it is." How about some *Glühwein*?"

I agreed readily, and we climbed down to the road and walked the fifty yards or so to the Gasthof Zum Turken, the only private German establishment on today's Obersalzberg. It was an old family hotel, she told me, that had been commandeered by the Nazis and converted into the headquarters for Hitler's elite, private Gestapo corps. The owner, an anti-Nazi who had spoken his mind, had died for it in a concentration camp, but now the Zum Turken was back in the hands of the family with the blessings of the American military administration.

"Ahh," I said, warmed by the first sip of the hot, spiced wine, "that's better." I stretched my legs, leaned back in the wooden chair, and looked appreciatively out at the stupendous Alpine view. "All right, this has been fascinating, and you've been very good, and now I'm ready to talk about art forgery."

"That's good," she said promptly, "because I've been thinking that you might have things all wrong."

I looked at her reprovingly. "Surely not."

"Chris, you've been assuming that the fake is either from the Hallstatt cache, in which case just about anybody might have been behind it anytime over the last forty years, or else it's in the collection from Florence, in which case you're pretty sure that someone on our own staff must have had a hand in it."

"That's true," I said. "What other possibilities are there?"

"Well, what if the forgery is from the Florence collection, but it was already there before it ever left Bolzano's house?"

I shook my head. "Peter would have seen it when he was there for the packing."

"How can you be sure? You've been looking for it for a week and you haven't found it yet."

"That's right, rub it in."

"Don't be sensitive. You know what I mean."

"Look, Bolzano's an extremely discriminating buyer. If there was a forgery in his collection—especially one that Peter could spot without scientific help—Bolzano would just about have to be aware of it too. Agreed?"

Anne thoughtfully moved the rim of the glass back and forth across her mouth, inhaling the pungent aroma. "Probably."

"Definitely. And why would he try to pass off a fake as the real thing? He's got enough genuine art to make his reputation ten times over without messing around with forgeries."

"I think there could be several reasons," she said earnestly. "Maybe he sold one of his originals a long time ago and replaced it with a fake that no one knows about— maybe he intends to try to sell it as the real thing himself someday."

"Why? If he ever needs money, he's got plenty of real masterpieces to sell. Why take a chance with a forgery?"

"I don't know why, Chris," she said exasperatedly. "I'm just guessing, like everybody else. All right, how about this: The forgery was bought by his father—I mean the older Bolzano's father—a long time ago, before there were all these fancy tests, and Bolzano—Claudio Bolzano—found out that his father'd been snookered, and he's ashamed to admit it. How's that?"

"Well, I suppose that's—"

"Or wait, wait! How about this?" She spilled a little wine in her enthusiasm and dabbed at the table with a napkin. "Maybe Bolzano was behind the storage-room break-in. Maybe the idea was that this fake—which everyone thinks is real—was going to be stolen along with everything else, and Bolzano was going to claim the insurance on it, but all the time he'd have the real one hidden away someplace where he could still enjoy it. Then Peter found out about it, and that's why he was killed."

I had listened open-mouthed, my glass held motionless. "Boy, you really get into this, don't you?"

She laughed. "You think it sounds improbable?"

"Just a little, but that doesn't mean it couldn't be true. But there are a few things that rule Bolzano out, I think."

"Like what?"

"In the first place, and most important, Bolzano very willingly OK'd the analysis of the paintings; never hesitated. Why would he do that if he had something to hide? And he gave me the micropattern on the copies without my having to ask twice for it."

"Yes, that's true."

"And Peter himself said he didn't know about the forgery; don't forget that."

"Mm. Well, what about the son, Lorenzo? Maybe he's trying to cheat his father. Maybe he sold off a real painting years ago and kept the money, and replaced it with a copy so his father wouldn't notice. Maybe—"

"I don't think so. Oh, it wouldn't amaze me to find out

he was trying to put one over on *il padrone*—there's a lot of tension between them—but if he had a guilty secret to hide, he'd hardly let it be shown in a public exhibition, would he? Too risky by far."

Anne nodded gloomily and finished her wine. "Yes, you're right. Back to square one."

"Back? I've never been off it."

Anne had a lunch meeting at the Zum Turken with a Bavarian state official to talk about an upcoming German-American friendship week, and I rose to go when he came in. But the middle-aged, jovial Herr Wecker was so gregarious and agreeable that I stayed to join them.

"Will you take your friend to see the night-shooting, Captain?" Herr Wecker asked, blotting his mouth with care after finishing his plate of roast beef and potatoes.

"I thought I would, yes," Anne said over the last of her chicken-salad sandwich. "The weather's lovely."

"The night-shooting?" I asked.

"Yes," he said, and laughed. "An old ceremony, quite famous. There is gun-shooting at midnight to welcome the Christ Child. It is done at several locations around Berchtesgaden."

"They welcome the Christ Child by shooting?"

He chuckled again. "That's correct—it was done in your country, too, until this century. A very ancient custom. You are interested to know more?"

I nodded.

Herr Wecker pursed his lips while he pared the apple he had ordered for dessert. "In olden times, the farmers used to make noises with pots and pans to keep away the evil spirits. Later this noise becomes an expression of joy to praise the Christ Child, and later yet the pots and pans are replaced by pistols. No one who comes here at Christmas should think of missing this. The Berchtesgadener Weihnachtschutzen."

"It sounds quite interesting," I said politely.

"It is, actually," Anne said with a smile. "They fire beautiful old black-powder pistols, and they dress in sixteenth- and seventeenth-century hunting costumes. They even hold a session up here on the mountain. We could drive to it in five minutes, or there's a trail through the forest if you're in the mood for walking."

Herr Wecker nodded while he meticulously quartered the apple and cored the segments. "Everyone shoots on signal from the leader. The flashes are so bright you would think it is daytime. You almost cannot look. It is marvelous." He carefully inspected the apple pieces. "Don't forget about your kidneys."

"Pardon me?" Anne and I said at the same time.

"It will be very cold at midnight. You must protect your kidneys adequately."

"Ah," I said, "we shall." I should have realized what he meant. From an American perspective, Europeans expend an exorbitant amount of energy figuring out how to protect their kidneys. That doesn't include the English, who spend their time worrying about their livers.

Herr Wecker ate his apple quarters with wonderful delicacy, holding them with two fingers in front of his mouth and reaching for them with his lips, as if they were juicy mangoes that might splatter his neat green Bavarian-style suit. When he finished the last one, he wiped his hands thoroughly on the cloth napkin, grasped my forearm, and delivered a final inducement. "The noise is so great you will believe you are going deaf."

Anne looked at her watch, then drained her coffee, sighed, and stood up. "Christmas Eve or not, Herr Wecker and I still have an afternoon's planning ahead of us. I'll see you for a late dinner, Chris, if you don't mind waiting. And we can skip the Weihnachtschutzen if you're not in the mood."

"Not in the mood?" I said. "I wouldn't miss it."

"*Gut,*" said Herr Wecker with approval. "You will enjoy it wonderfully."

He would have been surprised to know that the prospect of being blinded and deafened by gunfire held no appeal whatsoever. But the idea of a wintry Alpine walk with Anne under a black sky glittering with stars was another thing.

I spent most of the afternoon in shameless indolence while Anne and Wecker slaved over their planning. I wandered along piney, deserted trails, my mind contentedly emptied by the sparkling air and the stunning views of mountains, forests, and snowfields through the trees.

At about four I checked into the General Walker, the rambling U.S. military hotel that had originally been constructed as a "people's guest house," where the crowds who made the pilgrimage to the Obersalzberg could spend a full day and night within a few hundred yards of their führer for a single mark. From my room I called Jessick in Berlin.

"Did Kohler get in to look at the paintings?"

"Yes, sir, he came and went already. He said to tell you that—wait a minute, he left a note. . . ." Paper rustled near the telephone. " 'Piero della Francesca,' " he read slowly, " 'was originally painted in tempera. Restored at least four times, three in tempera, once in oils. Never extensively. No reason to doubt attribution.' He said if you call him he'll explain what he did."

So that was that, and I can't say I was surprised. Now I was down to the three paintings from the cache: the Vermeer, the Titian, and the Rubens. That should have made me feel that I was getting closer, but it worried me. None of them was really a credible fake, if it makes any sense to put it that way. I still had some checking to do on them in London, but I had a stomach-sinking conviction that they would all turn out to be the real thing; that I'd been pursuing something that wasn't there.

And where would that leave me? Would it mean that Peter had been wrong, that perhaps he'd spotted what I had on the Piero, and had jumped to a false conclusion? Unlikely. Or maybe the forgery was there, all right, staring me in the face, but I was too dense to see it. Or did it mean that there had never been a forgery in the first place; that

Peter, with all his oddly cagey talk, had been trying to tell me something else? But what? And if there were no forgery, why had he been so elaborately murdered?

Whew.

"Hey," Jessick said, "—er, sir—how's Berchtesgaden? Boy, I love it down there at Christmas."

"It's beautiful. And Conrad, 'hey' is fine."

"Yes, sir. Are you going to the shooting? It's fantastic."

"I think so. Conrad, has Harry Gucci tried to reach me there? I've been trying to get him since yesterday."

"Uh-uh. He's supposed to be back here tomorrow, but."

"Good. Will you ask him to give me a call? No, tomorrow's Christmas; you won't be in the office, will you?"

"Gee, I'd be glad to," he said sadly, "but I won't be here. It's Christmas."

"Oh, is it? Well, merry Christmas, Conrad."

"Thanks. Uh, sir . . . ? Remember when you asked me, where was Colonel Robey the day before the meeting, and I said Heidelberg?"

My ears pricked up like a dog's. "What about it?"

"Well, was it important?"

"Kind of, yes."

"Well—it wasn't exactly true. He was in Frankfurt; that is, Sachsenhausen, right across the river."

"Oh," I said without expression, "how do you happen to know that?"

"I guess you're wondering how I come to know that."

"Now that you mention it, yes."

"Well, I got his airline tickets for him. I know this guy at Lufthansa and I can get a good deal, so I usually get him his tickets whenever he goes."

"Whenever he goes? To Frankfurt?"

"Yes, sir, uh . . ."

"Conrad, it really is important. If you know some more about this, I need to know."

"It's kind of personal," he said uneasily. "I don't feel right about—"

"Let's hear it, Conrad!" Jessick was the only person in

Berlin on whom the Norgren command presence had any effect.

"Yes, sir. He's got a girlfriend in Sachsenhausen."

"A *girlfriend*?"

"Well, a lady friend. He goes to see her whenever he gets a chance." He seemed to interpret my silence as disapproval. "It's not as if he's got a wife somewhere, sir. He got divorced, like, five years ago."

"Why so secret, then?"

"Well, she's not exactly divorced yet herself, and I guess he doesn't like—"

"OK, Conrad, thanks for telling me. Don't worry, this won't make any problem for Mark, and I won't tell him you told me. And Conrad? Call over to Harry's office right now, will you? Leave a message for him to call me whenever he gets in."

If nothing else, at least I knew where Robey's mind was all the time.

A late dinner with Anne in the hotel dining room, and then coffee and vintage port (at fifty cents a glass) in the grand bar, where big, relaxed Americans, still in their ski outfits, sprawled in comfortable chairs at the foot of imposing columns made of Hitler's favorite pink Utersberg marble.

Anne poured more coffee for both of us from a ceramic pitcher and leaned back to sip. "So where do you go from here?"

"As far as the forgery goes, you mean?" I shook my head dejectedly. "I don't know. We may have to run all of them through a lab yet, but the show'll be over before that ever gets done."

"But you've already said you're sure the pictures are all the right age. How can a laboratory tell you any more than that? If *you* can't tell if something is really by Vermeer, how can an X-ray machine?"

"It can, as a matter of fact—if the operator knows what he's looking for. For example, Vermeer worked without drawing in the outlines first. Nobody knew that until we looked at one with an X-ray machine. That means that any old Vermeers with a drawing under the paint aren't really Vermeers." I took a long swallow of the velvety wine and licked the sweet stickiness from my lips. "Titian also worked without outlining, which was no secret from his contemporaries—but why would anyone faking a Titian a hundred or two hundred years ago bother doing it the hard way? No one else could possibly know what was or wasn't under the surface."

"I see," she nodded. "An X ray actually shows you the way an artist worked."

"And not only X rays. A good lab will put a painting through a mass spectrometric analysis—"

"Yoicks! What?"

"Don't ask me to explain it; I wasn't even sure I could say it. But it isolates chemicals, which can tell you interesting things." There was a long pause while I tried to think of an interesting thing. "Well, Dürer, for instance. For a while he was using copper blue under the impression that it was ultramarine. Even careful forgers didn't know that—and still don't—so their failure to make the same mistake proves the forgery. Clever, what?"

"Very. You think that might be the case with our Dürer?"

"No, I'm sure it's real. I'm down to the Vermeer, the Titian, and the Rubens now. And if they check out . . ."

"Don't look so glum. If Peter said there's a forgery, there is. And you'll find it, my good man. I have complete confidence."

"Good, I'm glad one of us does."

She stood up and held out her hand for my glass. "I think you can stand one more round of cheer before we face the shooting. And I'll buy."

"You will? I'm already more cheerful."

16

Midnight on the Obersalzberg.

There is a painting by Pieter Brueghel the Elder, *The Return of the Hunters*, in which three muffled men breast a snowy hill. Before them stretches a great plain rising to grotesque, jagged peaks in the far distance. Below are everyday people engaged in everyday activities on the plain, and snug houses with smoke coming from the chimneys, and yet the effect is—and this was certainly Brueghel's intention—of man dwarfed and trivialized by an awesome and indifferent Nature.

That was very much the feeling on the mountain. No moon, but starlight reflected from the snow made it bright enough to see across the valley to the mountains of Austria: ghostly blue-white snowfields; black, dense clumps of forest; monumental crests and ridges—everything windless, silent, sweeping, immense. For a while it was enough to subdue the crowds that had gathered in shivering little clumps, but after a time the Class VI vodka, gurgling steadily from flasks and bottles, had created a hum of conversation and laughter.

There were German spectators too, and they and the milling shooters had been at their schnapps, so the mood was pretty lively all around. Most people had brought flashlights, the beams of which bounced playfully from group to group.

By the time the shooting began, things were starting to get rowdy. The way it was supposed to work was that the senior marksman would give the order, and the others

184

would then fire in rapid sequence, sounding like a string of Chinese firecrackers. They would then load up again, ceremoniously knocking their powder into the pistol barrels with little wooden hammers, and await the next signal to fire.

And that, more or less, was the way the first series went, but each succeeding one got a little sloppier, until there were flashes going off out of sequence in all directions, generally followed by giggling screams from the women and laughter from the men. Good thing, I thought grouchily, that the weapons weren't loaded. Which was more than you could say for the people.

"Kind of boisterous, isn't it?" Anne said. "I've never seen it so wild."

"Dangerous too," I said, shielding my eyes against the jabbing flashlight beams. "Even without bullets, those flashes must be able to burn you. Or can't they?"

"Oh, yes. People get hurt every year. If you're ready to go, I am too, Chris. All this tipsy *Gemütlichkeit* is getting to me."

"Me too," I said with feeling, despite my head start of three ports. "And welcoming Christmas with a shooting spree still seems like a rotten idea, no matter how old it is."

We had been sitting on a log conveniently lying at the base of a thick pine that had served as a backrest, and although we were behind a group on blankets and air mattresses, we'd been too comfortable to move. We still were, so getting up took a special effort.

"One . . . two . . . *three*," I said, and shoved myself up, tugging Anne along with me, or trying to. I got her halfway up, lost my footing in the snow, and went over backward just as another ragged volley exploded.

"Ouch!" I said, at a small, sharp stab of pain in my left hip. I wound up flopping flat on my back, legs in the air, like a lassoed calf, while Anne tipped back over the log and landed in much the same position.

"They got 'em," somebody observed. "Good shootin'."

The twinge in my hip had only been momentary—a minor strain, I assumed—and we both roared with laughter, neither of us, it seemed, being so very far above the general level of tipsy *Gemütlichkeit* after all. I scrambled up, brushing the snow off, and hand in hand we trotted down the incline, working our way through the crowd. A turn in the path after a hundred yards put a great wall of rock between us and the shooting, and we stopped to listen to the sudden silence. The sound of our weight shifting squeakily in the snow was all we could hear.

"Aah," we said together, letting our eyes adjust to the dark again, our ears to the quiet. When I put a hand to her shoulder, she moved willingly into my arms to the noisy rustle of our nylon jackets.

"Tell your jacket to keep out of this," she said. "This is our affair. Oops."

Abruptly tongue-tied, I said nothing. I brushed my lips over her eyebrows, against the grain to feel the roughness, with it to feel the smoothness, and I felt her lids flutter against my chin. Her cheeks were cool, fragrant with winter. We kissed gently, quietly, and she bowed her head to my shoulder. Her hair stirred against my face when I breathed. There again was that cool, clean scent of citrus.

"Anne—"

"Shh." Her hands went to my sides and pulled me closer still.

"Ow!" I said.

"Sorry. When I get like this, I don't know my own strength."

I laughed. "I must have landed on a rock when I fell over back there."

She tilted her head back and regarded me. "No, you said 'ouch' before you hit the ground. I remember distinctly."

"I did?" I worked my hand under my jacket and explored the top of my hip. "Ow!" I said again. "Damn."

"Chris? Are you all right?"

"Oh, sure. It just stings a little. And it seems to be a little stiff."

"I think we ought to go inside and sit down," she said, and I complied happily, basking in her concern.

The bar was open late for the après-Weihnachtschutzen crowd, and we both ordered hot chocolate, which the creative bartender had to make from Kahlua, and a very warming invention it was. My hip stopped smarting by the third swallow.

I can't remember what we talked about, but we spent half an hour at it, until Anne finished her drink and stretched. "One-thirty. Time to call it a day."

"I guess so." I stared into the bottom of my cup, listening to my heart race. "Like to join me for a nightcap? I've got some cognac in my room."

"Could you really stand a nightcap?"

"No." I smiled and looked up. "All right, then; care to join me just for the company?"

She looked at me for a while, her eyes soft. "No," she said finally. "I don't think so."

"No?" This courting business was coming very hard to me, as must be obvious, and here was another unnerving development. I'd thought I was reading the signals correctly.

She covered my hand with hers. "You don't need to look embarrassed. I'd like to, Chris, very much. I just don't think you're ready."

"I'm not ready!" I laughed. "If I got any more ready I'd—well, I'm ready, believe me."

She smiled. "I don't mean that way. Chris, I'm kind of old-fashioned. . . . I don't mean that I need a commitment or anything—"

"Anne, it's OK. You don't have to justify—"

"No, let me finish." She spoke hesitantly, rotating her empty cup slowly between her hands and staring down into it. It was a side to her that I hadn't seen before: uncertain, diffident, tentative. "Chris, when you and I . . . if we . . . well, I just want you to *be* there for me, not off somewhere else." She shrugged, still not looking up at me. "I don't feel that you're ready to do that."

And I guess I wasn't. I didn't protest; I didn't tell her that she was so lovely it made my throat ache to look at her. I just sulked like any wounded male.

"Don't be angry," she said.

"I'm not angry," I said, and snarled, and we both laughed.

"And not embarrassed?"

"That's different; I'm embarrassed as hell. Did you think my forehead always glistened like this? And now can we stop going on about it, please?" I held out my hand to her. "Come on, I'll walk you to your room."

Later, alone in my own room, I had to admit it was a good thing. The pain in my hip had sharpened, and all I wanted to do was keep it still. I stripped gingerly, but all I found was a kind of crease, an angry red furrow, just below the crest of the hip bone, as if an object the size of a pencil had been pressed hard against the flesh for a long time. There had been some bleeding, and there were black specks on my skin that felt greasy when I touched them. I'd never had a bruise anything like it.

When I took a look at my clothes I discovered a tear just above the hip pocket of my pants, and a small hole with signs of a smudgy ring around it through all the layers of my jacket.

No strain had done that. Was this what a powder burn looked like? The pistols had gone off while I was pulling Anne up, I remembered, but I had been a good forty feet from them. Still, these were ancient, primitive weapons, and when they were fired, they produced great flaring volcanoes that very well might extend forty feet, for all I knew.

I know, I know, if it were you, you would have figured out long ago that someone was gunning for you. Easy for you to say, just sitting there, but I wasn't thinking along those lines. Admittedly, the possibility of danger had crossed my mind before, but not very seriously and not for very long. It was true that Peter had most certainly been murdered, but it was hard for me to give credence to the idea that anyone was out to kill *me*.

Wait until you find yourself in a similar situation, and see if you don't feel the same way.

By the next day my hip was better; still tender, but more of a dull, aching bruise than anything else. The same went for my ego.

I met Anne for breakfast, during which we both were restrained and awkward, with little to say. Then she drove me down the mountain in a blue air-force car to the railroad station, where we had another old-comrades embrace (not so satisfying this time). And then I was off to Munich, there to make my way to the München-Riem airport, whence to London via Heathrow and the tube.

17

London is the one city where I do splurge on accommodations, whether I'm traveling on my own money, the museum's, or the Defense Department's. I used to stay in Bloomsbury, in a pleasant little hotel on Bedford Street, just off Russell Square ("in the shadow of the British Museum," as they like to say in those parts). Every self-respecting person with intellectual pretensions has a favorite small hotel in Bloomsbury, especially self-respecting intellectuals who are traveling on a budget. After a few years, however, I admitted to myself that most of Bloomsbury was pretty grungy, that its literary gloss was long-dulled, and that it was a long way from the places most of my business took me—Christie's, Sotheby's, the Wallace Collection, the National Gallery, the Witt Library.

So I willingly waived my intellectual pretensions, and on my last few visits I'd stayed in Mayfair, surely the most civilized section of the most civilized city in the world. And, happily, within easy walking distance of Christie's, Sotheby's, and the Witt.

I didn't quite have the nerve to check in at Claridge's or the Dorchester on taxpayers' money (not that I doubted what Robey's reaction would be: "Good, fine, no problem"), so I went instead to the Britannia on Grosvenor Square, hardly a major sacrifice on my part. In any case I deserved it, to make up for my depressing love life.

It was 5:00 P.M. when I got there, and I called Harry in Berlin as soon as I'd washed up and poured myself a Scotch.

"Hey, Chris, where are you? I tried to get you in Berchtesgaden."

"I'm in London, at the Britannia. Harry, listen, I've been talking to people, and there are a few things you need to know. In the first place, I know what Robey was doing on that flight to Frankfurt. He's got a girlfriend in Sachsenhausen."

"How do you know that?"

"Jessick told me."

"How does he know?"

"Don't ask me. Jessick's the kind of guy that knows those things. This means Mark's in the clear, doesn't it?"

"Maybe, or maybe he just made it up and told Jessick, knowing good old Conrad would pass it on to you. And even if it's true, that doesn't mean he couldn't have arranged the whole thing as an alibi, to make it look as if he had some reason for being in Frankfurt that night just in case someone found out he was there. Or—"

"Harry, I think you've been a cop too long."

"You and me both. Well, I'll check it out."

"Here's something else to check out. The Heinrich-Schliemann-Gründung is one man. And that man ..." I paused dramatically.

"Is Earl Flittner."

"You knew?"

"Well, sure."

"Why didn't you ever tell *me*?"

"I just figured you already knew. Jesus Christ, isn't it obvious?"

It was, now that I thought about it. "You don't think it's important?"

"Why important?"

"Because maybe Peter knew even though Earl says he didn't, and maybe he was killed to keep him from talking."

"You really believe that?"

"Well—"

"Because if it's true, there goes your forgery theory again. How's your investigation going, anyway?"

No worse than yours, I thought meanly. "So-so," I said. "Incidentally, I found Peter's calendar."

That got a rise out of him, especially when I told him it was waiting for him in the Columbia House safe.

"Great! I'm on my way."

"Wait, there's something else." I sipped the Scotch, looking out over Grosvenor Square, which looked more gray than green in the dismal light of a wintry, misty London evening; at Roosevelt's statue on the lawn, so arresting and odd because he is standing unsupported on his feet; at Saarinen's jarringly modern American embassy with its tangle of metal barricades across the front; at the sedate, symmetrical red-brick buildings that border the rest of the square.

It was Christmas, and strange to see London without automobiles. Ordinarily, no city in Europe is noisier and more crowded with cars than London, and it is a mark of just how civilized it is that people don't go around shooting or even shouting at each other out of sheer frustration. That much traffic in Rome, or Madrid, or Paris, and the streets would be war zones.

"You still there?" Harry said.

"Harry, can an unloaded gun hurt you when it's fired? Not just powder burns, but . . . well, could it put a hole through a few layers of clothing?"

"If what you mean by 'unloaded' is that it's shooting blanks, you're damn right it could. It could put a hole through *you*."

"It could? But how? What is there to make a hole?"

"Oh, well." He cleared his throat. "Well now. A lot more comes out of the end of a gun than a bullet, you know. There's always some gas—which comes out real fast and real hot—and there can be some primer fragments. And even the wad can do a hell of a lot of damage."

"What's the wad?"

"What's the wad? Boy, you don't know anything about firearms, do you?"

"No."

"All right, let me start from the beginning. What *you* probably think of as a bullet is actually a cartridge, okay? Now a cartridge has three parts: the primer—that's what explodes when the hammer hits; and *that* detonates the propellant; and *that* explosion shoots the bullet—which is the lead slug in front—along the barrel and out. . . . Hello? Anybody there?"

"I'm with you, sort of."

"All right. Now, what makes a blank cartridge blank is that it doesn't have that lead slug in front—but it's got the powder charge in back. The wad is, like, a cover that holds the charge in place when there isn't any bullet in front. People get killed by blanks all the time. There was this TV actor a couple of years ago, fooling around with a prop pistol between scenes—held it to his head, you know, and pulled the trigger. Killed him. Let me tell you, blanks can be as lethal as live ammo from close up."

"How about thirty or forty feet?"

"Usually no problem, but there's this case where a guy watching a show in the balcony had his hand blown away by some balled-up newspaper they were using as wadding in a little cannon on the stage. Oh, God, then there's this really horrible case—"

"Please, no more cases. I believe you."

"Tell me, Chris, why are we having this particular discussion? No holes in you, are there?"

"No, just a groove," I said, and told him what had happened. "From what you said," I concluded hopefully, "it sounds like it was just an accident."

Harry let that sink in for a few moments. "I don't know," he said soberly. "Could be. See, here we're not talking about cartridges at all, just loose black powder, and that puts out a lot of burning crud. It could maybe do what you said at thirty, forty feet, especially if it was really rammed in there. But maybe somebody ought to go back and look at the place and see if there's a ball, a slug, imbedded in a tree or something."

"I did that this morning, first thing. There's nothing.

Look, let's say somebody really wanted to kill me. Why get so damn intricate? Why not just shoot me with an ordinary .38 on a dark street?" I startled myself by breaking into sudden laughter. "I can't believe I'm saying these things." I took a long gulp of Scotch.

Harry wasn't laughing. "You're right; killing somebody is pretty easy. But killing somebody and making it look like an accident—that's harder."

"Shooting me would look like an accident?"

"Yeah, your *particular* death would look accidental, if you know what I mean. Beside the point."

"Oh, beside the point. My particular death. I see."

Now he laughed. "Hey, cheer up, buddy; we're just thinking out loud, right? I don't think there's really any reason to get worried; it probably was an accident, considering all the boozing that was going on."

"I'm glad to hear you say that," I said, somewhat relieved. "Anne told me that there are a few every year, so—"

"On the other hand, it wouldn't be such a bad idea to sort of exercise some caution, you know? Don't go where they're firing guns anymore. Don't fool around on the edges of cliffs. Avoid standing directly underneath glaciers."

"I'm in London, Harry. No glaciers."

"Oh. Well, then, keep your ass the hell out of Soho."

Five minutes later, as I was finishing the drink and trying to remember whether that basement pub with the terrific steak and oyster pie was on Davies or Duke, the telephone rang.

"Chris? Who knew you were going to that shooting thing last night?"

"Why? I thought it was an accident."

"I said it was *probably* an accident. Did anybody know?"

"No, I didn't know it myself until a few hours before— Well, there was a German, Herr Wecker, but he's some kind of Bavarian official; he's worked with the Americans here for years."

"Uh-huh. Nobody else?"

"No, I told you. I hadn't even heard—wait a minute. . . ."

"I'm waiting, I'm waiting. Who?"

I put the glass slowly down on the pad of embossed Britannia notepaper on the desk.

"Jessick," I said. "Conrad Jessick."

The next morning was damp, gray, and cold—London's reputation for awful weather is well earned—but the walk to 20 Portman Square, where the University of London's Witt Library is located, was a pleasure. Portman Square is at the border of Mayfair and Marylebone, in a part of London dotted with little green plots around which are two- and three-story Georgian town houses of mellow brown brick, with white-painted ground-floor exteriors and black wrought-iron balconies one floor up. Whenever I think longingly of London, it's not of the great monuments of Wren or Inigo Jones but of these plain, tasteful, quietly elegant squares, where it's easy to imagine yourself in the eighteenth century. Especially on a foggy Boxing Day morning, with the ferocious traffic still reduced to a purr.

The Witt Library, housed in a fine old Robert Adam building, is the largest collection of photographs of paintings, drawings, and engravings in the world—a million and a half black-and-white copies, all annotated, in thick green file boxes stacked ceiling-high in every available inch of space. In the basement is the Dutch section, and it was there I went first, where "J. Vermeer of Delft" is given a four-foot shelf along the wall of a long, narrow corridor. This may seem rather a lot for a painter with forty works at most, but the Witt, as its director once told me with admirable British nonchalance, "is uncritical as to attribution." What that means is that the files include many copies—a great many copies—of paintings of doubtful authenticity or outright fakery.

And that is what makes it so useful. "We provide,"

Dr. Rowlande had further explained, "not so much a catalogue raisonné of an artist's work as a quarry of information to be discriminatingly mined, so to speak." At the Witt, and nowhere else in the world, it is possible to look at most of the dubious paintings that have been successfully put forward as Vermeers at one time or another, and to compare them with the entire small body of unquestioned Vermeers. It is also possible to mine the quarry for factual information—provenances, cuttings, sales records—that is impossible to get anywhere else.

I probably ought to explain that the three paintings from the cache required a different approach than the one I'd used on the others. That is, my initial premise for the pictures from Florence had been that the forgery, if there was a forgery, was an old copy of an already existing painting; that there were *two* identical Dürer self-portraits for example, one fake and one real, and that the fake was masquerading as the original. That avenue had turned out to be a blind alley.

But for the cache there were other possibilities. They had been purchased by Bolzano's father between 1930 and 1939—when only the most primitive scientific techniques for assuring the authenticity of paintings were available, and they had been out of sight since 1944. If one of them was a fake, it was not going to be a copy of an actual Vermeer, Rubens, or Titian, but a centuries-old painting in the *style* of one of them. Possibly it hadn't been intended as a forgery (what would be the point of forging the unknown Vermeer in the seventeenth century?) but had been altered later on. In any case, it had gotten by the experts of the 1930s.

If one of them was a fake. And if I couldn't find that out in the Witt, I wasn't going to be able to find out anywhere.

It always takes me a while to get used to the filing system. The materials under an artist's name are not arranged chronologically, or artistically, or by "period," but in the way that's most helpful to the people who use the place. Most of those who come are on errands like mine: They have an old painting whose authorship they doubt, so they want to look at every picture they can find with a similar composition, to see what it might be—other than what it's purported to be.

So Vermeer's pictures, for example, are organized under headings such as "Single Figures, Male, Full Length, Turned to Left" and "Males, Less Than Full Length, Without Hands." I found *Young Woman at the Clavichord* under "Single Figures and Portraits, Women, Less Than Full Length, With Hands, Turned to Right."

There was only one version, and it was identified as Bolzano's, and it matched the one in the exhibition perfectly. I turned over the large gray card to which the photograph was attached, hoping to find a provenance, and I did:

> *Young Woman at the Clavichord* was perhaps in the collection of Diego Duarte, Antwerp, 1682, or in an anonymous sale (Jacobus Abrahamsz, Dissius of Delft?), Amsterdam, 16 May 1696, or in an anonymous sale, Amsterdam, 11 July 1714 (Lot 12). It was apparently in the collection of Graf von Schonborn at Pommerfelden near Bamberg, allegedly by 1746, and passed with the greater part of his collection to the Lacroix family, Paris. After several anonymous sales, apparently purchased by Charles Sedelmeyer in 1892 and sold by him to Lawrie and Co. in London in February 1893. Lent by T. Humphrey Ward to the Royal Academy, 1896. Acquired by the Bolzano family, Florence, in 1933. Expropriated by German government in 1944, present whereabouts unknown.
>
> Also attributed to G. ter Borch, q.v.
> Also attributed to J. van Cost, q.v.
> Also attributed to K. Dujardin, q.v.
> Also attributed to P. de Hooch, q.v.

I'm not sure what I'd expected to find, but I'd hoped for something more useful. This is a pretty typical provenance for an old master, and as you can see, it raises more questions than it answers, with lengthy gaps, and "apparently," "allegedly," "anonymous," and "perhaps" sprinkled throughout. And then there was that mess of "Also attributed's," all of which except the de Hooch were news to me.

I looked in the files of the other three painters as instructed by the *q.v.*'s, but came away with no reason to think that any of them had anything to do with it. No surprise.

Then I went rapidly through all the Vermeer files, glancing at each picture. I was searching for parts of *Young Woman at the Clavichord* that might show up in other pictures. There is a common kind of fake, of a Vermeer, say, in which the forger borrows a pair of hands from *The Music Lesson*, a mouth from *The Geographer*, eyes from *The Love Letter*, and so on, and weaves them into a single picture that thus has many Vermeer touches, even if it lacks the unity of a Vermeer whole. The great artists, on the other hand, while they repeated themes or entire paintings, rarely cannibalized little pieces of their own work.

As expected, I found nothing to suggest that *Young Woman at the Clavichord* was anything but an original and thoughtfully integrated composition. And I was more than ever convinced—almost certain now—that whatever Peter meant by "Down your alley," he didn't mean that anyone but J. Vermeer of Delft had painted this one.

That left Titian's *Venus and the Lute Player* and Rubens's *Rape of the Sabines*, and although the Rubens files were only a few yards from Vermeer's, I was freezing down there in the stony cellar, so I climbed up two flights to where the Italian collection is, and where the temperature is kept almost livable. (Years ago I complained to Dr. Rowlande about the Witt's heating, and was given a lecture on the pitiful American dependence on central heating instead of sensible underwear.)

The bright oval room in which Titian's files are stored was once the house's dining room, and in its center is an elegant twenty-foot-long Adam table, probably the original one, now just a comfortably worn worktable. On it I spread the contents of a folder labeled *Venus With Musicians*. Bolzano's *Venus* was there, along with a lengthy provenance and an envelope full of cuttings. The provenance told me nothing, but one of the cuttings quickly solved the riddle I'd come with: Why was this relatively early Titian painted in a style not associated with the artist for another forty years?

The cutting was from a 1951 paper by a Yale professor:

> The Firenze *Venus* has long been ascribed to the year 1583. Clever biographical extrapolations by Sabrioli, however, now suggest that the correct date may be 1538, with the earlier ascription being attributable to an accidental transposition of digits in the seventeenth century. The current observer, though no art historian, finds Sabrioli's ingenious deductions thoroughly convincing.

Well, *this* observer didn't. With no disrespect intended to Sabrioli's biographical extrapolations, they were wrong. And the fact that all the post-1951 cuttings used the 1538 date merely meant that they were wrong, too. On stylistic grounds, *Venus and the Lute Player* was 1583, not 1538, and that was that. Sabrioli made a mistake. Case closed.

But the Titian had other problems, the main one being that there were six different versions: the one from Bolzano's collection, the well-known one in the Fitzwilliam Museum, one in Dresden with a doubtful provenance, one in Berlin with a black organist substituting for the lute player, and *two* in the Prado, also with organists, but white instead of black, with one of the two lacking the customary Cupid smirking nearby.

All different, but all very much the same. So much for Norgren's dictum about great artists never repeating themselves. I made photocopies of the other five versions to take back to Berlin, but I can't say that I expected much to come from them.

By this time it was one o'clock, and I was bleary-eyed

from staring at photographs. I went out to eat in a fish-and-chips restaurant on Oxford Street, marveling as every foreigner does at how it is that the British can fry their haddock so deliciously and their potatoes so wretchedly. A Liverpudlian once told me that they like them that way, and I suppose it must be true. Reasonably fortified by the fish if not by the chips, I returned to the basement of the Witt to tackle Peter Paul Rubens.

But the Rubens situation was hopeless. There was not just a folder but an entire file box devoted to "Rapes of the Sabines and Reconciliations of the Romans and Sabines" (with very little to tell them apart). Lest you think that Rubens was obsessed with this subject matter, I will tell you that the man has 114 file boxes devoted to him—and these are sizable containers a foot and a half high and three inches thick; fifty-seven linear feet of densely filled shelf space.

By five o'clock I had gone through almost half the boxes, although the last ten had been a blur. The attendant was wandering around nearby, straightening things, coughing politely, and looking pointedly at the clock. I capitulated, closing the box before me with a peevish snap and giving up for the day. And since I was due in Frankfurt the next morning to play my part in the Byzantine plot to get the El Greco out of Frankfurt, I would not be back.

Not that I wanted to come back; fifty file boxes was enough. The Rubens, I decided, would just have to be given to Kohler to look at, if need be. But truthfully, I couldn't see spending the money. There were a few touches on our *Rape of the Sabines* that were questionable, but there are a few touches on most Rubenses that are questionable, and I would have bet that we had something which was at least ninety percent by Peter Paul's own hand. By my definition, it was authentic.

And so, I was more and more certain, were the Vermeer and the Titian.

Whatever came before square one, that's where I was.

18

My flight to Frankfurt the next morning was delayed, so I arrived at the Kunstmuseum over half an hour late. I went directly to the basement workroom, as agreed, to observe the crating of the El Greco and to document the various nicks and scratches in it. That done, I dashed upstairs to Emanuel Traben's office, still twenty minutes late, but as it turned out I needn't have worried. I found him, more dyspeptic than ever, talking to an American major.

"Sorry I'm late, Herr—Harry, what are you doing here?" I hadn't recognized him at first. I don't think I'd really believed he owned a uniform.

Traben explained. "Major Gucci is commendably cautious. He has convinced me that the truck should leave later than the scheduled time and should follow a route other than the agreed-upon one. Another truck has left as scheduled, empty except for two of your soldiers, to provide a . . . a decoy, as the major calls it." He frowned painfully, digging with two fingers at the area below his sternum, and looked up at a wall clock. "And now perhaps we should get underway with the painting?"

In the hallway, he scuttled along in front of us, giving me a chance to talk to Harry.

"A *decoy*? What's going on? What do you expect to happen?"

"Who knows?" he said happily. "Nothing, probably. But I figured we already had enough trouble; why take chances? They always do it this way in the movies."

"Oh well, then; of course. Forgive my asking. How're you doing with Peter's calendar?"

"I've been through it. Can't say it did me any good. Also did a little more checking on Robey and Jessick."

"And?"

"Robey really does have a girlfriend in Sachsenhausen. A very nice almost-divorced lady with two kids. As for Jessick, it turns out Robey and Gadney walked in about five minutes after you talked to him on the phone, and he told them all about your going out to that midnight shooting—so he wasn't the only one who knew."

"Mm. And where does that leave us?"

He scratched briefly at his cheek and smiled serenely at me. "Who the hell knows?"

At the loading bay in the cobbled courtyard, while Traben gave instructions to the sleepy-looking workmen who would load the crate onto the truck, a soldier approached Harry hesitantly. "Major, I'm not sure if it's anything, but there's something funny here."

He took Harry to the back of the truck some thirty feet away, where they both knelt to peer underneath it, inside the right wheel. Harry straightened up instantly and the two of them walked rapidly back to us.

"Get that painting out of here," Harry said, his face set. "And everyone out of the courtyard."

"Really—" Traben ventured.

"Now!"

Traben jumped, and within five seconds he, the painting, and the now-wide-awake workmen had all retreated behind the swinging glass doors.

"All right, Abrams," Harry said, "get on the horn to the Frankfurt bomb squad."

"A bomb?" I said. "That's crazy. Are you sure—"

He spun around, justifiably brusque. "No, I'm not sure. Now, did you hear me tell you to get the hell—"

My attention was diverted by an extraordinary sight. The latched back doors of the truck were bowing slowly outward toward me, like an inflating balloon. "Harry," I wanted to say, "will you look at that," but I didn't seem to be able to find the words.

"Chris, are you all right?" he shouted suddenly. *"Chris!"*

"Well, of course," I said irritably. "Don't yell in my ear like that."

Only I didn't say that either. I think I may have made a small croaking sound, but that was all. What was happening? Something hard was pressing against my back, and my head was wedged uncomfortably against something rough and cold. Stone? Was I lying down? How could that be?

"Chris!"

"Harry . . ." I realized I couldn't see him or anything else. Were my eyes closed?

They were. I opened them and laughed, then shut them quickly as a surge of nausea welled up along with a sudden if incomplete grasp of what had happened. What with my newly exciting life, I now could recognize that sickening, heaving billow that goes with coming back to consciousness after a blow on the head. I was lying down, all right.

"Did the bomb go off?" This time the words made it all the way out.

"Did the bomb go off?" he repeated, and laughed, a squeak of pleasure. "Yeah, the bomb went off."

"I didn't hear it."

"I wish I didn't," the soldier's voice growled. "Jesus H. Christ."

Tentatively, I opened one eye and then the other. The nausea had receded. Maybe one developed a tolerance after a while.

"Are you all right, Chris?" Harry asked.

"I don't know." I was lying on my back on the cobblestones, my head propped against the rough granite wall of the building. I moved to shift the pressure onto my shoulders, and touched my head gingerly. Nothing broken there, and only one painful spot, behind my left ear. And a sore neck. "Yeah, I'm OK." Just another insignificant concussion.

I pushed myself up to a sitting position and felt my

limbs. Bloodied knuckles, bruised knee, torn trousers. "Yes," I confirmed, "I'm all right." I looked up suddenly. "What about you two?"

"Fine."

"Traben? The workmen?"

"Everybody's all right. You're the only one who got zapped. The painting's OK, too."

"Nobody else got knocked down?"

Harry shrugged. "Explosions are funny. I guess you were standing in the wrong place. If you'd moved your ass when I told you to—"

"Believe me, next time I will."

"Major," the soldier said, looking over Harry's shoulder, "that must be the bomb squad."

Harry turned around. "Yeah."

"Already?" I said. "How long was I out?"

"Five minutes, a little more." He straightened up. "If I were you, I'd just sit there for a while. Need anything?"

I shook my head. While he went to meet the German unit, I leaned back against the wall, feeling my pulse hammer at about twice its normal rate, and waiting for my mind to reassemble itself.

Ten minutes later I was on my feet, waiting impatiently for Harry and Herr Knopp, the dour leader of the bomb squad, to conclude their discussion just inside the now-shattered glass doors. I realized that I was very, very lucky to be alive. The bomb had gone off at about 12:40, at which time I should have been sitting directly over it, halfway to Rhein-Main. I suppose I should have been weak-kneed with relief, but I wasn't; I was tense with excitement.

I grabbed Harry's arm as Knopp turned to snap orders at his men. "It's the El Greco," I whispered. "It's got to be the El Greco."

"What?" He was understandably distracted.

"The forgery, the forgery," I babbled. "Don't you see? Peter said he found it a week ago—I mean a week before he was killed. Well, he was *here* a week before he was killed, trying to work out the insurance." I shook my head wonderingly. "I just automatically assumed it was one of the ones in Berlin. I forgot all about this one. It was as if I had blinders on."

"Yeah, maybe."

"It's staring us right in the face. They tried to blow it up before we found out."

"That's one explanation."

"What other explanation could there be? That's why," I said, not above a little self-justification, "I haven't been able to identify a forgery in Berlin. It wasn't there. I've been wasting my time."

"Could be," he said, his eyes on the green-uniformed Germans and the American soldiers in mottled field dress now beginning to sift through the wreckage of the truck and to pick up unrecognizable fragments scattered throughout the courtyard.

The wooden crate was standing near the wall. On a bench next to it Herr Traben sat, pale and trembling, staring into space, the red spots on his cheeks as vivid as lipstick. I put my hand on the heavy wooden crate. "Harry, do you have any objection to my opening this up and having a look?"

"I do!" said Herr Knopp, materializing from somewhere and speaking fluent English. "I goddamned well do!"

Harry made a little motion assuring him it wouldn't be touched, and waved him off. "Me too," he said to me.

"But why—"

"Because *I* want to have a look at it first."

"But—"

"Look, Chris, for all we know the crate itself could be booby-trapped." On its own, my hand jumped quickly off it. "I think that's what Knopp's worried about. Me, my mind runs more to drugs."

"Drugs!" I said, startled. "Where the hell did that come from? Why should there be drugs?"

He sighed. "I guess it didn't sink in yet, what would have happened if that bomb had gone off the way it was supposed to." He turned me gently toward the glass doors opening into the courtyard. "Look at the truck."

I looked, through a border of glass shards hanging from the doorframe. Not only at the grotesquely twisted ruin of the chassis, tipped awkwardly onto its wheel-less rear corner, but at the truck-size cavity gouged out beneath it, and the blackened halo scorched onto the concrete all around. For the first time I noticed that the two heavy back doors really had been blown off and now lay, caved in but still locked together, some ten feet away, like a monstrous tortoiseshell on its back. There were black metallic chunks and vicious splinters all over the courtyard. Now my knees did go just a little soft.

"There were supposed to be two guards in the back," he said. "And you. Maybe the driver would have made it, but there would have been three dead guys for sure, in a whole lot of nasty pieces. You're lucky you're alive."

"Thanks to you; never mind the luck."

"You're welcome. What I'm getting at is that blowing up trucks—and throwing people out of sleazy hotel rooms in Frankfurt, for that matter . . . Is that the kind of thing you expect from art forgers?" He answered himself with a shake of the head. "Nah. They don't go in for that stuff. Besides, it's not worth the risk or the expense. But dope—you're talking big bucks, and you're talking the lousiest, most vicious creeps in the world."

He was undoubtedly right about drug criminals, but he was off-base about art crimes. Art involved a lot of money too, and the vicious creeps had found out about it. Art crimes were no longer the undisputed province of the well-bred gentleman crook.

"But why would anyone want to hide drugs on a famous painting going from a major museum to a big U.S. Army show? It's not the most inconspicuous place in the world."

"I'm only guessing, but the show's going from here to Holland, and then to England, right? Can you figure a better way to smuggle drugs from one country to another? How keen do you think customs inspectors are going to be on fooling around with nailed-up, irreplaceable paintings shipped by DOD and guarded by OSI?"

"All right," I admitted, "that could be. So why blow it up?"

"A lot of reasons. Maybe they thought we were onto them, and they needed to destroy it. Maybe it was one gang getting even with another. . . . Who knows? But this whole thing revolves around dope. I can feel it in my bones."

"All the same, there's a forgery somewhere in The Plundered Past, and I'm willing to bet this is it. So if it's all right with you, I'll stick around while you go over it. There's a lot I can do while you're looking for your drugs."

"Chris, I'm usually a patient guy, wouldn't you say? Amiable, easygoing?"

"I'd say so. Usually."

"Well, I am. But I've got a lot to do here, and your company—delightful as it is—is starting to bug me. No offense? Good. So Abrams here is going to drive you to Rhein-Main and get you checked out at the hospital—"

"I don't need a hospital."

"And then he's going to check you into a room in the BOQ, and tomorrow morning we'll all fly back to Berlin with the painting, and you can look at it when we get there."

"Tomorrow's the reception," I protested, knowing it was a lost cause.

"You'll have time before the reception," Harry said, the delicate way he set his teeth together indicating that he was done being amiable and easygoing. "You don't mind waiting until then, do you?"

I did, but what was there for me to say?

We flew back to Berlin in the cavernous, windowless belly of a C-130 cargo plane, seated on flimsy seats mounted backward on steel rails. Harry was grumpy. He had found no drugs, even with the assistance of Wolf, Frankfurt's famous dope-sniffing beagle. And Knopp had found no explosives. No terrorist organization had claimed responsibility.

No one knew what was going on.

"What about insurance?" I asked helpfully. "It was insured for two million dollars."

Harry shook his head glumly. "Who'd wind up with the money? Bolzano. And he doesn't need it; I checked that out a long time ago."

"All right, then consider this: If that thing *is* a forgery, then someone still has the original, and—"

"Chris, I've got theories coming out of my ears. Why don't you find out first if it is a fake, and then we'll talk." He tilted his head upward and scratched vigorously under his bearded chin. The activity seemed to refresh him. "You know what I keep wondering?" he asked brightly. "I keep wondering if the painting was just incidental. Maybe there was something else they were trying to explode into little pieces."

"Something else? There wasn't anything else on the truck."

"Sure, there was. You."

"Me? *Me?*"

Abrams and another soldier, seated a few feet in front of us, looked up. I lowered my voice.

"Harry, this is getting to me. Why do you keep saying things like that? Why would anyone want to explode— kill—me?"

"Why would anyone want to kill van Cortlandt?"

"That's a terrific answer."

"Look," he said with weary patience, "you keep telling me he got killed because he found a forgery, right?"

"Probably the El Greco."

"OK, whatever. Well, whoever killed him has to be worried about you finding it, too, since you go around telling everybody in reach that you're looking for it and you're gonna find it. I mean, it only makes sense."

I sat back and stared at the plane's stark interior, turning over this unpalatable thought, which I was having such a hard time accepting.

"You're going to have to start being careful, Chris," he said gently. "I mean really careful. From now on, no more trips out of Berlin without talking to me first. I even want to know when you leave Columbia House."

"OK."

"I mean it; I'm serious."

"All right, I promise." After a while I said, "Harry, I just realized: Traben has to be involved, doesn't he? That whole ridiculous transportation scheme was his idea."

Harry looked over at me and smiled tiredly.

"No, listen," I said. "Let's assume the El Greco *is* a forgery. Isn't it possible Traben substituted it after making off with the original—which he could probably sell for thirty or forty thousand dollars—"

"I thought it was worth two million."

"It is, but stolen art's no different from stolen anything. You can't sell it for full value. Anyhow," I went on, growing more excited, "blowing up the truck would be a master stroke—it'd destroy the evidence, and it'd also kill me, the only guy around who'd be likely to know it for a fake. His worries would be over. . . . Harry, are you laughing for any particular reason?"

"I think you've got a first-rate hypothesis there, Chris. Only one small problem."

"Which is?"

"Traben was planning to ride in the truck with you."

"Oh." I slouched moodily down into the uncomfortably upright chair. "The hell with it. I'm going to get some sleep. Maybe everything will be clear when I've looked at the painting."

"Yeah," Harry said. "Sure."

19

Purification of the Temple, purportedly by Doménikos Theotokópoulos, called El Greco; the Greek. Painted about 1598 and certified by Major Harry M. Gucci to contain no explosives or contraband.

At the center stands a red-robed Christ, willowy, ethereal, dispassionately resolute. In his gently upraised hand is a flail, held aloft so languidly that its thongs trail straight down, limp and unthreatening. Nevertheless, there is consternation in the writhing knot of people before him. They fling themselves wildly away to escape the drooping lash, tilting their bodies far to the left, so that everything is disturbingly off balance. The figures are elongated or bizarrely foreshortened, the shifts in perspective violent and unnatural, the colors acid and eerie.

I stood frowning at it and working the kinks out of my back after a long, meticulous examination. I was feeling rather crabby. I wouldn't argue with El Greco's genius, but, speaking for myself, four hours of staring at those twisty, febrile fanatics was about three hours and fifty minutes too much.

"The damn thing's genuine," I grumbled. "I'd bet on it." Fortunately, Harry, who had heard my willingness to bet the other way not many hours before, was off somewhere else.

I didn't have much doubt about my conclusion. The painting was quintessential El Greco: thick pigments, tempered with mastic and then vigorously laid on with rough, hatching strokes, not so very different from the way van Gogh would do it three hundred years later. But anyone else painting in 1590 would certainly have used a more fluid medium and laid it on with a soft brush to get the smooth, unbroken glaze that was standard at the time.

It was even signed in Greek characters, not Roman, which is how El Greco did it until almost the end of his life—a minor detail that many El Greco forgers never bothered to learn, assuming that all they had to do was paint some religious-looking men with long faces and pointy beards and they could get away with it. And a lot of them did, leaving many a red-faced curator in their wake.

No, it was an El Greco, all right, probably worth more than its two-million-dollar appraisal. So what was going on? Between Harry and me, we'd come up with no answers. Where was there for me to go from here? Tiredly, I rubbed the hot, aching area at the nape of my neck.

I was startled by another, gentler touch on the back of my neck, but I recognized it quickly as Anne's. I stood there with my head bowed and my eyes closed, luxuriating in the warm pleasure of having my shoulders massaged by her soft, firm hands.

"Poor baby," she murmured, "you've been through a lot lately, haven't you?"

Earlier we had managed a quick lunch together, and she had warmed me with her concern over the story of my narrow escape from the bombing (made only a little narrower in the telling, purely in the interest of dramatic narrative). Even now, when I turned to look at her, there was a tiny crease of worry between her eyebrows.

I touched it with my fingertips. "Hey," I said guiltily, "I'm fine. Really."

The crease smoothed. "But from the look on your face, I gather you still haven't found the forgery."

"No, this is an El Greco for sure, and I'm ready to give up. There isn't anything else to look at."

Gadney came in, looking armored and stiff in a tightly buttoned blue suit instead of his usual tweeds. He seemed a little tense, but then he was overseeing the arrangements for the reception, and the usual sorts of things had been going wrong all day.

"So," he said, without much interest, "is it a forgery? No? Well, that's good. I *think* that's good. I'm not quite certain just what you hope to find. I'm sure it's none of my affair."

When this was not contested, he sniffed. "Mark would like us all to avoid saying anything just yet to Bolzano about what happened yesterday."

"What do you mean?" I asked. "Is Bolzano here?"

"Of course. Oh, didn't Mark mention it to you? It appears he recovered more quickly than anyone expected, and he flew in for the reception after all. Mark's with him now."

"Why shouldn't we say anything?" Anne asked.

"Well, you know how excited he gets. Mark seems to think it might be the last straw; that he might simply explode and call everything off."

He just might've, and I wouldn't have blamed him, but I thought he had a right to know that someone had very nearly vaporized his El Greco. I said as much.

"Yes, true," Gadney said. "Exactly what I told Mark."

"And?"

"Mark pointed out that it would be better to tell him after the reception. That way, he'll be more publicly committed; he'll have had his ego soothed by some important people—General Shea will be here, after all, and Ambassador Wheeler, and Mayor Grumbacher, and so forth—and he should be in a far more positive mood by then. I must say, I think Mark has a good point."

"What about Mr. Traben from the Kunstmuseum?" Anne said. "He'll be here. He's sure to—"

Gadney shook his head. "No, Mark's already spoken to him. He thinks it's a good idea to put it off, too."

"I'm sure he does," I said, smiling. "He's probably afraid Bolzano will strangle him when he hears about it."

"Be that as it may," Gadney said by way of closing the discussion, "I have to get back downstairs now. The caviar isn't here yet, if you can believe it, and we may have to do without." The thought brought a steely compression to his lips. "By the way, you might want to know that Lorenzo Bolzano is here with his father."

"Great," I said. "At least the conversation will be lively."

It was. Lorenzo was in classic form, voluble and opaque. "All of our old constants of 'objective reality,' " he piped, pushing a canapé farther into his mouth with one lank forefinger (the caviar had arrived in the nick of time, so that crisis, at least, had been averted), "all of our old constants—space, matter, time—we now recognize as nothing more than constructs of cultural consciousness." He smiled brightly at the group of six or eight people gathered around him, and gulped some more from the glass of Schloss Johannisberg Riesling wrapped in his other hand. "They are no longer valid."

"No longer valid," murmured a dazed one-star general, edging surreptitiously backward.

"No. Reality is, in reality—ah-ha-ha—a multidimensional and, in the end, an ambiguous invention, of no significance to the artist. In my paper 'Rembrandt, Warhol, and the Synthetist Manifesto' . . ."

The reception was a little over two hours old, and Lorenzo, having established a station within arm's reach of one of the food tables, had been going on like that for almost the whole time. Following Robey's instructions to mingle, I had wandered in and out of his ongoing discourse several times, finding myself entertained, as always, by his inexhaustible resources of learned goofiness.

I had also talked briefly with his father. Claudio Bolzano, looking happy and healthy, broke away from a circle of generals and diplomats to come and talk with me.

"So," he said, "here I am, after all." His alert black eyes glittered with life. "You're progressing in your investigations? Why don't I hear from you?"

"I'm afraid there's been nothing to report, signore."

"You're *afraid*?"

"Well, I only meant—"

He threw back his head and laughed. "I understand. I should tell you, signore, that as soon as I arrived, before the reception began, I went carefully through the collection, and my conclusion was this, signore: To search for a forgery among these paintings is to waste your time. They are authentic, all of them; I stake my reputation on it. And the three masterpieces from Hallstatt are even more wonderful than I remember." He smiled suddenly, his whole face alight. "Surely you must agree?"

I nodded. "I do."

Bolzano laughed good-humoredly. "I hear a scholar's disappointment. You're sad because you have no earth-shaking discovery to report to the world of art. Well," he said generously, "it's all right; I understand your long face very well."

But he didn't. I didn't give a damn about earthshaking discoveries. My friend and teacher had been killed because of something he'd found in the show. He had told me about it, and I'd been too dense to understand or even to follow his lead. And so his murderer was still walking around free. There were other compelling things to worry about, too, as Harry had pointed out; since I'd gotten involved I'd been beaten, grazed by a bullet (a doctor at Rhein-Main had confirmed it), and knocked silly by a bomb. And without a doubt I was *still* on somebody's hit list.

And I still didn't have a clue. I'd gotten absolutely nowhere at all.

That's why I had a long face.

"And so," Lorenzo was saying, "the subjectivist, essentially postexistential viewpoint opens to our minds a *third* reality, the astructural, nonfunctional, purely relational reality of an interior, many-layered system of reference. . . ."

I managed to hide a yawn under cover of finishing my Scotch and water, and let my eyes wander over the room looking for Anne. She was musing before the Vermeer, her arms folded, an empty wineglass cradled against her cheek.

It was the first time I'd seen her that afternoon without some panting male—or two or three—drooling over her. And no wonder. She looked marvelous; tawny-haired and glowing with girl-next-door prettiness. And she was in mess dress uniform, a knockout outfit of dark mess jacket, white shirt and cummerbund, and ankle-length skirt slit up to the knee. I hadn't been able to keep my eyes off her.

I went to her and took the glass from her hand. "I could sure stand a break. Why don't I get us a couple more, and we can find someplace to sit down for ten minutes."

"I don't know," she whispered. "I have orders to amuse the VIPs. I'm not sure if I'm allowed to talk to you."

"Well, couldn't you pretend I'm a VIP?"

Lorenzo, unfortunately, had noted my absence, and his voice, shrill with wine, cut effectively through the racket of a successful cocktail party well underway.

"Christopher, come over here and settle a fine point for us! We'll soon see," he said to his circle, "what the eminent Dr. Norgren has to say."

Anne took the glasses from me. "Duty first. Go be entertaining. I'll get your drink."

"Make it fast," I said out of the side of my mouth. "I think I'm going to need it."

"So, Christopher, ah-ha-ha," Lorenzo said, welcoming me with a comradely and unsteady arm across my shoulder, "tell us: If we accept—and how can we not—de Chirico's *pittura metafisica*, must it not follow that an *inner* reality— that is, the expectations and values which we impose upon our world—is infinitely more persuasive, more *real*, than the exterior world itself, which we can know only through our senses? How would you answer?"

"Uh, well." I looked for help to the group around us, but they simply looked back with that expression of stunned astonishment that ten minutes of Lorenzo invariably produced. I cleared my throat. "It's an interesting question. . . ."

Lorenzo rescued me, as I hoped he might. "It is a *vital* question, and not only for art. Heidegger, Kafka, Proust . . ."

He burbled merrily on, forgetting me again, as Anne came with the drinks.

"Thanks." I sipped, and then I must have frowned.

"What's wrong?"

"Nothing, the Scotch just tastes a little peculiar. Maybe they put mineral water in it." I laughed nervously. "Or maybe I'm getting paranoid." I took another tentative sip. "I guess they just changed brands, that's all. No taste of bitter almonds or anything like that."

"Are you serious?"

"About what?"

"It's wine, not Scotch. That's some educated palate you've got there."

"Wine? Why did you get me wine?"

"That's what I thought you were drinking. You had a wineglass."

"No, they just ran out of highball glasses, that's all. Is this really wine?" I tried it again. "Of course it is. Funny that I'd think it was Scotch."

"Not really. Other things being equal, you see what you expect to see, hear what you expect to hear, taste what you think you're going to taste. Didn't you know that?"

"So that's what you learn in career counseling."

"That's what *you* should have learned in Psych 101. It's an elementary principle of perception: expectancy."

"Expectancy! Yes!" Lorenzo burst out. "Exactly my point! Do you see? It's why you didn't recognize the wine!"

It wasn't the first time I'd observed his ability to take in other conversations even when he was in the middle of one of his own harangues. Presumably it was due to his being unable to follow what he was saying any better than anyone else could.

"You see?" He grinned triumphantly at his glassy-eyed audience. "One's expectation overrules the evidence of the senses. You expect whiskey, and although your senses tell you you have wine, your 'inner reality' constructs a complex rationale to protect itself, to convince you that *it* is right and your senses wrong. 'They put mineral water in it'; 'It's a different brand.' Anything to maintain the integrity of your preconception."

"Yeah!" one of the somnolent listeners said suddenly. "That makes a lot of sense."

Lorenzo's button eyes blinked in surprise. It wasn't the sort of thing people generally said to him. "Well," he mumbled gruffly, "I was merely speaking in concrete terms."

Anne and I seized the opportunity to move on, but after three steps I froze on the spot.

"Anne . . . ? I just realized—preconceptions—expectations—the integrity of—of—"

"I think," she said gravely, "you've been talking to Lorenzo too much."

"No." I shook my head impatiently. "Remember what Peter told me? To look at everything without preconception? Well, I haven't done it. I haven't done it!" I laughed, no doubt a little wildly.

"Chris—"

"Come on." I grabbed her wrist and broke toward the neglected alcove where the eleven copies of the missing paintings were.

"Dr. Norgren, a little decorum, please!" she yelped, tripping after me. "Remember, we represent the dignity of the government of the United—"

"Screw decorum! Anne, if I'm right . . . if I'm right—!"

I was right.

"Chris," Anne said, looking uncertainly up at my face, "you're making me nervous. What's going on?"

"Nervous?" I said, barely hearing her. "Why?"

"For one thing, because you're staring at that picture with a look on your face like that orangutan with his banana, only you're sort of chortling and oinking—"

"Oinking?" I repeated, not taking my eyes off the painting. "I don't think I'm oinking."

"Well, you are, and before that you practically yanked me off my feet, which isn't like you. You also said 'screw,' which also isn't like you—"

"Did I say 'screw'?" I asked dreamily.

"Yes," she said, "you did. Christopher, what . . . is . . . going . . . *on*?"

"Yeah, what?" Harry appeared at the entrance to the alcove. He, too, was in mess dress and looking uncomfortable, as if he longed to stick a finger down his starched collar and tug. "You practically ran me over getting here. What's the big deal?"

"The deal," I said slowly, relishing this moment so much I didn't want to move on. "The deal is, I've found Peter's fake."

In real life, people don't do double takes very often, but they both did one now. From vague, uncomprehending stares at the painting, their eyes jumped to me and then leaped again to fasten on the smallish, modestly framed picture we stood before.

"This?" Harry said in a squawk of surprise. "This?" He leaned closer to the identifying plaque, a neat white rectangle of cardboard on the brown wall covering, a few inches from the picture's bottom right corner.

" '*A Woman Peeling Apples,*' " he read, " 'Jan Vermeer, sixteen—' "

"I don't understand," Anne interrupted. "How can this be a fake? I mean, it already *is* a fake." She gestured at the other ten copies in the alcove. "These are *all* fakes. That's what they're *supposed* to be."

"Yes," I said, "but this is a fake fake." I know I chortled; maybe I even oinked.

"Listen, Chris," Harry said evenly, "it's real nice to see you having such a good time, but I think maybe you better let the rest of us in—"

"It's real."

Silence.

"It's a genuine Vermeer," I said.

Silence.

I finally looked away from the painting and at the two of them. "This is Peter's 'forgery.' That's why he was so funny about it. It's not a fake that everyone thought was an original, it's an original that everyone thought was a fake."

"Are you sure?" Anne said in a bewildered whisper.

"Absolutely. Look at the *pointillés*, look at the wall texture with all those incredibly tiny color variations; who else ever understood enough to do that? No question about it. It's obvious." I shook my head, not sure if I were more pleased with how clever I was or distressed with how stupid I'd been.

"Well, what the hell are you looking so smug about?" Harry asked almost angrily. "And if it's so obvious, what in the goddamn hell took you so long to find it?"

"What took so long was that I wasn't looking for it. Not here, anyway, among the copies. They were supposed to be fakes, so I saw them as fakes, and I didn't pay any attention to them. Damn, I should have figured this out weeks ago, but I didn't do what Peter said—I didn't start without preconceptions. My inner reality—"

"Inner reality!" Harry exploded, and looked at Anne. "Do you know what he's talking about?"

"Sure. Expectancy. The imposition of our values and expectations on the supposedly objective exterior world. Kant. Kafka. Heidegger. Ask Lorenzo; he'll explain it to you."

"You're getting weird, too," Harry muttered. "All right, it's real. I'll take your word for it." He folded his arms, pulled at the side of his beard, and stared hard at the simple homely scene on the canvas; a seated, house-jacketed woman peeling apples from a basket on her lap, with a little girl standing at her side, both figures bathed in Vermeer's wonderful, clean light pouring in through the window on their left.

"A Woman Peeling Apples," he said musingly. "This is why van Cortlandt got killed? Because he figured out what you just figured out?"

So much for chortling and oinking. In the excitement of discovery, I'd actually forgotten the point. "It's got to be that," I said, sobered. "And I think that's why somebody's been trying to do me in, too, before I figured it out as well.

I'm supposed to be a Vermeer expert, remember?" I shook my head ruefully again. "Down my alley, Peter said. Right smack down the middle of my alley."

"No, wait a minute," Anne said. "Why you and only you? If it's so obvious, couldn't someone else have found it, too? What about Earl, for instance? He's also an art expert. Why hasn't someone been trying to kill him before he—" Her eyes widened. "You don't—do you really think he might be the . . . *Earl*?"

"No, I don't. What motive could he possibly have? Even if he believes that junk he wrote in those letters, how would substituting a genuine painting for a copy help him?"

"All right, forget the letters," Harry said. "What about simple greed? Maybe he stole the real one—the real fake, I mean—and switched . . . No, what kind of sense would that make?"

"None," I agreed. "Stealing an original to sell it off and substituting a copy for it is one thing, but stealing a *fake* and substituting a genuine three-million-dollar masterpiece for it—why would he want to do that?"

"Why would anybody want to do it?" Anne asked sensibly. "It doesn't sound like a very good business proposition. Harry, what do you think?"

"I think we better get back to the other room. Somebody's going to notice we've been in here a long time, and they're liable to figure out what we've been talking about."

"You're right," I said. "Let's go." But I didn't go. I stood there looking at the picture, chewing on my lip. "Come to think of it, where did this come from? It's been missing since 1944. That's why it's here in this alcove. I mean that's why the copy's supposed to be here in this room."

"It just doesn't make sense," Anne murmured. "No sense at all."

But it was starting to make sense to me. Just a glimmer of sense, a hazy vision of the threads that bound it all together; the hoax, the murder, everything. Even the storage-room break-in.

"No," I said slowly, "I think maybe it does make sense ... but we're going to have a hell of a time proving it."

"Proving what?" they said together.

"Harry, I've got an idea. It'd involve using one of the security guards and—well—staging a sort of incident. Would you be game to go along with it?"

"Let me hear the idea first," Harry said warily, but I saw his dark eyes glint.

20

After the reception about a dozen of us sat tiredly in a closed-off section of the Columbia House dining room awaiting a private dinner, courtesy of the Defense Department. The senior staff was there, and the Bolzanos, and Emanuel Traben from the Frankfurt Kunstmuseum. There were some others too: a youngish air-force one-star general, somebody from the American ambassador's office, and a Bundestag member. An uneasy-looking Conrad Jessick was crimped into a corner chair, trying to look inconspicuous among all the brass.

Each of us held a half-filled cordial glass. Robey had somehow acquired a bottle of brandy from recently discovered stores laid down by Göring forty-five years before, and he thought this would be a good time to open it.

"First of all," he smiled drowsily, "I want to offer a toast to the man whose generosity has made this magnificent exhibition a reality." He nodded in Bolzano's direction. I could tell that he hadn't yet gotten around to breaking yesterday's news. Maybe this was the final phase of the softening-up process. Robey raised his glass. "To signor Claudio Marcello Bolzano."

He heard Flittner mumble "Hooray" as he lifted his glass. He had been as sullen and unsociable as ever during the reception, but I'd been surprised to see him there at all, since he had only three more days to put in.

The brandy was watery, but all of us made the silly faces people make to each other to show they've just tasted something special.

"I'd also like to express our appreciation," Robey continued, "to the German government for its extraordinary—"

He was interrupted by the noisy busting in of a guard who came galumping breathlessly over the hardwood floor in his heavy combat boots. It was quite dramatic. Anne, Harry, and I exchanged quick glances and settled back to watch.

"Sir!"

Robey turned, frowning. "What is it, airman?" His glass was still raised. He was the only one at the table who was standing.

"Sir, there's been a—we've had a problem. In the Clipper Room—one of the paintings—it's . . ."

It was as if we were all in a movie and the projectionist had pressed the stop-frame button. All the little sounds and movements of people seated around a table stopped. No squeaking chairs, no scraping feet, no breathing as far as I could tell.

"All right, airman," Robey said with pointed calm, "what's wrong? Nothing to be afraid of."

The guard glanced nervously around the table, as if he didn't know whether he ought to speak in front of us. Harry had picked a good actor. "One of the paintings, sir— somebody got in there—I don't know how—the C-system was alarmed as soon as the reception was over—"

"God damn it, airman!" Robey shouted, surprising all of us. "What the hell happened? Spit it out!"

"Somebody's slashed one of the paintings, sir. It's in shreds—"

I leaned forward and tried to watch everyone at once.

Lorenzo cried "No!" and stood gawkily up in uncoordinated segments, like a camel, his hands on the table bunching the cloth, his Adam's apple going crazy. His father sat deathly still with his eyes closed. Gadney's mouth opened and shut, but I don't think anything came out. Flittner's mouth just opened and stayed open. Next to me, I saw Robey grope behind himself for a steadying grasp on his chair. Jessick shrank more invisibly into his corner. Traben

I couldn't see, but I heard a soft hiccup followed by a distressed burp.

"And, sir, they scrawled something on the wall—in blood, I think—some kind of political message."

"Political message?" Flittner croaked. "What message?" He shot a furious, frightened glare at me, filled with outraged innocence. *Not me!* his eyes shouted.

I was as interested in the guard's answer as he was. There wasn't any bloody message in the script; it appeared that our airman was indulging a flair for improvisation.

"Sic semper tyrannis," he said, deepening his baritone. Not bad. "I think—"

"Never mind," Robey interrupted with a panicky glance at Bolzano. "Which painting was it, for God's sake?"

"I—well, I don't know. It's the second one from the door, in the little room at the back. You know—"

"The little room?" Lorenzo repeated, his voice cracking with strained laughter. "The little room? You mean it's a *copy*?" I thought he was going to faint with relief. He sank back down. "A copy," he said shakily to his father.

"Second from the door," Flittner said. "The Vermeer."

Bolzano jumped up so abruptly that his chair clattered over backwards. "The Vermeer? The Vermeer is slashed?"

"No, no, Father," Lorenzo soothed, "only the copy."

And that did it.

"Only the copy, only the copy," Bolzano hissed, his black eyes snapping, his head waving from side to side like a cornered wolf's. I half-expected a lolling red tongue to slide out between his jaws.

"Yes, only the copy, signore," I said. "Why get so excited over a copy?"

"You . . . fool!" He glared at me, choking on his emotion.

"Father," the mortified Lorenzo whispered, *"please.* You don't understand. . . ." He reached a hand upward toward his father, but Bolzano easily swatted his gangling arm out of the way, and then, in a surge of sudden rage, backhanded him in the face with his closed fist. The sound of his

blocky gold ring against his son's soft mouth was shocking and embarrassing, and Lorenzo's tall forehead blushed a brilliant pink almost before the blow struck.

"Idiota!" Bolzano snarled. "You don't know the difference—"

He spun and took three quick strides toward the door, then stopped as violently as if someone had jerked a leash.

He turned, staring directly at me, breathing heavily, saying nothing. His tongue emerged, not like a wolf's, but quickly, like a lizard's, twice darting in and out over his lips.

"A trick."

"Yes," I said, "a trick."

"And the picture is really all right?"

I nodded.

"I'd sure like to know what's going on," Robey said mildly. "I'd really like to know what's going on."

Harry stood up, scraping his chair back along the floor. "Mr. Bolzano, I'm going to have to ask you to come with me."

Bolzano looked at him. "I'm not coming with you."

"Yes, sir, you are," Harry said. "By entering these premises you place yourself within the jurisdiction of United States military authority. I think we'd better go now, please."

"It was a cruel trick, signore," Bolzano said to me. "Of all people, you should have realized how cruel."

I pressed my lips together and said nothing, fighting the urge to pity this small man with the big, hurt eyes, who was aging and shrinking in front of us. You tried to kill me twice, I said silently. You didn't hesitate over blowing up innocent guards. And you murdered Peter van Cortlandt, snuffing out that good man's life in the most vile, repellent way imaginable.

"I realized," I said.

Harry took Bolzano's arm. "Chris, I'm gonna need you too. You mind coming along?"

The last words I heard as the door swung closed behind us were Robey's.

"Will somebody please tell me what the hell is going on?"

21

"I understand most of it," Anne said, shaking her tea bag up and down over her cup to discharge the last droplets, "but—damn!" The paper tag at the end of the string had come loose and the bag had plopped into the cup. She fished it out with a pencil and dumped it into an ashtray. "I understand that Bolzano had Peter killed because Peter found out about the Vermeer, and he was trying to do the same to you, and I sort of understand why, but there's a lot that still doesn't make sense, Chris."

"All right, shoot. I think I've got it all straight."

I should have. I'd just spent six hours in police offices, first at Tempelhof Security, then at *Polizei* headquarters, giving and gathering information while a numbed Bolzano went through the dismal process of interrogation and detainment.

The high point of the evening had come when I was asked if I could identify two muttering, arrogant hoods who had just been herded in by a squad of grim, efficient *Polizei*. I could, with ease and with pleasure. Skull-face was just as ugly and mean-looking as I remembered, No-neck just as awesomely houselike. Simply looking at them brought a dull ache to the kink in my nose.

Finding them had been a personal coup for Harry. In looking through Bolzano's things he had seen the brief notation *10* in that day's space in a pocket calendar. He had suggested that the *Polizei* send men to the Inter-Continental, Bolzano's Berlin address, to see if anything turned up at 10:00 P.M., and the two thugs had walked in, finally justifying Harry's obsession with calendars and nicely wrapping matters up. In the nick of time, too; Harry was sure the subject of the meeting was to have been my overdue demise, which Bolzano had come to Berlin to oversee personally. When the two men were shoved into his presence, Bolzano, who had been contemptuously defiant until then, gave up, and it was all over.

It was after 1:00 A.M. when I got back to Columbia House, where I found a note from Anne asking me to call her whatever the time. When I did, she sleepily asked me to give her ten minutes to change and then to come over for something to drink and to tell her everything.

I asked for an additional ten minutes so that I could shower and change, too. I even managed a fast shave, but the cozy fantasies I'd begun to hatch didn't last any longer than it took me to walk the hundred feet of curving corridor between our suites. She had put on jeans, a blousy denim shirt, and tennis shoes, and not—of course not—the silky shift I'd been dreaming her into, and in which she would have looked smashing. And the drinks were tea, coffee, or hot chocolate.

As a matter of fact, hot chocolate sounded great after those long, grubby hours at police headquarters, and she looked smashing just the way she was. Which is not a bad way to look at things when nobody's given you a choice anyway.

"OK, first of all," she said, "what was the *point* of it all? Bolzano had that micropattern drilled in a real Vermeer, and a fake provenance made up, and all the rest of it. Why, exactly?"

"Because he couldn't afford to let anyone know he had his old painting back," I said, stirring the contents of the cocoa packet into the hot milk and contentedly sniffing the friendly aroma.

"But *why*? Had he collected some insurance on it that he didn't want to give back?" She shook her head. "No, that doesn't make sense. Why would anyone that rich need to go around killing people over insurance money?"

"It wasn't insurance money; it was self-preservation. They'd have put him away for the rest of his life if word had gotten out that he had his old Vermeer back."

"For the rest of his life? Are you serious?"

"He got it back on his own, you see, from an ex-Nazi in Potsdam, and he broke a lot of East German, West German, and Italian laws to do it. And apparently there was another murder at that time, too, aside from a few waggeries like smuggling and bribery. They would have had enough to lock him up for a hundred years."

She shivered. "What a horrible little man. Chris, what was going on in Peter's mind? Why did he tell you Bolzano didn't know anything about it?"

"Well, consider: Here's Bolzano, fiendishly proud of his collection and loving Vermeer above all other painters. Does it seem likely he'd pretend a beautiful, fantastically rare Vermeer was just a second-rate copy and stick it away with a bunch of old fakes that he obviously didn't give a damn about? There have been plenty of cases where collectors pretended their fakes were originals, but this is the first one I ever heard of the other way around."

I took a swallow of the chocolate. "I'd have said the same thing Peter did: Of all the people in the world, he'd be the last one likely to know."

"But what did Peter think was going on? After all, he knew the picture was supposed to be a copy of a real one that'd been looted. If *this* was the real one, then where did he think . . . I mean . . . I'm confused."

"I don't think Peter had that quite figured out, either. But he knew what he knew."

"And it killed him." She was holding her cup in both hands before her face. "And it almost killed you," she said quietly into it.

"You call that almost getting killed? Broken nose, bullet crease, bomb that missed by a whole thirty feet? Nah, those are just the usual curatorial contingencies. 'Other duties as required.' "

She laughed, but not very enthusiastically. "You know, I

can understand why Bolzano tried to get rid of you; you're a Vermeer expert—"

"Who's been staring at a Vermeer for two weeks," I muttered, "without knowing it."

"But why Peter? Wasn't his field nineteenth-century art? How did he know Peter had found out?"

"Oh, he called him that night—from Frankfurt."

"I thought you told me he *didn't* call him."

"I told you Bolzano told me he didn't call him. But he did. Peter beat around the bush, I guess, but Bolzano was able to figure out that he was onto it." I shrugged. "He had him murdered the same night, before he could come back and talk to me or anyone else connected with the show. And then he staged the break-in in the basement."

"The break-in in the basement," Anne said, putting down her cup and leaning forward. "That part I think I understand. He was stealing his own Vermeer before you got a good look at it."

"Exactly."

"But he couldn't take *just* the Vermeer, because that would have seemed suspicious—since it wasn't even supposed to be real."

"Right."

"So those men were going to take everything?"

"No, because then he'd have to keep them all in hiding from then on. No, they were just going to steal the Vermeer, plus a few of the copies, and one or two originals to make it look good."

"Pretty devious."

"To say the least. And then when the theft didn't come off, he tried to use it anyway as an excuse to pull out of the show. He used Earl's ridiculous Schliemann-Gründung the same way."

"Vile, clever man." She uncoiled her long legs and stood up. "Are you hungry? Have you had anything to eat?"

"I'm starved."

She went to the waist-high refrigerator, crouched, and peered inside. "Blueberry yogurt, apples, sliced ham, bread.

What sounds good? There are a couple of bottles of beer too."

"How about a ham sandwich?"

"Coming up."

She stood at the refrigerator, her back to me, making up the sandwich on a plate. The living room was a duplicate of mine, but she had the knack of making even a hotel room look homey and personal. Some of the chairs had been rearranged; a couple of family pictures were on the desk along with her portable typewriter; and magazines, newspapers, and working files lay in healthy disarray, of which my friend Louis would have vigorously approved. No anal-retentive, Anne.

I stretched out my legs and leaned back, hands clasped behind my neck. I was comfortable and relaxed, and happy to be there, right there in her personal space, as Louis might have put it. It was lovely to have her making a sandwich for me.

"And a beer too," I called masterfully.

"Righto. Want a glass?"

"No thanks." A glass? I was ready to drink it in my undershirt (if I'd had an undershirt) and wipe my mouth with the back of my hand.

"Chris," she said over her shoulder, "what in the world ever possessed Bolzano to put that painting in the show in the first place? If he'd just left it in Florence, none of this would have happened."

"He didn't put it in the show; Lorenzo did, while Bolzano was in the hospital. He wanted desperately to get it out, but of course I summoned all my charms to pressure him into leaving the copies in. So I guess he figured it'd be safer to kill me than to keep making waves."

"All right, then, why was he so ready to let you investigate the pictures? Wasn't he worried?"

"No, what harm could it do? It just focused my attention in the wrong direction: on the originals instead of the copies. He figured I'd never waste my time studying fakes— which I didn't—and it would give him more time to do something about me before I accidentally stumbled onto the Vermeer. Which is what I did, with Lorenzo's help, of all people's. How'd Lorenzo take things, by the way?"

"He stayed around biting his fingernails with the rest of us until Harry called Colonel Robey to let us know what was happening. Then he seemed to pull himself together—I think he realizes he's the head of the family now. He said The Plundered Past is going to continue, by the way, whatever else happens."

"That's great. I think Lorenzo's going to be all right."

She brought the sandwich and set it down on the coffee table along with a bottle of Beck's. "No mustard or butter or anything. I suppose I could smear it with blueberry yogurt."

"No thanks, this'll do fine."

She settled down a cushion away, pushed off her tennis shoes with her toes, and turned sideways to face me, one arm over the back of the sofa, one leg tucked under the other, the pale blue denim tight against her thighs. Some women have legs that seem to catch your eye no matter what they're doing with them or what they're wearing on them. Anne, happily, was one.

"Only two more questions," she said, after waiting for me to take a couple of bites and have a swig of beer. (I wiped my mouth with a paper napkin.) "First, if Bolzano is such a great art lover, why would he be so cavalier about blowing up his El Greco to get at you? I mean, if he'd do that, why not just have one of his thugs destroy the Vermeer in the first place? Wouldn't that have been easier than all this killing?"

"Good question," I said, chewing. "I'm just guessing, because no one thought to ask him, but I assume he figured he could live without an El Greco—especially with two million dollars' insurance to soothe him—but he couldn't stand the idea of losing his Vermeer. I know that's the way I'd feel about it."

"Oh? Vermeer over El Greco? Is that an objective art-historical judgment or personal preference?"

"Personal preference. Of an objective art historian. What's your other question? Last one, mind you."

"How Bolzano knew you were going to be at the Christmas shooting. Did he have somebody following you?"

"Nope, that was me telling Jessick telling Mark telling Bolzano. Bolzano came up with some excuse to call Mark and just casually asked him what I was doing over Christmas. And you know how he found out I'd be on the truck with the El Greco?"

"Traben told him?"

"Nope. Bolzano paid a guy that works at my hotel in Florence to tape my telephone calls—one of which was from the Kunstmuseum—and send the tapes to him."

"Like in the movies."

"Uh-huh. Wait'll that rotten Luigi sees what kind of a tip he gets from me next time."

She watched me finish the sandwich, her head tilted to one side, a look in her eyes that I hoped I was reading correctly for once. "I'm glad you didn't get killed." She shrugged and gave a small, shy laugh. "I just thought you might like to know."

"I'm very glad to know." I put my hands on either side of her face, pulled her head closer, and kissed her gently on the lips. Her hair, soft and warm and tousled, tingled against the backs of my hands. "I'm extremely glad to know. You don't have any idea how glad I am to know."

She pressed my hands to her face for a moment, then let go and sank back down on the sofa.

"Chris, has it ever struck you that for a couple of mature adults we're having a remarkably chaste, old-fashioned sort of romance? If this is a romance."

"Oh, the thought may have crossed my mind. Once or twice. And yes, I believe this is a romance."

She put her hand on my knee and I covered it with mine. "I'm sorry about the other night at the General Walker," she said. "I kicked myself the minute you left."

"No, you were right. I realized it later; it wasn't the right time."

"No." And then, softly: "Not then."

I leaned across and kissed her again, getting up on one knee to do it. "I want to ask you something."

She looked mutely up at me, her clear violet eyes huge and shining.

"Do you mind if I use your telephone?"

She laughed.

"No, I'm serious."

"You want to make a telephone call right now? This minute?"

"Yup, this minute."

I charged the call to my room and waited for it to go through. If I'd ever felt happier in my life, I couldn't remember it.

"Rita? Chris Norgren."

Rita laughed ropily. "I don't believe it. You're actually returning a call after only eight days? Hey, it must be the middle of the night there."

"It is. Listen, I'm calling about Bev's last counteroffer."

"Okay, just a sec." I heard her scrabbling for my file. "It's been so long I . . . All right, here it is: nine-and-three-quarters percent of *Jan van der Meer van Delft*, including the advance; fifty percent of proceeds from sale of house—sorry, she reneged on the forty—car to her, Murphy to you, but she gets visiting—"

"Fine."

"—privileges. Library to . . . What?"

"It's fine. I accept."

"But—but there's more—"

"That's fine, too. Let's go with it. It's gone on way too long already."

A hiss wooshed out of her chair all the way from San Francisco as she fell heavily back into it. "Do my ears deceive me? Don't you have a counteroffer? Don't you want to think it over and call me right back, like next month sometime? Don't—"

"No sarcasm is necessary, Rita. Just send it. I'll sign it."

"Well, well, well," she said. "Well, well."

When I put back the receiver, Anne was watching me with a quiet, luminous smile, very still and alert, sitting with both feet tucked up under her, her forefingers steepled against her mouth.

I smiled back, feeling as if an enormous weight that had been strapped to my shoulders for years had finally been lifted, which indeed it had.

I was finally ready, in every sense of the word; ready to give my full and wholehearted attention to Anne, ready to move forward again with my life, ready to take on a significant new dyadic interrelationship.

Louis will be glad to hear it.

Coming to bookstores everywhere in July 1994 . . . OLD SCORES by Aaron Elkins. Published in paperback by Fawcett Books. Read on for the opening pages of OLD SCORES . . .

"My treat," Tony said, reaching over my extended hand to pick up the check. "This is on me."

Oh-oh, I thought. Watch out now.

This is not to imply that Tony Whitehead is a devious type, or one in whom every generous action implies some ulterior motive. It's just that Tony usually doesn't do things without a reason. Sometimes it's to your advantage, sometimes it's not. And it's been my experience that when he picks up the tab—it's not.

Tony is my boss, the director of the Seattle Art Museum (or SAM, as we insiders call it). I'm Chris Norgren, the curator of Renaissance and Baroque art. We were lunching a few blocks from the museum in the stylish, dark-wood elegance of a trendy new dining spot called Palomino. Our table was at a railing overlooking the spectacular glass-and-granite atrium of the Pacific First Centre building four stories below. As befitted a restaurant that described itself as "a Euro-Seattle bistro," Palomino was neoeclectic all the way. The furnishings were vaguely Art Deco, the wall hangings and open brick ovens vaguely Country French, the massive round columns and mauve walls vaguely Aegean.

It was all very handsome and inviting, and certainly of the moment, but it wasn't a choice I would have expected from Tony, who prided himself on ferreting out little hole-in-the-wall "finds" under the Alaskan Freeway. He'd surprised me by suggesting it. And made me wonder what was up.

Not that I didn't trust him, you understand. As a matter

of fact, I do trust him. And I like him a lot. He works hard and he has high standards for himself and his staff. He's a skilled administrator and a formidable Trecento scholar, and more than once I'd seen him stand up for his people when the chips were down. He'd been particularly kind to me at a critical time in my life.

All the same, there was an occasional whiff of snake oil in his nature, and he had a history of getting me involved in things I should have known better than to get involved in. Always for the greater good of the Seattle Art Museum, of course, or in the interests of art itself. But not always in the interests of my personal comfort and convenience.

"How was the meal?" he said amiably.

"Delicious," I said. Which was true. I'd had a spit-roasted-chicken pizza, thereby taking advantage in one dish of both the Milanese *girarrosto* that roasted the fowl, and the alder-fired Roman pizza oven. The famous applewood-fired oven had made its contribution in the form of *bruschetta*, delicately charred chunks of Italian bread coated with olive oil, garlic, and bits of sun-dried tomato. I hadn't figured out a way to try the hardwood grill, too, but whatever I'd had was excellent.

"How about some dessert?"

"No, thanks."

"Why don't we have some salad? You know, a palate-cleanser."

I agreed. We ordered green salads. Did we wish fresh Gorgonzola and walnuts on them, the black-shirted, black-trousered waitress wanted to know. We didn't. Would we care for another glass of wine?

"Go ahead, Chris," Tony said expansively. "No hurry getting back. We've got all the time in the world."

"No, thanks, Tony. Gee, I wonder why I have this feeling I'm going to need a clear head?"

"Ha, ha," he said reassuringly, "not really. Although, you know, there is something I wanted to tell you about. Don't look so edgy, Chris. I think you're going to find this interesting."

I didn't doubt it.

He reached for the bruschetta and broke off a piece. "As it happens, there's a collector who wants to give us one of his paintings," he said off-handedly. "It'd fall in your bailiwick if we take it."

"What painting?" I asked warily.

"Oh, it's just a portrait. By, what's his name, you know, Rembrandt."

Well, there in a nutshell was why no one had ever accused Tony of not knowing how to get someone's attention.

"What's-his-name Rembrandt," I said thickly, once I got my voice going again. "Tony, this is . . ." I frowned. "What do you mean, *if* we take it?"

"Well, we do have a small problem. The man we're talking about is René Vachey."

"René . . .?" I stared at him. "And he just . . . just up and offered us this old Rembrandt he happened to have lying around?"

Tony continued his placid chewing. "That's about it. One of his lawyers called me this morning to tell me about it."

"Just like that? Out of the blue?"

"Just like that."

I sat back against my chair, not sure just what my feelings were. "Mixed" would be as good a way as any to describe them, I guess. A Rembrandt portrait. Any red-blooded curator of Baroque art who says he wouldn't be salivating for it sight unseen would be lying through his teeth. I mean, after all, Rembrandt is—well, Rembrandt. The fact that SAM didn't own a single one of his paintings was something I regarded as almost a personal affront, but I'd long ago given up the idea of getting one any time soon. And now, suddenly, there it was, in my mind's eye, gilded seventeenth-century frame and all, hanging in the Late Renaissance and Baroque Gallery on the fourth floor, in pride of place on the west wall. I was dazzled.

At the same time, the mention of the donor's name had made me thoroughly leery. For although I'd never met the elderly René Vachey, I knew who he was. A successful

237

French art dealer as well as a collector, he was one of the art world's more eccentric characters (take my word for it, that is saying something), unpredictable, controversial, notorious. To some, an unscrupulous and self-serving scoundrel; but to many others a welcome gadfly in a field cram-full of self-puffery and faddishness. I could see both points of view.

The most spectacular of his escapades had occurred about ten years earlier, when the morning shift at the Musée Barillot in Dijon had walked in to discover to their horror that six of the museum's most-prized possessions had vanished during the night, frames and all. Among them were paintings by Tintoretto, Murillo, and Goya.

The usual tumult followed. The police were called in and got to work grilling museum employees and other suspicious characters. Photographs and descriptions of the stolen works were given to Interpol. Accusations of lax security were flung at the museum director, who responded by wringing his hands and bemoaning the sad state to which French morality had degenerated. He also fired his security chief.

Then, exactly four weeks later, René Vachey opened a public exhibition of works from his own excellent collection, mounted in his own gallery, three blocks from the museum. This was something he did occasionally, but this time there was a difference. Featured proudly and prominently in their original frames were the six pictures missing from the Barillot.

More tumult. Vachey, one of Dijon's most prominent citizens, permitted himself to be arrested and charged in what was almost a public ceremony. Afterward, he held a news conference well-attended by the Parisian press corps (whom he had taken care to invite). Yes, he said, he had taken the pictures from the museum, or rather caused them to be taken; the responsibility was entirely his. But *stolen* them? No, he had not stolen them. To steal, he pointed out, was to take the property of another, was it not? But whose property *were* these paintings? Did the Musée Barillot *own* them? He thought not, and he thought he could prove he was right.

Now I ought to point out that we are not talking about timeless works of art here, despite the famous names. Artists are like anyone else; they have off-days. Usually they themselves destroy or paint over their less successful efforts, but often enough these works survive. And there are certain small European museums, and some American ones, too, that have capitalized on this, picking them up relatively cheaply and amassing collections rich in great names but lacking in great works. This is not my favorite approach to developing a museum, based as it is on the belief that the average museumgoer is too dumb to know or care what he or she is looking at as long as the label says Picasso or Matisse. Worse, that's precisely the kind of museumgoer it helps to create. ("Ooh, look, a genuine Picasso! Isn't that *beautiful*?")

Anyway, the Musée Barillot, I have to say, was just such a museum. In fairness, it could hardly have afforded a first-rate collection of paintings. Containing a modest collection willed to the city by a wealthy physician named (surprise) Barillot at the turn of the century, it had since received little support beyond that required for maintenance. It had, in fact, made almost no acquisitions since the late 1940s. Just how it had managed to acquire the pictures in question was something that was buried in the remote past. They had hung there as long as anybody could remember, that was all.

And it was just this point that had started the clever Vachey thinking. He did some research, tracing them back to their appearance in the country in about 1800 as Napoleonic loot from Italy, Germany, and Spain. With thousands of other plundered artworks they had been destined for the Louvre, but they were among those the experts pronounced unworthy of basking in *la gloire de France* and had found their way into the French art market. Eventually, one or two at a time, the museum in Dijon had picked them up in the early years of the twentieth century. They had done so legally, paying the going price, and they had the papers to prove it (although it had taken them a while to locate them in the dusty vaults of a bank in Beaune).

Vachey shrugged this off. How could paintings or anything else be purchased legally from sellers who had no right to them in the first place? But French law didn't see it that way, and a much-publicized court case ensued, with Vachey cheerfully questioning the French legal system's authority to rule in cases involving non-French property.

Yes, cheerfully. For the whole thing was a sensational stunt. There had never been a question of it being anything else. Certainly these second-rate products of first-rate artists had no financial or aesthetic appeal to Vachey. His own collection was infinitely more valuable than the Musée's. He had simply decided to call attention, somewhat ahead of time, to the enormous and tangled question of Who Owns Art?—and perhaps to make some waves and ruffle a few feathers in the sober, snooty French art establishment along the way.

This he did brilliantly, for three well-publicized weeks, until the court began to make threatening noises. In the end, the paintings went back to the museum, as Vachey had always claimed—and I believed him—was his intention. He also paid the museum's legal expenses and voluntarily donated from his own collection, as a goodwill gesture, a fine Goya charcoal study that was worth more than all six "stolen" pictures put together.

From beginning to end, he had clearly considered the whole affair an enormous lark. Whether you conclude his basic motives were altruistic or self-serving depends on who you talk to. There was little doubt that he accomplished something useful by focusing attention on an important issue. On the other hand, he also became for a while the world's most celebrated art dealer, which couldn't have been bad for business. But whichever way you felt about that, the fact remained that he did it by burglarizing a museum, and anytime you load pictures in and out of trucks you subject them to frightening risks, especially when you do it through windows—in a hurry and on the sly. I've already said that these weren't among the Western world's great masterpieces, but Tintorettos are Tintorettos, and as far as art people are concerned, you don't mess with them to prove a point.

He'd also caused an art museum, and by extension, art museums in general, to look foolish, and that was what was worrying Tony and me right now.

So that was the man who wanted to give us a Rembrandt. Who knew what he was up to this time? The only thing I was sure of was that any gift horse from René Vachey required a long, hard look in the mouth.

"This picture," I said to Tony, "what does it look like?"

The salads had come. Tony began on his. "I told you," he said. "It's a portrait. Oil on canvas."

That struck me as a rather laconic description from a man who can get every bit as overheated about old paintings as I can.

"But what kind of a portrait? Of whom? Group or single subject? What kind of condition is it in? How much restoration has there been?"

Tony hunched his shoulders and chewed, the implication being that his mouth was too full of arugula and fennel to reply at the moment.

I leaned forward, eyes narrowed. "You haven't actually seen it, have you?"

"Well, not exactly—"

"Have you?"

"Well, no, nobody has."

"Not even photographs?"

"Well, n—"

"So we don't really know for sure it's what he says it is."

Tony swallowed and put down his fork. "Hell, we don't know for sure it exists. This could be some hoax, some game he's playing. It probably is."

I sat back and looked at him, thoroughly deflated. "So why are we even talking about it? Why are we bothering?"

"Because," Tony said, "he just might be on the level. What do you want me to do, tell him we're not interested?

241

Tell him to go find some other museum for his lousy Rembrandt? Tell him to go ahead and give it to the Met?"

"No, I guess not."

"Of course not. How'd you feel if the next time you walked into the Met, *your* Rembrandt was hanging on *their* wall?"

I laughed. "Not good."

"Well, neither would I. So let's not jump to conclusions."

"Agreed. But something's clearly fishy here, Tony. Look, why would Vachey donate anything to us? Why not some other museum? Why *not* the Met? That'd give him a bigger public arena, if that's what he's after. Or why not a French musuem, where at least he'd come away with some tax benefits?"

"Makes you wonder, doesn't it?" Tony agreed.

"We've never had any kind of association with him, have we?"

"Well, in a way, yes. You know who Ferdinand Oscar de Quincy was?"

It wasn't a name you'd be likely to forget once you'd heard it. "Sure, he had your job back in the fifties."

"That's right. Well, before that, in the forties he was with MFA & A. You remember what that is, don't you?"

I nodded. MFA & A—Monuments, Fine Arts and Archives—was the U.S. Army unit that had tracked down so much of the stupendous German art plunder of World War II and gotten it back to the museums and individuals it had been taken from. It had been the biggest and most successful recovery of stolen art in history, a well-deserved feather in the cap of the U.S. military. Afterward, most of MFA & A's experts, like Rorimer of the Met, and like de Quincy of SAM, had returned to the museum world from which they'd been recruited.

"Anyhow," Tony said, "according to Vachey, de Quincy was personally responsible for getting a dozen of his paintings back to him, and he swore then that he'd repay him someday by giving something worthwhile to de Quincy's museum." He shrugged. "That's us."

"What took him so long? It's been almost fifty years. De Quincy's been gone for forty."

"You've got me. According to his attorney, Vachey's getting on in years, he's getting sentimental. Wants to set his accounts in order before he passes on. He's taking care of old obligations, settling debts, redoing his will, all that kind of thing."

I picked abstractedly at the salad. What I'd heard so far was not abundantly convincing. From what I knew of Vachey, I didn't think he was the sentimental type, or at least not sentimental enough to give away something worth millions just to discharge a half-century-old obligation. There was surely something peculiar going on here, something we hadn't been told.

"Tony, let's assume the painting does exist. Let's assume it's really a Rembrandt. How positive are we that he's got legal ownership? How did he come by it? What does the provenance look like?"

Now provenances are tricky things. A provenance is the pedigree of a painting, the record of its ownership from the time it left the artist's hands. Since paintings change hands often, works as old as the ones we were talking about tend to have long provenances. Often they have gaps; for one reason or another, pictures disappear for a while and then turn up again, often fifty or a hundred years later. When this happens, there are always questions. How, after all, can people be absolutely certain that a long-lost Titian that is discovered in the living room of an Atlanta townhouse is the very same picture last seen or heard of in 1908 when it disappeared from the wall of a church in Pisa? (Answer: they can't, not absolutely.)

Even when there aren't gaps, there are often questions about authenticity or ownership. But a reasonably solid-looking provenance, capable of being at least partially verified, is a necessary place to start. Without it, no museum curator in his right mind would touch a so-called Old Master.

"There isn't any," Tony said.

My fork stopped halfway to my mouth. "No provenance?"

"Not to speak of, no. He says he got it from, well, from a junk shop in Paris. It was grimy, almost black. Naturally, the seller had no idea what it was."

"Well, how does *he* know what it is?"

"He says he knew the minute he saw it. He bought it, had it cleaned, took a good look at it, and satisfied himself that he was right."

"What do you mean, satisfied himself? Are you saying he authenticated it himself?"

"That's it."

I laughed. "Come on, Tony, this is a joke. An art dealer authenticating his own picture? What kind of authentication is that? Especially René Vachey, for God's sake."

He shrugged. "What do you want me to say?"

"Well, what do the French experts have to say about it?"

"I told you, nobody's seen it. He's setting up a big show at his gallery, and this is going to be the centerpiece. Critics, press, everybody's invited. I hear it's already making a huge flap over there. He's practically challenging the experts to prove his attribution's wrong, and people are starting to choose up sides before they even see the damn thing. Vachey has a lot of enemies, and, as usual, he's right in the middle of it. He called Edmond Froger a *dilettante ignorant*, in *Le Monde*."

"Oh, wonderful."

Tony shrugged. "Well, the guy is a horse's ass."

This was starting to have an ominously familiar ring. Several years before the Barillot affair, Vachey had gotten together about fifty of his own paintings to form a well-publicized exhibition called the Turbulent Century: 1860–1960. It ran for a month at his gallery in London, and was scheduled to go to Switzerland, Belgium, France, and Holland, where eager museums had been squabbling with each other for the privilege of getting it. This was quite a show, including works by Gauguin, Seurat, Braque, Picasso, and Kokoschka.

244

Except it didn't, not according to some reputable critics and reviewers who pronounced most of the collection to be questionable or downright spurious. Others, equally distinguished, supported Vachey's claims of authenticity. Battle lines were drawn. There was another flap, with epithets a lot more colorful that "*dilettante ignorant*" being hurled back and forth. In this one, Vachey stayed away from center stage, enjoying the fireworks while the experts fought it out. In the end, the museums scuttled for cover and pulled out with much huffing and puffing. Not, however, before they—and by extension, art museums in general, and by further extension, art experts in general—had been made laughingstocks. There were a lot of people who thought that just might have been the iconoclastic Vachey's aim in the first place.

And right now I was starting to wonder if it wasn't time for us to think about scuttling for cover ourselves.

"He can't expect us to accept the offer without seeing it, can he?" I asked. "Because if so—"

"No, you've got yourself an invitation to the opening. You can examine it to your heart's content. Okay?"

I considered. The odds were about a hundred to one against the trip accomplishing anything. An unknown "Rembrandt" discovered in a junk shop by a man with an offbeat sense of humor and a quirky history, to put it mildly. No provenance, no reliable authentication. Not a very good bet. On the other hand, for a hundred-to-one shot at this particular reward, yes, I was willing to take a trip to Dijon.

"Good," Tony said heartily, "so it's settled. I'd better send Calvin along with you. He's at the Return of Cultural Property Conference in The Hague, anyway, so he can pop over to France easy. He can take care of details, check the fine print, that kind of thing—his French is even better than yours. That'll leave you to concentrate on the painting."

"Fine." Then, after a second: "What do you mean, you'd *better?*"

Calvin Boyer was the museum's public affairs officer, formerly known as the marketing director. I enjoyed his

245

company—well, most of the time—and he seemed pretty good at what he did, whatever it was, but I couldn't see his being much help in this.

"Well, you know," Tony said, just a little cagily, "you're absolutely tops at what you do, and you know that I trust you completely to handle anything that comes up—"

"Right. But?"

"But, you know, sometimes you're, well, you're not too swift when it comes to people. And Vachey is a very tricky customer."

"Oh, I'm gullible, is that it?"

This was an old complaint from Tony, who was given to wondering aloud how a naive soul like me had survived as well as I had among the sharks of the art world.

"I'm just saying you maybe trust people a little too much," he said. "You're not suspicious enough, you don't have a devious mind. You take people at face value, you don't always look under the surface of things. This is not a criticism, Chris."

It sure sounded like one to me, and I started to climb up on my high horse, but caught myself in time. As a divorced man whose very first clue that his marriage wasn't everything it might have been came when his wife moved in with another man—this was after she'd been seeing him for a year without my noticing a thing—I figured I was in no position to tell Tony about how sharp I was at seeing under the surface of things.

Besides, I have a friend named Louis who from time to time has told me pretty much the same thing Tony just had. Louis says that I tend to resort to the secondary repression of ego-threatening perceptions for fear of bringing to the surface the primal hostilities and id functions that I long ago denied by means of primal or infantile repression.

At least I think that's pretty much the same thing Tony said. Louis is by trade a Freudian-Marcusian psychotherapist, and not always as lucid as Tony.

"Calvin's an M.B.A., Chris," Tony explained further. "You're an art historian."

"Okay," I said, not quite grasping his logic, but letting it pass. "Actually, I'll be glad to have him along. And he can help work out the logistics for getting the painting analyzed. We'll want to have Taupin, from Paris, run it through infrared and X ray, don't you think? And there's that outfit in Lyons—what's its name?—that can do laser microanalysis. I've got it somewhere."

"Mm," Tony said, and pushed his salad plate away. He'd finished his salad. I'd hardly looked at mine. "Come on, let's head back."

We took the escalator down to the lobby, passing under a "Baroque" stone arch that had come from a 1920s theater that had stood on the site. Once out on Fifth Avenue on a mild October afternoon, we threaded our way through shoppers, bemused tourists, and fellow late-lunchers getting back to work. While we walked, Tony told me more.

The Rembrandt, it seemed, wasn't the only centerpiece of Vachey's show. Vachey, no piker when it came to gall, was actually claiming to have come up with a *second* "newly discovered" painting; this one by the Frenchman Fernand Léger, who was, with Picasso and Braque, one of the foremost proponents of Cubism in the early years of the twentieth century. The Léger, it was understood, would be going to a French museum, as yet unnamed.

"Is that right?" I said. "Where'd he find this one, at a garage sale in Toulouse?"

"Strasbourg, actually," Tony said. "A flea market," and then he couldn't help laughing. "Now don't jump to conclusions here, Chris. Whatever else you can say about Vachey, he has a hell of a record for stumbling on masterpieces nobody even knew were out there." He started counting them off on his fingers. "There's that Constable that's in San Francisco now, remember? And that Francesco Guardi that wound up in, where was it, Budapest, and don't forget the Lebrun—"

"Well, yes, I know, but—"

"All those authentications were verified later—beyond

247

any doubt, Chris. Sure, he's made a few that didn't hold up, but that much you have to admit."

"I suppose so," I said. "Well, there's one thing to be thankful for, anyway."

"What's that?"

"I was just thinking: He might have given the Rembrandt to a French museum and stuck us with the Léger." I put my hand over my heart. "Whew, it's too awful to contemplate."

I say such things primarily for the fun of annoying Tony, who has a thing about me being too enamored of my specialty. He thinks I need to be more eclectic. He says I put the Old Masters up on a pedestal (he's right), and that I look down my nose at anything after the eighteenth century (he's wrong, but not wildly wrong).

But this time he wouldn't bite. He merely gave me one of his superior, pitying looks and went on with his story. According to the terms, both pictures were to be displayed for two weeks at Le Galerie Vachey, after which they would go to their respective new owners. Vachey would pick up all transportation and insurance costs. He would even provide a continuing fund to cover future conservation and insurance.

"So what do you think, Chris? Too good to be true?"

"By half," I said.

In Seattle, you can't walk very far without passing an espresso bar, and most of us are addicted to the stuff. Tony and I, exercising our iron wills, ignored two of them, but finally succumbed at the third, a plant-filled, conservatorylike Starbucks on Fourth near Union. We got on the end of a line of five or six people at the counter.

"Uh-uh, no, it *is* too good to be true," I muttered while the attendant went through her steamy routine at the espresso machine. "There's a catch somewhere."

"Um, there is a sort of catch," Tony said.

I looked at him sharply. I didn't like the sound of that *um*. "What catch?"

"Two catches, you might say."

"What catches?"

"Well, remember what you were saying about getting that X ray and microscopic analysis done?"

"Yes—oh, Bussière, that's the name of the lab in Lyons. I have the number in—"

"No dice," Tony said.

"What?"

"No labs. No X ray, no ultraviolet, no cross-sectional analysis, nothing but the naked eye. You can look at it all you want, but no scientific stuff."

"Why not, for God's sake?"

"That's the way he wants it, Chris."

"But *why?* Tony, he knows it's a fake, that's the only possible reason."

"Not necessarily. He says they're fragile. He's worried about damaging them."

"With X rays? That's ridiculous, you know that."

"Apparently he doesn't."

I shook my head. "I don't buy it. You know what it is? He's got a good fake, that's all, and he's giving it to us because he thinks Seattle is probably located just west of Dogpatch, and what could we know about art? He thinks he can get it by us, and after he does, he's going to announce that it really *is* a fake, and so once again he'll show us all up for the greedy, ignorant idiots we are—don't ask me what his point is this time."

Tony listened to this harangue, visibly and somewhat smugly amused. "And could he?"

"Could he what?"

"Get it by you?"

"By me?" Oddly enough, the question caught me by surprise. "I don't think so," I said honestly, after a moment.

"So there's no problem."

"Well, yes there is. First of all, there's the question of why he won't allow tests—he knows damn well they won't hurt the picture, and he knows equally well that museums *always* run them before they buy something."

"True, but we're not buying anything, are we? He's giving it to us."

"What's the difference? Why not allow them? And there's a second problem. Sure, if it isn't real, I think I could spot that, but a lot of other so-called experts have thought the same thing and wound up making big mistakes. What if I made a mistake?" I shook my head. "I don't like seeing us put anything in our collection without adequate testing."

"But you're not a 'so-called' expert, Chris," Tony said simply. "If you tell me it's a fake, we won't touch it. If you say it's real, that'll be plenty good enough for me. We'll take it in a flash."

I was flattered, even touched. I cleared my throat. "Thank you, Tony. I appreciate that."

"Besides, we can test the hell out of it after we get it here."

"Right," I said, laughing. Tony wasn't the sentimental type either.

Tony smiled in return; somewhat weakly, I thought. "Well, actually, even that's not true, Chris. You see, this is a restricted gift."

"A restricted gift? You mean we're not allowed to sell it later? Even if we decide we don't like it?"

His expression was one of bottomless forbearance. "Chris."

"Tony?"

"Museums are not in the business of 'selling' works of art," he said softly. "You know that."

"Oh. Right. Sorry. I don't know what I was thinking of. I meant we're not allowed to de-accession it?"

I suppose I was getting back at him for getting me into this—for despite all my reservations, I knew perfectly well I was in it up to my eyebrows.

"That's better," he said, fractionally mollified. "But not only can we not de-accession it, we have to agree to keep it on permanent exhibit—well, for five years, anyway— properly labeled *as* a Rembrandt, and displayed in a manner befitting a Rembrandt."

He exhaled, long and soberly. "So, my friend, it we decide to take it, we better be damn sure it *is* a Rembrandt ahead of time."

In themselves, restrictions like these are not extraordinary. Donors are always sticking little riders on their bequests that tell you what kind of case something is to be displayed in, or when or where it's to be placed, or what should be next to it, or how it ought to be lit. That, as far as it goes, isn't usually objectionable. These things are gifts, after all, and the people donating them usually love them every bit as much as we do. Why shouldn't they care about what happens to them after they go to a museum?

But this was different. The proscription on testing made it different; the absence of provenance made if different; above all, the presence of the unpredictable René Vachey pulling the strings made it different.

"You mentioned two catches," I said. "Was that the second one?"

"Actually, no; that was still part of the first."

"What," I said, gritting my teeth, "is the second?"

"Um, it'll hold. I'll tell you about it when we get back."

Um again. "Tell me now."

"Patience. Let's have our coffee first."

"Tony—"

"Here, Chris," Tony said generously as we got to the cashier, "let me pick up the tab. This is on me."

A GLANCING LIGHT

What should have been a pleasant interlude in Italy for Chris Norgren, curator and art expert, turns into a bizarre odyssey into shady art-world doings and deadly secrets.

by

Aaron Elkins

Published by Fawcett Books.